true blue

true blue

Jane Smiley

with illustrations by Elaine Clayton

ALFRED A. KNOPF
NEW YORK

THIS IS A BORZOI BOOK PUBLISHED BY ALFRED A. KNOPF

Visit us on the Web! www.randomhouse.com/kids

Educators and librarians, for a variety of teaching tools, visit us at
www.randomhouse.com/teachers

Library of Congress Cataloging-in-Publication Data
Smiley, Jane.
True blue / Jane Smiley ; with illustrations by Elaine Clayton. — 1st ed.
p. cm.
Summary: In 1960s California, eighth-grader Abby Lovitt has trouble with True Blue, the newest horse on her family's ranch, a beautiful dappled gray who is so often spooked, Abby wonders if he is haunted by the ghost of his deceased former owner.
ISBN 978-0-375-86231-1 (trade) — ISBN 978-0-375-96229-5 (lib. bdg.) —
ISBN 978-0-375-89416-9 (ebook)
[1. Horses—Training—Fiction. 2. Ranch life—California—Fiction. 3. Family life—California—Fiction. 4. Christian life—Fiction. 5. California—History—1950—Fiction.]
I. Clayton, Elaine, ill. II. Title.
PZ7.S6413Tru 2011
[Fic]—dc22
2010035975

The text of this book is set in 11.5-point Goudy.

Printed in the United States of America
September 2011
10 9 8 7 6 5 4 3 2 1
First Edition

true blue

Farm Gate

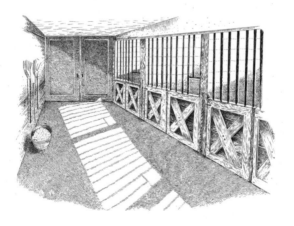

Row of Stalls

Chapter 1

I HAD GONE INTO THE HOUSE TO CHANGE MY JEANS, AND I WAS only about halfway out of my boots—which were very muddy—when the phone started ringing. And it kept ringing, all the time I was pulling off my boots and hanging up my hat and pushing my hair out of my face. I was really wet—I'd been riding Happy in the arena when the rain fell out of the sky like water out of a bucket, and we were drenched so fast we just started laughing. Daddy was in the barn, and Mom jumped off of Jefferson and ran in there with him—she was right by the gate, so she didn't get as wet as I did. I could barely see my way across the ring, the water was coming down so hard. But Happy didn't care. All of our horses lived outside anyway. Rain was just a bath to them.

And then it all stopped. There we were, standing in the aisle of the barn, looking out at the clouds blowing off and the sun shining through the misty air. Mom said, "Oh, I love California. The weather just comes and goes. And there are no tornadoes. I love that the best." Back in Oklahoma, where Mom and Daddy had grown up, there were tornadoes every day, or at least that's how they made it sound when they talked about it.

But I had to change my jeans at least—my jacket had kept my shirt a little dry.

The phone rang and rang, and I knew because of that it would be Jane Slater, and it was. Jane was a trainer at the big stable on the coast; she had helped us sell a horse there in the fall. She said, "Oh, Abby! How are you? I do so miss talking to you. What's it been?"

I said, "We saw you at New Year's. How—"

But she was excited about something, so she interrupted me. She said, "Then I didn't tell you that Melinda is back, did I?"

"No, when . . ."

"She hasn't grown an inch, and Ellen Leinsdorf thinks she's her worst enemy! Their lessons are back to back, and they're both riding Gallant Man, because, you know, there's been a big brouhaha about Melinda's parents' divorce, and they have to half lease him to the Leinsdorfs to afford the board, which is fine, but, goodness! What am I talking about?"

Ellen and Melinda were two students she taught; I'd helped her with them from time to time. Melinda was older—about ten—but Ellen was tougher. I laughed to think about them and said, "I don't know."

"Oh, Abby, I miss you. I feel surrounded by little little girls!"

I said, "I miss you, too."

2

"Well, why don't you come over here and look at this horse, and I can see you."

"What horse?"

"Such a sad story. But he's a nice horse. His name is True Blue. Very pretty dappled gray, black mane and tail, black points. Is your dad around?"

Just then, Daddy came in. I handed him the phone and ran upstairs. That was the first I heard of Blue. While I was looking for a clean pair of jeans, the rain came again, and by the time it was over, the arena was too soaked to ride any more that day, because even if there was no more rain for the rest of the weekend, it would take twenty-four hours ("Only a day!" Daddy always said) for the arena to drain. This meant that our work in the winter could be a little intermittent, but at least there were no blizzards. Back in Oklahoma, whenever there weren't tornadoes, there were blizzards, and Daddy and Mom had to walk through them for hours on end to get home from school, without mittens or buttons on their coats (at least, that was what my brother, Danny, always said when they started talking about how lucky we were to be living in California). "And uphill both ways!" When he said that, I always laughed. Of course, I went to Oklahoma myself from time to time, and the weather was fine.

So instead of waiting around and maybe going over to the coast "at some point" (it was a half-hour trip each way, and more than that if we were pulling the horse trailer), we decided that we had nothing better to do than go look at True Blue and then shop for groceries. We left Rusty, our dog, sitting inside the gate with that look on her face that she always had—"Don't bother to call. I've got everything under control here."

The rain might have skipped the coastal part of the peninsula, because even though there wasn't a horse show, the stables were busy with lessons in all the rings, and grooms, riders, and horses were walking here and there. I looked around for my old horse Black George and that girl, Sophia Rosebury, who had bought him, but I didn't see them in any of the rings. I made myself stop looking. I had had tremendous fun on Black George for a whole year. I thought about him often, but I hadn't seen him since they'd driven away with him in the Roseburys' trailer before Thanksgiving. In fact, I was a little afraid to see him, not because I thought there would be anything wrong with him, but because I thought that seeing him would make me miss him more.

Jane ran over to meet us when she saw us parking the truck in the little lot. Daddy said, "You didn't get all the rain?"

Mom laughed. "We got buckets. It drove us out."

"No rain," said Jane. "Just fog fog fog. Did I say fog?" She lowered her voice. "Our golfers don't allow that sort of weather disturbance around here."

We all smiled. It was fun to see Jane.

The horse, True Blue, was in the nicest part of the barn, and he was standing in his stall, looking out over the door toward the rings with his ears pricked. He saw Jane right away and tossed his head. She said, "He's such a sweetheart. Listen to this."

We must have been about fifty feet from the stall still; she called out, "Blue! Blue! How are you?" and he let out a tremendous whinny. She said, "He always answers."

"He's a poet and don't know it," said Mom.

4

"Absolutely," said Jane.

By this time, we were at his stall, and I let him sniff my hand, which he did, then I started petting him down the neck. He liked it. But he wasn't spoiled, because he didn't all at once start looking for treats the way some horses do.

"How old is he?" said Daddy.

"We think he's about seven. No tattoo, even though he looks like a Thoroughbred."

Since our adventure with our yearling, Jack, in the fall, I had learned more about Thoroughbreds, and one thing I'd learned was that they get tattoos when they are about to go in their first race, on the inside of the upper lip, so that you have to lift that up and read the letter and the numbers, which isn't always easy. But the tattoo lasts the horse's whole life, so every horse that races can be identified forever after. The letter comes first and tells what year the horse was born.

Daddy continued, "Doesn't the owner . . . didn't the owner . . ."

Jane shook her head.

I could see that there were things Daddy and Jane had talked about while I was changing my clothes. I said, "Did something happen to the owner?"

Mom and Daddy and Jane all glanced at one another the way grown-ups do when they think you are too young for something. Since Mom was now shorter than I was, if only by half an inch, I thought this was silly, but instead of rolling my eyes or scowling, the way Stella and Gloria did, I just kept petting True Blue, and right then, he looked me in the eye. Horses do that, and when they do, it makes you feel like they are seeing something that you didn't realize was there. Finally, Jane said, "Well, yes, Abby. It was very sad. Not long after she got here with Blue, maybe five weeks? She got into a car crash and was killed. No one else was, thank goodness. It was a one-car accident."

"Very tricky road for newcomers," said Mom. "Down the coast."

"They say she was swerving to avoid a deer. I don't know. . . ." They shook their heads, and I could tell that was all I was going to hear about it. "Anyway," said Jane. "Her name was Mary Carson, and she was from Cleveland, Ohio, and she had made no friends here that I can tell, at least none who've come forward to claim the horse and pay the board. The Colonel has called all his Cleveland horse friends and no one there knows her, or knows where she was stabling him. My guess is that she could have been recently divorced and changed her name. Anyway, she wasn't terribly ambitious—she would get him out and take him on the trail every day or so. He seemed okay doing that, and he's lovely. Here, let me get him out."

She took the halter off the hook and slipped it over his head. He came out like a prince, his ears pricked, his neck arched, his feet stepping lightly, and his tail lifted, but not excited or nervous, or even full of himself. Like a prince was how he was. Mom and Daddy and I stared at him, then Daddy stepped forward and ran his hands along True Blue's spine and over his flanks, then down each of his legs. He was careful about this, feeling for swellings and warm spots. One of the things he always said was, "There's no such thing as a gift horse." And then he looked the gift horse in the mouth. Horses' teeth grow their whole lives, and they keep wearing them down by eating. Daddy said that if they had the right pasture, and they ate it all year, they would go from eating lovely sweet moist grass in the spring through tougher grass in the summer, right into gnawing old dead shoots in the fall, and their teeth would wear down in just the right way all their lives. Hay isn't as good for that.

At any rate, True Blue had a full mouth, which meant that all of his baby teeth were gone and all of his adult teeth were grown in, so he was at least a five-year-old. He also had canine teeth, which are little sharp teeth that stick down about an inch behind the front teeth. They aren't for anything, and usually only stallions and geldings have them. Canines meant that he was at least five. And if you looked at the biting surface of his lower teeth (which he allowed us to do without trying to get his head away), you could see that the indentations in the lower front teeth were worn away in the middle teeth but not in the two outer teeth. Daddy said, "I'd say seven. Not much older, if that."

Jane nodded. "He's healthy and in good shape. Trot him out. He's completely sound."

We took him out into the parking lot, and my job was to run and his job was to trot after me, going fairly fast. Lots of horses think this is an incredible waste of time, and so you have to cluck to them and pull them and get someone to move them out, but True Blue just came with me—away and back, away and back, with Daddy watching the way his feet hit the ground from the front, the side, and the rear.

Jane said, "He's a correct mover." She meant that his feet didn't go in any weird directions and his trot was even.

Daddy said, "Not very big, though." He meant that True Blue didn't have much lift, and that his steps weren't very large. Jack was our big mover—he sprang all over the pasture every chance he got, in a kind of show-offy way. Thinking about him made me smile, as always. He was thirteen months old now, and something of a handful.

Jane said, "We are full of lesson horses, and I don't have time to train him myself, but I hate to send such a beauty to the auctions. You never know where they'll end up."

She and Daddy stared at each other, but I knew there wasn't any disagreement, really. True Blue was a gorgeous horse with a perfect head and a big, kind eye. The only thing holding Daddy back was that superstition about gift horses. I put my hand in my pocket. There was a dollar there, along with some coins. I took my hand out of my pocket and held it toward Jane. She held out her hand, and I dropped the money into it. Turned out the dollar was a five-dollar bill, and the coins were two quarters and a dime. Jane looked at the money, then smiled. She said, "Well, Miss Abby, you beat out the other bidder and now you've got yourself a horse."

Mom stepped up to him and patted him and said, "He seems very sweet." Daddy pretended to be scowling. Then he said, "I'll give you ten," and Jane laughed and said, "Sorry, sir, the bidding has closed." I still had True Blue's rope in my hand, so I led him over to a patch of grass and let him graze. I could see Daddy and Jane keep talking. I petted Blue again, this time along his shoulder and flanks. I knew we were playing a game, and that Daddy would have taken Blue—he was sound and nice and no reason not to—but even so, I felt like I had bought myself a horse, and it was a wonderfully scary feeling.

Blue cropped the grass in a leisurely way, and then Daddy waved me over. Jane took the rope. She said, "Actually, the horse has six more days on his boarding contract, so you don't have to pick him up right away."

Daddy said, "No reason to keep him here. I'll come back Monday. Abby will owe me five cents a mile."

That's why there are no gift horses.

Jane put him in his stall, and we started to walk away. When we had gone about thirty feet, I turned around and called out, "Blue, Blue, how are you?" And my new horse lifted his head and whinnied loud and clear.

It was late when we got home—time for Mom to make supper and for Daddy and me to feed the horses and put things away. The sky was clear, but everything was still pretty wet. Happy, Jefferson, and Jack were covered with mud—they had gone to a puddle and rolled around. But Lincoln, Sprinkles, and two horses we had gotten from Oklahoma over Christmas, Amazon, a big chestnut mare, and Foxy, a large bay pony mare, were completely clean, except for mud up to their ankles. And I had to oil my saddle because it had gotten caught in the rain, so that took me twenty minutes. While dinner was cooking, I had to clean my boots and oil them. Winter is a lot of work!

After supper, I did my homework. We had just started reading a book in French called *Le Petit Prince*. I was now on page two: *Les grandes personnes m'ont conseillé de laisser de côté les dessins de serpents boas ouverts ou fermés, et de m'intéresser plutôt à la géographie, à l'histoire, au calcul, et à la grammaire.* I translated this as "The grown-ups told me to leave the boa constrictors alone and pay more attention to Miss Geography, Miss History, Mr. Calculations, and Miss Grammar." I always called nouns "Miss" or "Mr." so that I would remember if they were masculine or feminine, because you couldn't tell just by what they seemed like. I was getting a B in French. It was okay. In algebra, we were doing a lot of square roots, such as does the square root of 49 divided by the square root of 64 equal the square root of 49 divided by 64? I thought about this and decided, well, why not? So I put yes. I actually had a harder time with the problem about whether or not the square root of 7 squared equaled 7. I thought it surely did, but then I thought I was being tricked, so I sat there for a while before I wrote my answer. In science, we had just had a test, so no homework, and in English, we were reading *The Adventures of Tom Sawyer*. They were painting a fence. Things weren't great for Tom, but he had a much nicer life than that boy Pip, in *Great Expectations*.

I took a bath and thought about my new horse, True Blue, and Miss Geography and her friend Miss Grammar just seemed to float away into the mist.

Truck and Horse Trailer

Bedded Stall

Chapter 2

On the way to church the next morning, Daddy asked me
what I was going to name the new horse.

"He's got a name."

Daddy shook his head. "We never keep their names."

"Why not?"

"Clean break, fresh start."

It was true, though I'd never thought of it before. It had always seemed to me that the horses we got from Oklahoma had
never even had names, but of course they had—Jack's dam was
named Alabama Lady, even though we'd called her Brown
Jewel (and even though I'd called her Pearl in my own mind).

Daddy said, "At some sale barns, the horses don't even
have names. They have numbers. Same at that Thoroughbred

auction they have in New York. It's very rare for the yearling to have a name."

Mom said, "What would you name him, Mark?"

"Oh, George."

"Ha!" I said.

Mom said, "How about Misty?"

I said, "That's a girl's name."

"Cloudy? Stormy? Foggy?"

I made a face.

Daddy said, "Spot."

"Spot! As in 'See Spot run'?"

"Well, he is dappled. Nicely dappled."

"Dap?" said Mom.

It was oh-so-tempting to roll my eyes. But I made myself not do it. Daddy hated sass and because of our conversation about the names, he was looking for it. But really, eye-rolling was contagious. First Stella had been doing it, and I knew she did it at home, because I'd seen her do it as soon as she got into the car when her mom picked her up. Her mom said one thing, maybe one word, and Stella's eyes started to roll. And then Gloria started it, though my guess was she was careful at home, especially with her dad. I must have sighed, though. Finally, I said, sweetly, I hoped, "What's wrong with Blue? And anyway, he knows it and answers to it."

When we pulled into one of the spots left in the parking lot in front of our church, Mom said, "Oh, there's Mrs. Lodge and Mrs. Nicks. They can hardly get themselves out of their car." She threw open the door of the truck and ran over to help them. Daddy and I carried in the pans of baked beans and fried

14

chicken. The great thing about Mom was that when she was helping these old ladies, she made it seem like she was just happy to see them and wanted to hear all about what they'd been doing since Wednesday night. Then, "Oh, watch that curb, Mrs. Lodge! So your granddaughter is in high school now! I had no idea. I'm glad she sent you those pictures!" She got the ladies into the church and settled into chairs without any mishaps or any complaints, either, for that matter. The long table where we arranged the food was already set up, with a stack of plates and another stack of napkins. I peeked at the two dishes that were covered by cloths—macaroni and cheese and green beans with some bacon, it looked like. Everything was so hot now, and wrapped in dish towels and cloth napkins, that after the first service, it would still be warm and nice to eat on a winter's day.

Within what seemed like a minute or two, everyone in our congregation was there—twenty-seven now. There were the three of us, the five Hollingsworths, the five Greeleys, Mr. and Mrs. Hazen, Mrs. Lodge and Mrs. Nicks, of course, plus Mrs. Larkin, who taught the kids Sunday school in the afternoon. Mr. Larrabee and his two sisters, Ethelyn and Marian, who were almost as old as Mrs. Larkin, but had never gotten married, so everyone called them by their first names. Mr. and Mrs. Brooks brought Mrs. Brooks's brother Ezra, who sat in the back and never said anything. He was the thinnest man I ever saw, and he wouldn't touch any of the food unless there were cookies. Sometimes he even read a book during the service, and no one said a word about it. Then, of course, there was Mr. McCracken, who came by himself, and lived by himself. The only time he ever looked happy was when he was singing, but he did a lot of preaching, too. Today, another couple named Mr. and Mrs. Good had also come. We hadn't seen them since before Christmas. Mrs. Good had a chocolate cake with her, and she put it on the table.

Mrs. Larkin said, "Oh, Sister Good, that looks wonderful," and everyone smiled, even Ezra.

It was Daddy's turn to start the preaching, so after we were all sitting down and the door was closed and the blinds pulled down, Daddy stood up next to me and let his Bible fall open. He put his hand on the page for a moment and looked at it, then said, "'Do not be like your fathers and brothers, who were unfaithful to the Lord, the God of their fathers, so that he made them the object of horror. Do not be stiff-necked, as your fathers were.'"

Daddy did it this way every time. I could tell that Mr. Hazen and Mr. Hollingsworth, and maybe Mr. Greeley peeked into their Bibles ahead of time, and marked the page they were going to open to, so that at least they sort of knew what they were going to talk about. Mr. McCracken was so old and had been doing this for so long that he could pretty much tell his Bible to open where he wanted it to, but with Daddy it was like cutting a deck of cards—whatever card came up, he had to make something of it. For instance, just the week before, he had read out, "'You who ride on white donkeys, sitting on your saddle blankets, and you who walk along the road, consider the voice of the singers at the watering places. They recite the righteous acts of the Lord.'" It was easy to see in your mind what was going on in that passage, but it was hard for Daddy to make much of a lesson out of it.

He cleared his throat and settled himself and said, "I look around me here, at my brothers and sisters, and I feel my heart swelling in gratitude for such good and faithful friends in the Lord."

We all said, "Amen."

"I am especially thankful to see Bob and Sally Good, and their chocolate cake, of course."

We all laughed. Out of the corner of my eye, I saw Brad Greeley, who was three by now, jump out of his chair, but his mom grabbed his elbow before he could run.

"The garden of the Lord is open to everyone equally, no matter when they enter or how often they return. That may seem unfair to the children of the Lord, but how could it be any different, and still be truly holy? The Lord must be merciful. He can't be any other way. When one of his lambs comes to the door and asks humbly to enter, that lamb will be allowed to enter. And we are grateful for that. But our subject today, shown to us by the Lord himself, as he guides us to ponder his word—"

Brad Greeley was sitting in Mrs. Greeley's lap. I could see him fold up and start to slide backward. He got halfway out before she realized what he was doing. She straightened him up again.

"—is not those who ask to enter but those who refuse to enter. Who have turned their backs on the Lord and headed in the other direction. What are we asked to do with them?"

One thing I knew was that those who had turned their backs and headed in the other direction included almost everyone we knew, from my brother, Danny, who no longer went to church at all (because ever since Daddy and he had a big fight

17

over dinner one night and he walked out, he almost never came back, except when he was assisting our horseshoer, Jake Morrisson); to my uncle Luke, who sometimes went to a regular Methodist church back in Oklahoma, but not very often; to my mom's parents, also back in Oklahoma, who have been Baptists since before the Revolutionary War, so they aren't going to change anytime soon. In fact, you could be driving to church on a Sunday, talking about naming your new horse, and you could look out the window, and every car you saw driving on the other side of the road or turning off onto another road or stopping at the store, not to mention turning into the parking lot of another church, like a Catholic church, was carrying people who were turning their backs on the Lord and heading in another direction. Mom said that it wasn't their fault if they didn't know the truth, and Daddy kept his mouth shut when she said this, but I knew that he thought that it was their fault, at least if they were related to us.

Brad Greeley pushed off and jumped forward, right out of his mother's arms, but his dad was ready for him, and caught him about one second after his feet hit the floor. Daddy stopped talking and looked in the Greeleys' direction. I looked at Carlie Hollingsworth, who was my age and usually helped me with the Greeleys, but she was looking at her own feet. As far as Brad was concerned, her eyes were closed and she had her hands over her face. Mom, who was next to me on the other side from Daddy, gave me a little nod. I slipped past her, and went to the end of the room where there were a few toys. I picked up a Slinky train and a jack-in-the-box and waved them at Brad. Mr. Greeley let go of him, and he ran over to me. I knelt down and said, "Hey, Brad, let's take some toys outside and play with them." He nodded and put his hand in mine. I gave him a toy truck to carry in the other hand. If worse came to worst, I knew I could take him down past Longs, which was in the same mall as our church. There was a store that was closed on Sunday; he could run back and forth there. It was fine with me not to listen to Daddy talk about Danny without letting on that he was talking about Danny. I didn't want to hear about the punishments.

It was cloudy but warm outside. We played with the Slinky train on the curb for a minute or two, then popped the jack-in-the-box three times. Then I showed Brad the book I'd picked up, *The 500 Hats of Bartholomew Cubbins*, but Brad stood up and ran down toward Longs by the time I got to page three. I ran after him. I was glad I'd put the other toys inside the door of the church before I'd started reading the book. I caught Brad just by the door of Longs and decided to take him in there. I didn't have any money, but I thought we could at least go to the toy aisle and look at things.

Since it was Sunday morning and not raining (in fact, the sky had cleared in the time since we got to church), Longs wasn't very crowded—two checkers talking, a couple of people in the card aisle, a girl in the shampoo aisle, and someone stocking the makeup aisle. The toys were in the back, kind of in a corner. I picked up Brad and carried him there. He was a wiggler, so I kept saying, "Hey! Let's go look at the toys! Let's see what they've got!" At least he didn't scream. That was always the thing you worried about with a Greeley kid—if the kid had suddenly had enough, he or she (there were the two boys and Annie, who was two now) would let out a piercing roar of rage until you let him or her go. Daddy thought that Mr. and Mrs. Greeley were "allowing those kids to get away with murder," but I knew them better—I thought they were just born tough, fast, and single-minded.

One of the toy shelves was at Brad's level, and as soon as I put him down, he began reaching for the Buzzy Bee and the Snoopy Sniffer. On the higher shelves there was the usual stuff—Silly Putty, more kinds of Slinkys, Play-Doh sets, boxes of Crayolas and coloring books, and books of paper dolls. I looked for a minute at the dolls—I had one doll, a Raggedy Ann. I had never liked dolls much, preferring stuffed animals, but Gloria had lots of dolls, everything from Betsy Wetsy and Shirley Temple to Poor Pitiful Pearl, and about seven Barbies, along with a drawerful of clothes and one single Ken. I picked up a Barbie box and showed it to Brad, but he didn't even look at it. Good, I thought. He pointed to the Barbie car box, and I set that down beside him. It didn't look like he could get into it. There was one Barbie I had never seen before—Color Magic Barbie. You could brush something onto her hair and even her clothes, and they would change color. I took this box off the shelf and looked at it. Then I saw the Tressy doll—the reason she had such a weird name was that you could make her hair grow by pressing a button. I was trying to figure out how long you could make it grow by looking at the pictures on the package when I looked around and saw that Brad was gone. There were two Slinkys and the Barbie car and the Buzzy Bee sitting there in the middle of the aisle, but Brad was not playing with them.

You read in books about how it feels when something horrible happens, and it's always "My heart sank," or "My hair stood on end," or "I couldn't believe my eyes," but it was different from that. It was that it took me about six hours to lift my eyes from the toys and look down the aisle, and then it took another six hours for me to open my mouth and call, "BBBBrrrrraaaaaadddddd!" in what sounded like a moo. Then I felt both silly and terrified running down the aisle—almost silly enough to stop running and almost terrified enough to scream, but too silly to scream, and too terrified to stop running.

I came to the cross-aisle and looked all the way to the end of the store. No Brad, no one. At this point, I decided to trot down the cross-aisle, looking both ways down each aisle to see where he might be, so I did this. No Brad. I got all the way to the end, to hair dyes, and turned right, toward the front of the store, thinking he would be okay if he didn't get out the door. As a Greeley, he would have a nose for the door, and head there first. And then, of course, across the walk, down the curb, and out into the parking lot. I started to run.

The two checkers were still talking. I stopped and said, "Did you see a kid? Three years old, dark hair—?"

"Nope," said one, as if it weren't her business, but the other one, who was older, said, "You missing a kid? Where was he?"

She followed me past cameras toward the toy aisle. But he still wasn't there. Then we split up. I came to the wall and went left, toward the front, and she went right, along the potato chips toward the back. When I was almost to the front door, and really panicking—I would have been crying in about two seconds—the front door opened, and a woman came in with Brad in her arms. He was wiggling.

I said, "Oh, Brad!"

She said, "This one yours?"

"He is! He got outside?"

"Well, apparently, when I left the store, he was right on my heels, and then, when I stopped to look both ways before stepping into the parking lot, he took hold of my skirt. I've never been so surprised in my life as I was when I looked down and I had a kid looking up at me."

"I can't believe I lost him." But he was a Greeley. I could believe it.

"Well, I can't believe I let him out the door without realizing it. He could never have pushed it open himself."

Now my heart was pounding. Yes, it was. Brad struggled, so the lady put him down. I picked him up. He stared at me, opened his mouth. I put my finger in front of his face and said, "Don't you dare scream, you naughty boy!" and for those two seconds, he did not scream.

The screaming started outside Longs as I was carrying him back to church. He just put his hands on my chest and reared back, and opened his mouth and bellowed. It was like holding springs, because the whole time he screamed, he was throwing himself around trying to get down.

By the time we got to the church, I was just beginning to wonder what to do, but the door opened and there was Mrs. Greeley. She held out her arms, and I handed him over, but that was hard, too, because I didn't want to drop him. She smiled at me and said, "Oh, thank you, Abby, for taking him. I'll watch him now. Bob is preaching, but he'll soon be finished. I was glad to hear your dad—he had some interesting things

22

to say, and, of course, Brother Abner is a wonderfully wise man, so it's always worth hearing what he has to say." Abner was Mr. McCracken. This whole time while she was smiling and chatting, Brad was flapping his arms and kicking his legs. But she just held him as if it was no big deal, even when he whacked her in the eye (I think by mistake). She said, "Ouch," but not a word to him. She said, "Go on inside. They're almost done, and you don't want to miss everything."

I went inside. Mr. Hazen was on his feet, talking about Zachariah and John the Baptist, who was his son. I was exhausted, and sat down in my chair and closed my eyes. For a minute or two, I could still hear the screaming outside, and then it stopped. By the time Mr. Hazen was finished, Mrs. Greeley came in with Brad and sat down. Then we sang "Farther Along," and, of course, "Amazing Grace," and also "When My Name Is Called Up Yonder." Then we were finished for the morning, and we got up. Everyone stretched. Some of the brothers and sisters headed outside to the restrooms. Mom and Mrs. Larkin went over to the table and began to unwrap the dishes of food. I was hungry.

I have to say that while we were taking our plates, and Mrs. Lodge was getting out the silverware and then we were lining up to help ourselves (Mom's fried chicken looked really good, and so did that chocolate cake), Brad just stood there with his spoon in his hand, looking very cute, and completely as if he had been a well-behaved boy all morning long. I helped myself to a small chicken breast and some green beans, and I was just looking into a dish I hadn't seen before, au gratin potatoes, when I heard Ben Greeley, who was five, say, "What's that?"

and then Mr. Greeley said, "What is that?" I put the spoon back into the potatoes and looked over. Brad had a tiny little truck in his hand, a Matchbox truck, not the one I had given him when we left, which was over in a box inside the door.

Brad held the truck out, and Ben grabbed it. Mr. Greeley said, "Where did that come from?"

Daddy looked at me. I said, "I don't know."

Of course I knew that it came from Longs. Later, when Daddy said that I had not "lied," but that I had been "evasive," he didn't understand that what I was thinking of when I said that was that I hadn't given Brad any of the Matchbox cars, and I hadn't seen any of them on the lower shelves, only on the upper shelves, so how did he get that? That was all I meant. But everyone looked at me.

Mom said, "What were you kids doing?"

"We just went over to Longs. We were looking at the toys."

"You didn't realize he had that?"

Mrs. Greeley said, "I'm sure he put it in his pocket. He loves to do that. It's very small. I'll take him over there and pay for it."

It was when she came back, after talking to the older lady who was at the checkout counter, that everything about our trip to Longs came out. I guess the lady said how scared she was, especially when she saw that "perfect stranger" bringing him in the door, and she was so glad that he was all right, because that could be a very busy parking lot out there, and maybe the "little girl" who was in charge of him should be "given a bit of a talking-to." And so I was. It took most of lunch, and I had to apologize for letting Brad out of my sight, and Mom and Daddy were disappointed in me for being irresponsible AND evasive. Mr. and Mrs. Greeley weren't saying anything against me, but they weren't smiling, either, and the only people I could see who weren't shaking their heads at the whole thing were Brother McCracken, who always expected the worst anyway, and Brother Ezra, who never said anything. In the afternoon, there were several prayers of thanks that Brad had been saved by the mercy of the Lord from injury and possibly worse.

On the way home, Mom had her hand on my knee, but she didn't say anything.

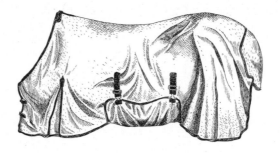

Fly Sheet

Rain Sheet

Chapter 3

I WAS STILL PRETTY UPSET ABOUT BRAD ON MONDAY MORNING. I was used to being the good girl of church, and having my head patted every time I turned around, so it was pretty shocking to be the one who was responsible for things that might have happened that no one even dared to name. So, I was glad to get to school, and even to sit in French class and have the teacher give us another page of *Le Petit Prince*, which we had to struggle through right there and then. My sentence was *C'était pour moi une question de vie ou de mort.* When it was my turn, I said, "This was for me a question of the life or the death."

"Of life or death," said Madame. "You should make it idiomatic."

In the back row, Bret Hatton said, "You should make it idiotic."

Madame ignored him, but a couple of kids laughed.

For physical education, we were now just starting tennis. The courts outside were still damp, but we were in the gym with our rackets and our balls, practicing bouncing them, first on the floor, then upward, then, in groups of five, against the walls of the gym, which had a line painted all along two walls that was the height of a tennis net. Barbie Goldman was in my class. Her twin sister, Alexis, was still taking volleyball. For some reason, Barbie did not like volleyball, and when she was told she had to keep taking it, she tried what she called "civil disobedience," which involved letting the ball drop all around her, and even hit her in the head. This made Alexis laugh so much that the teacher gave up and put Barbie into tennis.

Barbie had become my slightly better friend than Alexis, though Alexis was completely nice, too. I could tell them apart all the time now. For one thing, Barbie was left-handed, and for another, her eyes were shaped a little differently. But it was also true that they were just themselves. Once you got to know them, they were themselves.

As soon as she saw me, Barbie came over, and we stood in our places in the row of ball bouncers, bouncing our balls on our rackets, trying to hit the sweet spot and trying not to let the balls get away. The tennis teacher, "Mr." Tyler, who was really not much older than a high school kid and still had acne, was bouncing his ball on the rim of his racket. He didn't have that kind of control over the class, but he was nice, and even though we almost always talked, no one ever just walked out. Or not very often.

Barbie said, "So guess what."

"What?"

"My mom said that if you would agree to give me some riding lessons, she's happy to bring me over."

"You want riding lessons?" I didn't think I had ever heard the word *horse* come out of Barbie's mouth.

"They had *My Friend Flicka* on the late-night movie Friday night. I thought, 'Well, that's what Abby does all day.' It looked like fun."

"It is fun. But I never taught anyone to ride before. If you go out to the coast, there's a great stable where they teach people all the time. I have a friend there."

"Oh, I know that place. Dad plays golf there about once a year. But I want to ride western. And I want you to teach me."

"You girls! Barbara G.!" This was "Mr." Tyler, who had noticed that our balls were no longer bouncing. Barbie balanced her ball in the middle of her racket, then popped it up about two inches, then three.

I did the same thing, which made it hard to say, "What. About. Alex. Is."

"She's. Not. Inter. Ested."

We laughed. "Mr." Tyler gave us a look.

Barbie said, "I'll call you tonight." Then we had to go to our assigned places on the wall and hit above the line twenty-five times.

I didn't go home from school on the bus—I went out to the road that runs in front of the school and I waited for Daddy, who pulled up in the truck and trailer. We were going to pick up True Blue. As I got into my side of the truck, I glanced at

Daddy's face to see if he was still mad at me about Brad Greeley, but he didn't look it—he looked normal. As soon as I got in, he said, "We will just SLLIIDDE out of here as quick as we can to try to avoid all these buses and carpools." We drove along. I was still thinking about Brad, but I decided that if Daddy wasn't going to bring it up, why should I?

The day was rather dull—not bright and not gloomy, not cool and not warm. I took off my nice new sweater that I had bought before Christmas and put on an old jacket, then I took off my loafers and put on some jeans under my skirt. Then I took off my skirt and put on my boots. Then I folded all my good clothes and put them in a paper bag that Mom set on top of my riding clothes. I was ready for my new horse. We pulled into the stable courtyard ten minutes later.

Monday was not a big day at the stable—no lessons were given, and half the grooms got a day off. Usually, even Colonel Hawkins wasn't there. Jane was more or less in charge, and I found her in the main office, doing some paperwork. Daddy was opening the trailer—he wanted to get Blue home and settled in before dark, so he was trying to be efficient.

Jane and I went over to the section where my new horse was stabled. He was standing there, just the way I remembered him, with his chest pressed against the bottom half of the stall door and his eye out for everything. Some horses are like that, always surveying the horizon. Others always have their heads down, looking for bits of hay or grass. She didn't call to him, but he whinnied anyway, and she pulled a carrot out of her pocket.

She said, "I'm going to miss him."

I said, "I thought he's only been here for a couple of months."

"He has, and I've never even ridden him. But you notice we put him right here, in one of the prime spots. That's because he's so beautiful, and that's what I'm going to miss—just having a look at him every time I walk by. You're a good boy, aren't you, Blue?"

He nickered and she gave him the carrot.

It was then that I noticed all the things by his stall door. They were all blue.

Jane said, "And he has more stuff than any horse I've ever seen, and everything has his name on it." She opened one of the two navy-blue trunks. "Here's his rain sheet. Here's his fly sheet. Here's his winter blanket from back east; that's much too hot for around here. Here's his summer sheet from back east. Here's his bridle. See the tiny brass tag, 'TB'? His saddle is in that trunk. It's a Barnsby. Nice saddle. Also three sheepskin pads. Two sets of blue flannel bandages and some cotton sheets. A spare halter with a brass plate, two spare lead ropes. Never saw a horse with so much stuff. And the lady drove an old Ford, nothing fancy. My guess is that she spent all her money on this guy."

I petted Blue on the neck and ran my fingers around his eyes. Daddy had finished getting the trailer ready, and I could see him heading our way. I kept petting Blue, and when Daddy got to us, I said, "All of this stuff is ours, too. Blankets and saddle. Everything."

"You're kidding."

Daddy opened the second trunk and lifted out a very nice saddle. Underneath it was a pair of boots—black, tall boots. Jane said, "Oh, I forgot about those. I only saw her wear them once. I guess I thought she kept them at home."

31

Daddy set down the saddle on blankets that were folded on the first trunk and took one of the boots. He looked inside the top, then said, "These are, what is that, Dehner boots."

"Goodness," said Jane. "Custom-made. Dehner is in Omaha. Those are seventy-dollar boots."

We stared at the boots. It was one thing to take a woman's horse because there was no one else to take care of it, but I thought it was creepy that the horse didn't come in just a halter like all our other horses, stripped and ready for a new life. Daddy looked in the trunk again. He said, "Boot hooks. Some brushes."

Jane said, "My parents bought a lake house when I was a kid, up in New Hampshire. The people who sold it to us walked away without taking a thing. They didn't even throw away the old whiskey bottles or the half-smoked packets of cigarettes. It was like we were visiting there. It never did feel like our place."

Daddy said, "I've bought plenty of used equipment. . . ." But his voice trailed off. Then Blue whinnied, as if to say, "Look at me, I'm the main event here." And he was. He was beautiful and healthy and he needed a home. Jane said, "If you don't take it, it will just gather dust in that storeroom."

Daddy shrugged. He put the boots and the saddle back in the tack trunk and said, "Got a dolly?"

Jane nodded.

While they loaded Blue's belongings into the bed of the pickup, I got him out of his stall and let him eat grass at the edge of the parking lot. I petted him and said his name, and from time to time, he looked at me and flicked his ears. For some reason, all the stuff didn't seem like a bonus—it seemed like a reminder that there's no such thing as a free horse.

But Blue performed his first task kindly—he paused and sniffed the trailer before he got in, but then he got in, and didn't seem to worry when we lifted the ramp. You never know with a new horse if he's been properly trained to load or if he's been given some reason to worry in there. We drove home. My horse passed his first test. Or, that's what Daddy said. He said, "Well, your horse passed his first test." This made me uncomfortable. I did not want to think of Blue as my horse now that he had all this stuff. Somehow, he seemed like too big a responsibility if all of his blankets were embroidered with his name.

It wasn't that late when we got home, but late enough, with the cloudy weather, to be a little dusky and mysterious. When I backed Blue out of the trailer, he was much more nervous than he had been. His head was up, and his ears were as far forward as they could be. His neck was arched, and his tail was lifted, and I didn't have to touch him as he swept around me to see that he was tense from front to back. He stared at the mares, whose pasture was closer to the road, and whinnied something that sounded a little like a scream. Amazon and Happy answered him right away—I was sure Amazon was saying, "Who are you?" and Happy was saying, "Who do you think you are?" Then he whinnied again, and the geldings all came to the fence and stared at him. His ears went, if possible, more forward, and two of the geldings whinnied, Jefferson, who now saw himself as the pasture boss, and one of the others, I couldn't tell who. And Jack had something to say, too.

Daddy came over and took Blue's lead rope out of my hand and said, "Let's put him in the pen for a few minutes. He seems a little worked up."

He took him over to the training corral and opened the

gate. Blue swished through and barely gave Daddy a chance to unsnap the rope. After Daddy got out of there and closed the gate, he started whinnying and running from one side of the pen to the other, which got the other horses worked up, too, until we gave everyone their hay, which they were waiting for anyway. I also, of course, gave Blue his hay, and he put his nose down to it. I thought he was going to eat, but he only took a little bite before trotting away from it, across the pen again. Then he came back, and trotted right through the hay, scattering it, as though he didn't really care about it. By now the other horses were eating, and no one was whinnying, but Blue couldn't stop staring at them.

Daddy and I put his stuff away. We didn't empty the trunks, but we took them into the tack room in the barn and we hung up and stacked away the extra things that weren't in the trunks. I didn't open either trunk, but I thought again about those boots. When we came out of the barn, Blue was still trotting back and forth, and he was in something of a sweat.

Daddy shook his head. "Best to go inside and let him settle down on his own. They always do. Maybe he needs to stay out all night. Sometimes they prefer the close quarters of a bedded stall and sometimes that makes it worse. I don't know." He looked at me. "We'll pray about it. But he'll be all right."

The bad thing, I thought, was that Blue wasn't rearing and kicking up, or even bucking. Those things show at least a little playfulness. But just running back and forth—that isn't playful at all.

My ears were open all through supper, and I could hear both the hoofbeats and the whinnies—there got to be fewer of the whinnies, then, after a while, fewer of the hoofbeats. I went out when we were finished and gave him another flake of hay, since he had scattered what I'd given him before. After I threw the hay over the fence, I stood there for a while, hoping that he would come up to me and let me pet him, but when he did, he turned away almost before I could touch him. I talked to him anyway. "Hey, Blue. Hey, Blue. You are such a beauty. This is a nice place. Look at the others. Everyone is just eating or walking around. Look at Amazon. She's lying down taking a nap. Do you think if anything were really going on, Amazon would be taking a nap? Here comes our dog, Rusty. Hi, Rusty. Rusty watches for all kinds of things, including empty water troughs. Did you ever hear of that before? Last fall, we went away, and when we came back, it was Rusty who took me to the tipped-over water trough. See? You'll like it here. In a day or so, you can go out with the other geldings and be in a herd. Every horse likes to be in a herd." He wasn't moving around as much as before, but even when he was eating, his head kept popping up and looking here and there. Every little noise or movement attracted his attention.

And yes, I knew he would settle down. But this was a horse Daddy would not have chosen if he'd found him at By Golly Horse Sales, back in Oklahoma, where he went to look for horses to bring to California. He would have noticed his nerviness and passed him over, and that was why we didn't have much experience with this sort of horse. The other thing was that even though I knew the horse would settle down in a day or two—after all, he had been perfectly calm out at the stable— it was like his worries got into me. Everything was all right around the place. I mean, Rusty was just sitting on my left foot, letting me pet her, as relaxed as she could be, and Rusty's entire life's work was keeping an eye out. Happy, in the mare pasture, was dozing on her feet, and Happy always had her eye out, too. But the weird thing is that everything you know doesn't always stop you from having feelings. You get this prickly tension in your stomach or your shoulders, and then your mind, which was just a minute ago thinking about *Le Petit Prince* and the Oregon Trail, starts thinking, Well, what if there is something up on the hill? or, What if he runs so fast that he breaks the fence? or, What if he jumps out? or, What if he's always like this, and Jane Slater just gave him some sort of shot to calm him down long enough to get us to take him?

With that thought, I couldn't watch him anymore, and I walked around the barn and over to the gelding pasture. Rusty followed me. Jefferson and Lincoln were standing under the tree—hardly visible in the dark—but Jack came over to me right away. He was quite big now, and since we had done the string test right around his one-year birthday, we knew that he was going to get as big as Amazon, or bigger, maybe seventeen hands.

A "hand," as I had told the kids when I did my English report "The Language of Horses," is four inches, and horses are measured in "hands." I guess someone's real hand could be four inches wide, and you could estimate a horse's size if you bent down and moved your two hands upward along his leg, then his shoulder, to his withers, which is the topmost point, where the neck comes into the body. A horse is never five foot four; he is sixteen hands. I was five foot four now—the top of my head would be even with the top of the withers of a sixteen-hand horse. Five four isn't tall for a person, but sixteen hands is tall for a horse and seventeen hands—five foot eight—is very tall. That means that the bottom of his chest is about at my waist and I have to reach way up to put my hands on the saddle just to mount from the ground. Daddy, who was almost six feet, liked for a horse's withers to be about even with his collarbone. That meant he could mount easily no matter what, and also that the horse would be compact and athletic.

The string test was something I'd never seen before, because we'd never had a yearling before. It was simple. What you did was take a piece of string in your two hands, and set one hand against the yearling's fetlock (another word I told my class about—this is the joint at the bottom of the horse's leg where the leg makes an angle toward the hoof) and one against his elbow, which is right at the top of the foreleg next to the chest. Then you pivot the first hand around the second hand, and hold the length of string straight up. Where your top hand is (the hand that started out touching the fetlock) is where the withers of the horse will be when the horse is full grown. This is because a horse's legs are longer when he's born (so that he can keep up with his mother and the herd) and the body has to grow to catch up with the legs. When the string test showed that Jack was going to be seventeen hands, Daddy was not happy. As far as he was concerned, a seventeen-hand horse costs more to feed and takes more time to care for than a nice fifteen-and-a-half-hand horse and would not be nearly as useful. But I had noticed when we were showing Black George, before he got sold to Sophia Rosebury, that a lot of those jumpers and hunters were big, so I had already made up my mind that Jack was not going to be a cow horse, so he could be seventeen hands if he wanted to.

But here was the funny thing. Right after we did the string test and were talking about Jack being seventeen hands, we did a little geometry unit at school, and I saw why a seventeen-hand horse is so much bigger than a fifteen-hand horse—he's got lots more volume. He's one-sixth taller, but he's really one-third bigger. When I did an extra-credit problem likening horses to spheres, my math teacher gave me an A.

Jack looked in my hands for a treat, which really is not good manners. According to Daddy, horses are supposed to never know that you could have a treat, and to act like a treat couldn't possibly come their way, and keep their noses to themselves. But with Jack, I just opened my hands and let him sniff them and learn for himself that there was nothing there. Once in a while, he also licked them, but tonight he didn't do that. He stood next to the fence while I scratched his forehead, then smoothed down his forelock, then petted his neck and ears. Horses like petting, but not as much as dogs do—even a youngster like Jack, who was used to being brushed and rubbed with the chamois, soon got bored with mere hands. He put his nose over the fence and sniffed my hair, then looked over at Blue, who suddenly started trotting back and forth again. I said, "You are not going to be nervous like that, are you? No, you're not. Because we are going to raise you to be a good boy." Jack snorted, which I took as a "yes." Rusty, who had walked out toward the end of the fence line, now walked back toward me, yawning. Then she gave a little bark, and Jack gave another little snort, and I laughed. When Rusty first started hanging around, she had actually chased Jack down most of the length of the pasture—we never figured out if she was playing or attacking. But now she and Jack sometimes trotted around the pasture together, so whatever she had been doing that first time, now she was playing, or at least Jack thought she was.

I said, "Yes, Rusty. Time to go in."

I walked past Blue's pen without trying to talk to him again.

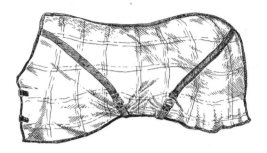

Winter Blanket

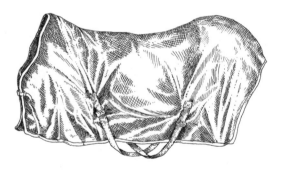

Summer Sheet

Chapter 4

WHEN I GOT INTO THE HOUSE, MOM WAS JUST GETTING OFF THE phone. She said, "Well, we've never done that before, but we'll talk about it. I'll let you know. That could be fun. We'll see. Byyye." The "bye" sounded extra long, as if she didn't know the person on the other end of the line very well. When she saw me, she said, "Guess who that was?"

"I don't know."

"Mrs. Goldman. Barbara wants to take riding lessons."

"She told me that."

"Is she serious?"

"Well." I thought for a moment. "She's never serious, but she's always serious. I mean, she loves to make people laugh, but she never says she wants to do something and doesn't mean it." I told her about the volleyball.

"It's such a responsibility," said Mom. "And Jane would be happy to teach her."

"I guess she doesn't want to go all the way out there."

"Does she always get what she wants?"

I thought about this for a moment, then nodded.

Mom grinned and said, "Well, maybe she should meet your dad."

"Maybe he should meet her."

Mom gave me a little squeeze.

I was about to go upstairs to do my homework, which was just some reading for social studies and a chapter of *Tom Sawyer*, when Daddy beckoned me into his study. He pointed to the Bible on his desk and said, "The Lord will provide."

I stood there for a moment, then walked over to the desk and flipped open the Book. Daddy said, "Read where your eye falls."

I said, "'The righteous perish and no one ponders it in his heart; devout men are taken away and no one under—'"

Daddy said, "Try again. Isaiah is a little scary."

I flipped some pages. Daddy had his eyes closed. I tried really hard to focus on the first word I saw, which was O. I paused for a moment, then read, "'O unbelieving generation,' Jesus said, 'how long shall I stay with you? How long shall I put up with you? Bring the boy to me.'" I looked up.

Daddy's eyes were open now, and he looked happy. He said, "That line always made me laugh. I love it when Jesus gets fed up." He cleared his throat. "Anyway, I know you're nervous about the gray horse, Abby. I don't quite understand how this turned into such a big deal, either for him or for us—"

"It's all that stuff. I feel like he's . . . haunted or something."

"He's not haunted. He's just a nervous type."

"How did she die?"

"I don't—" But then he pursed his lips and said, "She had had too much to drink, and I guess she saw something, or thought she saw something, in the road, and swerved to avoid it."

"What did she hit?"

"A tree. Flipped the car."

"When did they find her?"

"Early in the morning."

"Why do people do that?"

"Do what?"

"Get drunk and then drive a car?"

"I don't know, Abby. But we didn't know her. We can pray for her soul to rest in peace, as we would for the soul of anyone. The world is full of people who die every minute, and we can pray for all their souls."

"I thought when I opened the one trunk that there was a smell."

"What kind of a smell?"

"Like a perfume. Not bad. But not horsey or sweaty."

"There may indeed have been a fragrance. I don't know. I didn't smell it."

"Do you think that there are such things as ghosts?"

"No, I do not."

"But . . ." In fact, I hadn't thought about there being a ghost, or ghosts at all, before we started talking, and when I smelled that fragrance, I had noticed it, but I didn't think anything of it. Barns are full of fragrances—hay, straw, tack, the scent of

43

flowers floating in from the pastures, manure, of course, which is a good smell, not a bad smell. But now I said, "Why not?"

"Because when a person dies, his body is buried and awaits the Second Coming, and his soul goes to heaven or hell. There's no intermediate place, where ghosts wander around or anything like that."

His voice was easygoing, but I understood that this was a rule. NO ghosts. Daddy said, "Are they telling you at school that ghosts are real?"

"There was a ghost in *Julius Caesar*. Julius appeared to Brutus."

"That was a play."

"It was Shakespeare."

Daddy gave me a look that told me he didn't know where to begin.

"This is partly why you kids haven't been allowed to go to the movies. You get all of this nonsense in your heads and then you think—"

"My teacher said Shakespeare was the greatest writer ever in history."

"Well, other teachers might agree with her or not, but Shakespeare was HUMAN, and he was writing for MONEY, so he let people see things in his plays that would get them all excited and make them tell their friends about the play. That's the category that I would put ghosts into. There are no ghosts. That lady, Blue's owner, is not a ghost haunting him. He's a spoo—a nervous type of horse, and he will settle down, and we will make something of him, okay? I'm sure once he's been in with Lincoln and Jefferson for a week, he'll be completely fine. Do you understand?"

44

I nodded. I had noticed how he avoided the word *spooky*. But I didn't say anything.

"Jesus said, 'How long shall I put up with you?'" Then he stood up and kissed me on the top of the head.

"I better do my homework."

"I'll put Blue in a stall for the night, one where he can look out the door and see the mares. Since he's been in a stall, he might feel more secure in there. He's settled down quite a bit even since he got here."

"I guess. Yes, I guess he has."

But as I walked up to my room, I felt like the barn was full of ghosts, or *a* ghost, the ghost of Mary Carson. Then I thought, Maybe that will make Blue feel better.

I read more about Tom Sawyer, who by this time was interested in a girl named Becky, who gets sick, and stays home for what seems like weeks and weeks, or at least long enough so that his aunt gets worried and gives Tom "the water treatment," which is throwing buckets of cold water at him first thing in the morning, then scrubbing him down with a rough towel, then rolling him in a wet sheet and covering him with hot blankets until he sweats yellow. Then it gets worse. The book never says what's wrong with the girl, either, only that Tom goes out and sticks around her house late at night, so it seems like he does whatever he pleases. Then somehow after that, he poisons the cat, and after that, Becky Thatcher comes back to school, and Tom and his friends go out on the river and get a ham and build a fire. Even though they are about my age, no one pays any attention to a thing they do. It was hard to keep track of and put me to sleep. Which was good. I did not dream of Blue; I dreamt of the Mississippi River, which I had never once seen. I love that you can dream of things that you don't know about.

In the morning, it was still dark when I was getting up, but by the time I got around to feeding Blue, it was light enough for me to see him and for him to see me. I fed him last because he didn't know the schedule, and the others did. They could see the light go on in the kitchen, and they could see me come out the back door, and they could see Rusty come around the house to meet me, and from all of this, they knew they were about to get their hay, which of course they had been waiting for all night long, and just because every single one of them was sleek and fat didn't mean that they weren't starving to death. Amazon and Foxy were the whinniers; Happy snorted and nickered; Sprinkles tossed her head. In the gelding pasture, Lincoln and Jefferson walked around, and Jack went over to the gate, where he ran his teeth along one of the metal slats, making a grating sound. He only did it once each feeding, and I never understood where he learned it, but since making that sound always resulted in me throwing the hay over the fence, he must have thought it worked.

I took the last flake to Blue, who was standing against the door of his stall, staring out the doorway of the barn. I threw the hay right over the door, and he put his head down to it. He ate one bite, then lifted his head and looked at me and the mares. Then he took another bite. Well, two bites and one look was better than one bite and one look. Out of the corner of my eye, I saw a woman sitting on one of the tack trunks, but when I whipped around and stared, I realized it was just a shirt of Daddy's, hanging from a hook. Even so, my heart was pounding as though I had seen a ghost. It did not help that just at that moment, Blue gave a loud whinny and Rusty came in the door of the barn and dropped something on the floor. It squeaked. I said, "Rusty, what have you got?" and went over.

I knelt down and looked at it. It was a kitten—a black kitten, but with two white toes on each front foot. Rusty sat and looked at me, then looked down at the kitten again. She wagged her tail. I scooped the kitten up in my hands and brought it near my face so I could see it. It looked about three or four weeks old—fluffy and big-headed, but with its eyes open. It was not old enough to be away from the mother, but it was old enough to creep around. I stood up and put it under my shirt to keep it warm.

Mom was making breakfast when I went in the house. I lifted my shirt and showed her the kitten. "Rusty found it. She brought it into the barn and put it down on the floor." I could see Rusty out on the porch, watching us through the window. Mom petted the top of the kitten's head with her forefinger, then opened a drawer and took out a clean dish towel, which she made into a nest inside a big wide pot on the counter. I put the kitten into it.

Mom said, "I hadn't realized Bossy had a litter."

I said, "But it's black." Bossy was a gray tabby. We called her a barn cat, but really, she was a feral cat who sometimes came around. The other female barn cat, Doozy, had been spayed, but we hadn't ever been able to catch Bossy.

Mom said, "That's true, a tabby never produces a black. Isn't it cute?" The male barn cat was a tabby, too, but orange, named Clyde. I heard him in the barn more often than I saw him, but I sometimes saw him leaping or running out on the hillside.

By this time, the kitten was sitting up in its little nest,

mewing, but it wasn't trying to get out. The important thing with a kitten is keeping it warm. Mom said, "Rusty is such a busybody. The last thing I need right now is a kitten to raise." But she petted it on the head again and said, "Yes, you're cute. I'll find you a basket after breakfast."

I sat down at the table. She put my scrambled eggs in front of me and said, "At least it's pretty old. It'll be eating solid food any time now. What shall we name it?"

I said, "Spooky."

I don't know why I said that.

Rope Halter

Western Bridle

Chapter 5

BLUE DID SEEM TO SETTLE DOWN WELL ENOUGH. HE WAS BETTER in the stall than he was in the pen, though we put him in the pen to stretch his legs every day for two or three hours. After a couple of days, Daddy threw some extra hay into the pen and put Lincoln in there with him—Lincoln was the more easy-going of the two geldings. Daddy set out three piles of hay far apart from one another, and then when Blue was eating, he opened the gate and let Lincoln go in. Blue raised his head and pinned his ears. Daddy and I leaned against the gate and watched them. Lincoln inspected the two free piles, and then chose one and started eating. Blue lifted his head again, and pinned his ears again, but he didn't move toward Lincoln. All Lincoln did was switch his tail in a meaningful manner and cock his right hind foot. Blue was saying, "This is my pile," and Lincoln was saying, "Yes, but this is my pile."

There seemed not to be much disagreement. After a bit, Blue moved to the third pile, and Lincoln tried Blue's pile, and so on. By the time the hay was eaten, Daddy and I had ridden Foxy and Happy. The two geldings now seemed not friends but not enemies, so Daddy went into the pen and got them to trot around a bit together. Lincoln did as he was told, and did not seem to notice Blue, but trotted past him and in front of him and across his path. Every time he did, Blue moved out of the way or paused. Daddy said, "That's good. Always remember that the one who seems to be ignoring the other one is the boss. We want Lincoln to be the boss here, because he's already the boss of the pasture. We don't want Blue to go out there and challenge him."

"Blue doesn't seem like a very brave horse."

"He's sensitive and he's observant. That can be good and it can be bad."

When I put Blue away in his stall, I brushed him down, which he seemed to like.

The next day, it was time to ride him. As soon as the school bus dropped me at the gate, I ran in and threw down my books. I had been thinking about Blue all day, thinking about this first ride. I knew that Jane said he didn't do much, but he was so beautiful that I couldn't help feeling that he had to be one of the good ones, a horse like Black George, the one we sold to Sophia Rosebury, who loved his work and did it all so well that people just stared at him. All through my last class, which was math, I kept imagining going to the horse show on Blue and having everyone stare at us—what a beautiful horse he is; look at how he takes those fences; Abby Lovitt trained him; champion, best ever, perfect.

Blue had spent the day with Jefferson, and they were still in the pen together. They both came to the gate, and they didn't squeal or step out of each other's way, which meant that they had made friends, or at least accepted one another. Jefferson was the first to look into my hands, so he was the boss, but since he wasn't pushing Blue out of the way, he wasn't making absolutely sure that Blue understood every moment of the day that he, Jefferson, was the boss—at least of Blue—and would always be the boss. I went in and put a rope halter on Blue (not his leather one with the brass nameplate), and Daddy took Jefferson and crosstied him in the barn.

I did not open the blue trunk and take out Blue's saddle and bridle—I put my own saddle on him, with a nice thick blanket, and one of the simpler western bridles. I thought I would be safer for the first ride in equipment that was familiar to me and a little heavy. But I did put on my hard hat.

Daddy tacked up Jefferson, and we led them to the pen. I went in with my flag, which was a white rag tied to the end of a whip, and got them to go around me. There was no reason to think that Blue had ever done this before, but Jefferson had—I worked him in the pen every week or so, not because he was badly behaved, but because he needed to be reminded to get going from time to time. With Blue in the pen, he was happy to show off a little, and so he trotted around with his ears up and his tail up, and Blue trotted after him, doing what he was told. After they had gone around to the left three or four times, I stepped back and to the right, and Jefferson made a smooth turn and began trotting to the right. Blue stared at him, then followed him. In a moment, they were both trotting to the right. When they picked up the canter, I saw what the bonus was going to be.

Because Blue had a nice trot—even and steady and balanced, but nevertheless nothing eye-popping, nothing like, say, Jack's trot, which was huge and floating, or Happy's trot, which was exact and perfectly sure-footed. It was not a trot to remember. But his canter was so effortless and graceful that it was like a ball rolling. It made Jefferson look as though he was on a pogo stick, popping around the pen. Blue didn't push himself forward and he didn't hang back; he just folded and unfolded and glided along. I couldn't stop watching. Behind me, leaning on the fence, Daddy said, "If he's not a Thoroughbred, I can't imagine what he could be."

We watched him for two circuits of the pen, and then I stepped back, and the two horses slowed to a trot. Jefferson, knowing what to do, arced around and headed in the other direction. After a couple of seconds, Jefferson picked up the canter. Blue followed him. To the left, Jefferson stayed in front. Blue didn't pass him either by coming in toward the center or slipping by him on the outside—by not passing him, Blue showed that he respected him. But Jefferson didn't maintain a steady pace. You could see that he couldn't make up his mind. On the one hand, he was naturally lazy, but on the other hand, he wanted to show off for Blue, and he couldn't decide the best way to do that. Blue, though, was so easy in his canter that when Jefferson sped up, he lengthened his stride just a bit, and when Jefferson slowed down, he shortened his stride the right amount. There was even one point where Jefferson was trotting and Blue was still cantering, but so easy and collected (which was a word Jane Slater used for a small but not lazy canter or trot) that he stayed right behind him.

"Nice," said Daddy.

Now the horses both subsided into the trot, and then I let them slow down, which they did. Jefferson walked for a moment, then turned toward me, his ears pricked. Blue stayed on the fence, but he looked at me. Daddy climbed the fence and went to get Jefferson. I walked over to Blue. Daddy took Jefferson out, and I led Blue over to the fence and stood him up beside it. Then I climbed on.

Blue's ears went forward. He did not snort or actually move, but I could feel tension enter his body the way it does just before a horse DOES buck or DOES rear. I kicked him a tiny bit with my legs, and he stepped forward, first one step and then two. His steps were small. I pressed him with my legs again, and his steps enlarged a little bit. His ears stayed pricked forward, which was not good. When a horse is relaxed, his ears are relaxed, too, and when he's paying attention to his job and making a real effort, his ears sort of drop to either side, not limp, but more or less out of service, because he's more interested in what you, the rider, are asking him to do than the world around him—when you are riding a horse and his ears stay rigidly pricked, that means he is attending to something other than you. I urged him forward again, then asked him to turn in a half circle toward the center of the pen. He did it. We walked across the pen, and I asked him to turn again, along the fence. He did it. He was neither disobedient nor resentful, and we did this walking and turning for a few minutes. However, he did not relax. His ears stayed pricked, and I continued to have the feeling that he was on the watch.

In fact, the feeling got worse. It was like it swelled out of him, up through the saddle blanket and the saddle and into me, and pretty soon, I was looking to see who or what was coming, when I knew that just about the only thing that would or could come would be Rusty. Jefferson, whom Daddy was sitting on outside the pen, wasn't looking around at all, and neither was Jack, in the gelding pasture, normally the most observant of the horses. Jack was twitching his tail and splashing in the water trough with his nose, sure signs that he thought there was nothing to do and nothing to worry about.

Blue and I continued to walk around the pen, turning this way and that. He relaxed a little. Daddy said, "What do you think?"

I lied. I said, "He's fine. Let's go over to the arena."

Daddy unhooked the latch of the pen from Jefferson's back and the gate swung open. Blue and I followed him and Jefferson to the arena.

I would never have said that the arena was a frightening place, but now, as we walked through the gate, I saw the straw bale jump that we had never removed after Black George was sold—we had just pushed the bales over into a corner—and I saw the traffic cones Daddy had gotten somewhere so we could practice barrel racing, and I saw the chairs and the table on the other side of the fence that we sometimes sat in. I saw the jump standards Daddy had set along the railing over where a tree sort of overhung the fence and threw them into shadow. I saw some puddles with water in them, and the sunlight rippling on the water as a breeze picked up. I saw birds in trees and in flight. I saw Rusty take off across the hillside. And Blue saw all these things, too. As we went into the arena, he twisted this way and that, not exactly shying, but curving his body away from whatever it was he didn't understand. I lifted my inside rein, as my favorite trainer, Jem Jarrow, had taught me to do, so that I could control his shoulder (because, as I learned with Ornery George, or Rally, as we renamed him, where the shoulder is, is where the horse is about to be). He didn't resist this. We walked on.

I made him go past every scary thing, and he did it well enough. In the meantime, Daddy and Jefferson were trotting and then cantering figure eights. Daddy was teaching Jefferson to change his canter lead across the middle—he'd been working on that for about a week, and Jefferson was finally starting to get it. He was good to the left, not so good to the right. Daddy was using one end of the arena for his figure eights, so I went to the other and dismounted. Blue looked at me, so I stroked him along the neck and said, "Everything really WILL be all right, even if I have to get Jem Jarrow to come over and work with you."

Western reins are usually longer than English reins. Mine were roping reins, which were attached to the bit by leather loops. The end of the rein had a slit, which slipped over a little metal knob inserted into the leather. The idea was that you might need to tie your horse to something when you were out with the cattle, or you might need a longer rein, so you had to be able to detach one side or the other from the bit. So that's what I did. I detached the left side and stood by Blue's right shoulder, lifting and drawing the rein until he realized that the pressure on his bit and the left side of his face would go away if he stepped his right hind foot in front of his left hind foot and moved his haunches away from me. I tried this gently at first, because he was a sensitive horse and was paying attention to me, but I had to get a little stronger with him, because it soon became clear that he didn't know anything about his hind feet. It was like they were coming along with the rest of his body, but he didn't actually understand that he could operate them independently. It's funny how many horses don't know that. So I did what I had done with Rally: I made him step over and step over, first one direction and then the other, until as soon as I lifted the rein, he would soften his spine and begin his shift to the side. It took me about twenty times on each side before I felt that he was ready to try it with me mounted. I reattached the reins.

And then there was mounting. When I lifted my foot to put it in the stirrup, he turned his head and bent his body away from me. He had been fine when I mounted from the fence, so I realized that maybe his previous owner had never mounted him from the ground. And furthermore, he was suspicious of everything new. I led him around a couple of times to relax him, then started again. The first two times he still gave me that what-in-the-world-are-you-doing look, but then he must have put two and two, or one and one, together and decided that I was mounting. No big deal.

I worked on lifting and drawing his head and neck from both directions, and after a little bit, he put one and one together again and began to step his right hind in front of his left, and then his left hind in front of his right. I remembered again what a useful exercise this was, because Blue seemed at least a little more relaxed after we had done it. When we walked out along the rail again, his steps were bigger and his hind end swung back and forth a little more. The fact is, you want your horse's back end to swagger a little bit, because you want his hips to be nice and loose, and Blue managed to do that.

But because he did relax some, I could feel all the more when something made him tense up. It was like everything he saw (or heard, since he tensed when some crows started having an argument and squawking like mad), the tension rippled through him. I would then move his hind end over, back and forth, two or three times, because the tension rippled through, and then got stuck, and I had to move him over in order to let it flow away. When Daddy said we'd been at it for an hour, I could hardly believe it.

It was Happy who broke my arm.

Back in December, when it was time for the calves at the Jordan ranch, across the fence from us, to be branded, the foreman, Mr. Louis, called Daddy and asked if he was available to help, because two of his regular hands were working in Oregon for the winter. Daddy had sold Mr. Louis maybe his own favorite horse ever, a beautiful golden buckskin named Lester, a month or so before Mr. Louis called him. I always thought that for once in his life Daddy regretted selling a horse, and that maybe his usual motto—it's never too soon to sell a horse—did not really apply to Lester. But Daddy didn't say anything about it. He went to the branding for two days, and he rode one of the ranch horses—Happy wasn't well trained enough by that time to go.

After the branding, Daddy talked to Mr. Louis from time to time, and as the winter progressed, we climbed the hillside every so often to have a look at the blue Brahmas that had broken through the fence and come down the hill in the fall. They never broke through the fence again, and as they got bigger they got more beautiful and less cute, but they continued to be blue. I guess Mr. Louis told Daddy that he thought they weren't much use compared to regular old Angus and Herefords, and a lot of trouble to boot, but when Daddy reported this at the supper table, Mom said, "They are beautiful and unusual, and if I ever met a ranch manager who didn't think his owner was nuts, I can't remember when that was."

Daddy laughed and nodded, then he said, "But they are more active than the standard breeds, so even though they aren't bothering us any, maybe they're causing trouble elsewhere on the ranch."

The ranch was some six thousand acres, so there were plenty of places on it for the Brahmas to cause trouble.

After supper the night I first rode Blue, the phone rang, and as soon as Daddy picked it up, he started smiling, which meant that the person on the other end of the line was not any of our relatives. He said, "Sounds good. We will do that. Shouldn't be a problem."

We were invited to come on Saturday to help gather the cattle—not just the Brahmas, but the Angus, too, and drive them from the chewed-over pastures to the greener one. There were about two hundred head, plus the ten Brahmas, and after the work was done, there was going to be a barbecue. We were all invited—Mom was going to ride Lincoln, I would ride Happy, and Daddy would ride Lester. I guess Mr. Louis had about three horses that he used, including Lester, and he had only bought Lester because he couldn't resist, not because he needed a horse.

We were in the living room when Daddy told us about this. I was reading *Tom Sawyer* (Tom continued to be completely unsupervised—I wondered what Danny had thought about it) and Mom was feeding Spooky with a doll's baby bottle. Even in a few days, Spooky had changed and gotten bigger. His head was no longer as rounded over the top, which made it look as though his ears had moved higher. His tail had grown, too—it didn't look quite so much like a nail. He also made meows, or almost meows—more like "miaaas." Mom had gone from feeding him four times a day to three times, and she no longer had to stroke his belly after she fed him, because he was getting more active. Part of the reason I was reading in the living room was because it was fun to watch Spooky come out of his box and play around for a few minutes after his supper. Rusty liked to watch, too—when she could not see through the front door, she would stand on her hind legs and stare through one of the windows.

Mom finished with the bottle and said, "I think I'll leave him with some soft food on Saturday. I could be gone for five hours." She carried him across to the hallway and set him in the litter box, then petted him rather firmly down his back and sides. He sniffed the litter and walked around in it, and then finally squatted and did something. Mom said, "Good, good boy, Spooky." Then she deposited him in the middle of the living room floor. I put down my book and knelt in front of him. He saw me and came bouncing in my direction with his ears up and his tail high. It made me laugh. I put my forefinger on the rug in front of him and moved it around. This made Spooky jump up and down. Then I moved my finger toward him, and he jumped on it.

"Precocious!" exclaimed Daddy. "He'll be a ratter in a week."

"Poor Spooky," said Mom. "Out to the barn with you."

"Every cat prefers the barn," said Daddy. "Lucky to have a barn."

We didn't argue. The only cats I had ever known were the barn cats, and the only one that even came close enough to exchange a meow was Doozy. I said, "Well, at least when Spooky is living in the barn, maybe he'll come over and let me pet him once in a while." I moved my finger again, and Spooky jumped out of the way. Mom tossed me a toy she had made, an empty spool from her sewing box with thread tied through the center. I pulled it and as it rolled toward me, Spooky stared at it and then pounced on it and picked it up and flopped over on his back. Then he fought with the spool and got tangled in the thread for about ten seconds, until it broke. Then he bit the spool quite viciously for a moment. We all laughed. Mom got up to do the dishes and Daddy went back to his reading. Just then, Spooky sat, totally quiet, and looked me in the face.

This look probably lasted a few seconds, but for a kitten, that was a long time. I looked right back at him without thinking about it at first. It was only when Spooky lay down and rolled over on his back and looked across the room that it struck me that he had done something odd. That night, I went to sleep thinking about all sorts of things—Blue, and Jack, and the fact that it looked as though Barbie Goldman was going to take a riding lesson from me on Saturday morning at nine— Daddy had loved the idea, especially when Mrs. Goldman called and said that she wondered if $2.50 per lesson might be a fair payment.

But I woke up lying on my back, with the three-quarter moon in the window and the image in my mind (left over from a dream?) of Spooky the kitten staring at me. It seemed much bigger and longer than what really happened, and it sort of gave me the creeps.

Saddle Pommel with Horn

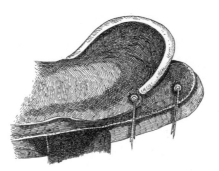

Saddle Cantle

Chapter 6

Since Lincoln was going over to the Jordan ranch that afternoon, I thought for a long time about whether to put Barbie on Jefferson, who was quiet, but big, or Foxy, who was a little less quiet, but hardly more than a pony, and so maybe not so scary. I decided to imagine that I was Jem Jarrow and make up my mind that way. I closed my eyes, and when I opened them, I went and got Foxy out of the mare pasture and brought her to the pen, where I worked her to the left and to the right, where I got her to move over in both directions, and where I had her step back about six different times, because Jem always said that if you ask a horse to step back and he does so willingly, then he's feeling obedient and cooperative—horses in the wild don't like to step backward. As for me, I was feeling pretty good, because I had ridden Blue the evening before, and he had seemed to relax, and I had already worked Jack, and he had been a good boy. When Barbie was finished (forty-five minutes, if she would take that much the first time), then I would get on Happy, whom I liked because she was smart and comfortable to ride, and later we would head to the "roundup." All we had to do was get on our horses and turn left out the gate and ride about a quarter mile down the road.

Foxy behaved herself fairly well, and just to be sure she understood her job, I went up to her and took her face between my hands and I said, "Foxy, you be a very good girl today and you will get three extra carrots." Then I moved my hands up and down, making Foxy nod "Okay."

Then I saw Mrs. Goldman's car at the gate. Barbie got out; Mrs. Goldman rolled down her window, said something, and drove off. Barbie turned and waved to me, then climbed the gate and trotted over. She was wearing new jeans, some oxfords I had never seen before, and a UCLA sweatshirt. She looked nice. I thought it was a shame to smash down her hair with the hard hat, but I took her in the barn and handed it to her. She put it on. It fit. That was lucky.

I pointed to the saddle. Barbie said, "I know, I carry it like this. My dad watches *Gunsmoke*." She picked up the saddle, propped the cantle on her hip, made her legs bow, and swaggered toward the pen. I walked behind her with the bridle. When we got to the pen, she hawked, bent to the right, and spat. When I laughed, she looked at me as if she couldn't imagine what I was laughing at. I could see right then that my biggest challenge was going to be keeping a straight face.

I had tied Foxy to an upright in the pen, and she gave Barbie a look. Barbie gave her a look, too, then said, "You know, I prepared for my lesson by reading a book."

"What book?"

"*The Black Stallion and Flame*."

"I never read that one." I showed her how to lift the saddle onto Foxy's back, a little up past her withers, then slide it backward. Foxy twitched her tail. She didn't like to be saddled, but she was good after that.

"The Black is in a plane crash and ends up on Flame's island, and just when they are going to fight to the death over the mares, Alec brings a rabid bat who is foaming at the mouth to the island, and then the two stallions kill it and are friends forever afterward." She said this with a straight face while adjusting the saddle blanket under the saddle.

I said, "That sounds exciting."

She said, "It reminded me of *Two Gentlemen of Verona*."

"What's that?"

"A Shakespeare play."

"You've read that?"

She looked at me over Foxy's back. "No."

We both laughed.

She said, "At least there wasn't an earthquake, where the ground opened up and the Black had to take Alec's shirt between his teeth and pull him out of the flames."

I said, "Maybe that's in one of the other ones. I've only read *The Black Stallion* and *The Island Stallion*. I like those."

We got Foxy cinched up, and then I showed Barbie how to put on the bridle. Then they were standing there, and I thought, What next? The fact was, I had been riding horses since before I could remember, so I had never had a lesson about how to sit on one. I decided to put this part off. I said, "First, you need to know how to lead her." I took Foxy's reins, just below the bit, in my right hand, with the other end in my left. I stepped out, and Foxy stepped along beside me. We walked about halfway around the pen, and Barbie walked with me. I stopped and turned to Barbie. I said, "Barbara!" I held up the reins where she could see them.

"What!"

"Never wrap the reins or a rope or anything at all that is attached to a horse around your hand or your foot—"

"Or your neck. I can see that."

"Good."

She took the reins and led Foxy around, turning this way and that. She said, "It's like heeling a dog."

And it was. She started and stopped a time or two, and Foxy stayed right with her. When they were finished, Barbie patted Foxy on the neck and said, "That was a good girl."

There are people who never think to praise a horse or thank one, any more than they would pat their car after parking it, but Barbie wasn't one of them.

I taught her to mount from the ground (checking the girth first) and to sit with her feet in the stirrups and her heels down, and to relax her shoulders and look where she wanted to go, and to hold the reins in one hand, with her hand just in front of the horn, and the reins flowing under her thumb and out over her palm, and I taught her to bang her lower legs lightly against Foxy's sides, just enough to ask for a walk, and I taught her to walk forward, and not let Foxy wander around. I taught her to let her hips move with the horse's hips and that if she felt insecure, she could hold the horn of the saddle. I taught her to count the beats of Foxy's front feet and feel the rhythm of her steps. When Daddy came out of the house and said, "Your mom called, Barbara, and I told her you're about ready," I couldn't believe we had gone ten minutes over the scheduled time and I hadn't even gotten her to trot.

Daddy headed toward us. It was only then that I remembered that he hadn't met Barbie before. He held out his hand and said, "Hi, I'm Mark Lovitt."

Barbie shook it just the way he liked, strong grip, looking him in the eye. She said, "Pleased to meet you, Mr. Lovitt. I am Barbara Goldman."

Daddy said, "Barbara Goldman."

"Yes," said Barbie.

Since Barbie was mounted on Foxy, they were about at eye level, and they stared at each other for just a second. Then Daddy said, "Well, your mom said fifteen minutes." Then he turned and walked to the barn.

I taught Barbie to dismount. The one I liked was the safest, once you master it—you take both your feet out of the stirrups, put your right hand on the pommel of the saddle and your left hand on the horse's neck, and rock forward, throwing your right leg over the horse's haunches and landing with your feet on the ground and your knees a little bent. Some people don't take their left foot out of the stirrup until they have the right leg over—then they hold both ends of the saddle and drop to the ground—but that takes a patient horse, and I wanted Barbie to get used to doing it the safer way. She was good and did it the first time. She said, "Alexis couldn't do this, you know."

"Why not?"

"She's always had the bottom bunk."

We led Foxy back to the barn and untacked her. Barbie forgot to swagger and spit this time. She had a piece of sugar for Foxy in her pocket, and out of the same pocket she pulled two dollars and two quarters for me. She said, "Do we have to wait until Saturday?"

"We'll talk about that Monday, after the stiffness sets in."

Her mom honked. She put her hands on my shoulders and kissed me on the cheek. That meant "thank you," and I felt thanked.

We didn't head to the Jordan ranch until almost two, because the plan was to move the cows to fresher pastures when they were resting around the water troughs after having come down from the hills for a drink. Daddy was on Amazon, and he had his chaps on, with his initials tooled into the belt, and Mom was wearing her good boots. I had on my favorite red and green plaid shirt and my leather vest that Uncle Buck sent me for Christmas—it had a sunflower tooled into the back. Mom and Daddy were wearing their cowboy hats, but Mom had insisted I wear my hard hat, and I knew better than to argue. When we got to the ranch road, the gate was open, and all sorts of trucks and trailers were parked along it, with horses tied to them, getting tacked up. Everyone waved to us the way cowboys do, just a little cock of the head, a smile, and a lifting of the hand. You wouldn't want to scare a horse.

Daddy's saddle had his rope tied to the horn, and some of the others did, too. We walked down the road, turning our heads back and forth, smiling and waving. Daddy's plan was to leave Amazon in the ranch corral and switch his tack to Lester, and there Lester was, up by the barn, shining and beautiful. When he saw us (when he saw Lincoln and Happy, maybe), he let out a loud whinny. Lincoln responded.

It was Mom who first saw Danny. He was mounting a black horse (two white feet and a narrow blaze), and as soon as he saw Mom, he waved like there had never been any problem in the world between him and Daddy. He settled into the saddle and trotted over. Daddy acted a little stiff, but for Mom, her day was made. I was happy to see him, too, and really interested in that black horse—I didn't know that he'd bought a horse.

Daddy said, "Lot of people here. Is it us gathering the cattle or the cattle gathering the people?"

Then he looked at Danny and said, "Hey, there. How ya doin'?"

Danny said, "Hey, Dad!"

Daddy could not help staring at Danny's horse, noticing his throatlatch and the size of his nostrils and the set of his neck and the depth of his shoulder and the angle of his hocks and the straightness of his front legs. I saw him do it. It took about ten seconds, and his nose twitched. I said, "Nice horse. What's his name?"

"He's lovely," said Mom.

"He's one of Jake's," said Danny. "I've been working with him. His name is Crockett." Jake was the horseshoer Danny worked for.

I said, "Davy?"

"Just Crockett. Crockett the Rocket. He's a great cutting horse."

"How old?" said Daddy. He sounded so stiff that Mom glanced at him—and then she rolled her eyes. I was amazed. But Daddy was staring at Danny and didn't see her.

Danny said, "He's eight."

Mom said, "Mark, you'd better get your horse, don't you think? Everyone's about tacked up."

Daddy nodded, and then trotted Amazon down the road toward the pen where Lester was staring over the fence. Lester whinnied again. Then Mom jumped off Jefferson, and Danny dismounted, and they hugged each other right there. I suppose that they hadn't seen each other since the last time Jake and Danny had come to shoe our horses. That would have been about a month. When Danny first moved out, Mom went over to Jake's ranch, where Danny was living in an old cabin up the mountain, maybe once every week, but then everyone got busy and all.

Hoofpick

Horseshoes

Chapter 7

The valley where the Angus cattle were living was toward the back of the ranch, about as far from our place as you could get on Mr. Jordan's ranch. It took us about an hour to ride there from where the trailers were parked. There must have been twenty-five of us, and we mostly walked and trotted a little, to save the horses. Happy was manageable, but I could feel that she knew something was up—she hadn't been off our place enough to be used to so much stimulation, but she didn't pull or jig; she just needed a reminder every so often that she was with me. Her ears were forward. As we rode along, I thought about how in Happy, I considered pricked ears to be a sign that she was paying attention and enjoying herself, while in Blue, I considered them to be a sign of anxiety. I could feel the difference in their bodies—Blue's body was tense and ready to flee. Happy's body was loose.

These cattle were an Angus-Hereford mix. Pure Angus are black from nose to tail. All of these were black, but had white faces, and also some other white markings, which were from the Hereford side. When we came over the top of the ridge, the cows were mostly lying down and resting. Some of the calves were walking around, and others were playing. Some were nursing, which wasn't easy, since they were pretty big. Others were grazing, but I could see why they were being moved—down by the water troughs, it was muddy; up on the hillsides, the grass was very short. I was so used to looking at the blue Brahmas, which were lanky, with long ears, big humps, and beautiful faces, that these looked a little fat and ugly to me, but I heard Daddy say to Mom, "Now, here's some cattle."

As we came down the hill, the twenty-five of us spread out until we made a long curving line. I was between Mom and Daddy, and Danny was over at one end. I could see from where I was that his horse was practiced and quick—a real cow horse. The new pasture was not very far from this one—just down the valley and over one small ridge into the next valley. No cattle had been in that pasture since the summer. Ideally, the cattle would see us (which they did), and slowly get up and bunch together, then amble ahead of us down the valley, then over the ridge, and through the part of the fence that was being taken down just for this. Ideally, the cows would say to themselves, "Oh, I remember this. We just do as we're told, and we get all new green grass." Ideally, the calves would say, "Well, Mom is headed out. She must know where she's going." However, from my experience of driving the Brahma cows and their calves up the hill in the fall, I did not suppose that everything would be ideal, and as much as I looked around, I could not see Rusty on the horizon, ready to save the day. Rusty was miles away from here, probably lying on the porch and wondering why she had to miss out.

We moved slowly. The hill was steep and I sat back to balance Happy as she picked her way. I glanced over at Mom—she was sitting back, too, and holding the horn of Jefferson's saddle. Jefferson was not as sure-footed as Happy, and he knew it—I could see that he didn't care much about the cattle, and was working on placing his feet and shifting his weight. Lester did care about the cattle—they were his cattle. But he and Daddy knew better than to push ahead. We all just came down the hill. Danny at his end and a man at the other end on a palomino rode just ahead of the others, slowly contracting our curve around the cows and calves.

One by one, the cows got up. They started mooing. The cows' moos were low and comforting in a way, rather harmonious with one another. The calves' moos were sharper and more worried. The calves who were already beside their mothers stayed there, and the other calves began moving around, looking for their mothers in the group. When the cows seemed to get a little worried, Danny and the guy at the other end slowed down, and the rest of the line slowed down, too. But we needed to keep moving, because we didn't want the cows to forget that they had to go somewhere.

After what seemed to me to be quite a long time, we were maybe two-thirds of the way down the hill, and the slope had flattened out. I no longer felt as though my horse would tip over if I made a mistake and leaned forward. Happy was containing herself, but was eager underneath me. The herd of cows was now fairly well bunched, and the ones in the lead seemed to figure out that they were headed somewhere good. The mooing increased, and the last lazy ones suddenly realized that they might get left behind if they didn't start. Our curving line had closed up—Mom was maybe ten feet from me on one side and Daddy the same distance from me on the other side. What we were doing was not terribly exciting—Daddy was chatting with the man on his other side about growing up in Oklahoma compared to growing up in South Dakota. It sounded like it was either blizzards alternating with tornadoes or blizzards all the time. I wished Danny was with us, just for the moment, but I could see him—our curve was more like a C now, and Danny was at the tip of one of the legs, making sure that the front cows didn't turn. Daddy and the man (who was on a pretty chestnut) were now talking about the barbecue. Best steaks in the valley, said the man.

And then Happy was out from under me, and I was landing on my rear end, with my hand stuck out behind me to break my fall.

Cowboy Hat

Cowboy Canteen

Chapter 8

THE FIRST THING I HEARD WAS MOM SAYING, "ABBY?" THEN I heard Daddy say, "What—"

I was sitting there on the hillside. Happy was running to the right, and she was after a calf who must have gotten separated from its mother. The stirrups were flapping and the reins were flapping, and Happy had her head down and her front legs splayed. She was staring at the calf. When he jumped to his right, she jumped to her left. I don't think she had any idea that I wasn't on her. That side of the line of drivers began to shift, but it was Danny who knew what to do. He turned Crockett and cantered toward Happy. When he reached her, he leaned over and grabbed her reins, but he didn't pull her off the calf— he let her watch the calf and drive it a bit closer to the herd.

Only when the calf had moved the way Happy wanted it to did Danny lead her away from it.

"How did that happen?" said Daddy. "What's going on?"

I held up my arm. My hand flopped. But it didn't hurt that much. Mom exclaimed, "Oh, no! Her wrist is broken!" and got off Jefferson in about one second. My hard hat seemed hot and tight. I reached up with my left hand to take it off, but it didn't work. The right hand worked. I was kind of dumbfounded. I set the hard hat next to me on the ground.

But the cattle had to keep moving. Danny trotted over with Happy and gave the reins to Daddy, then said, "Sorry, sis, gotta go. I'll call you." He cantered Crockett back to his spot, and the rest of the people on the line closed in front of us and everyone pushed the cattle farther down the valley. I said, "It's my left wrist. I can ride."

"Of course you cannot," said Mom.

"It doesn't hurt." I looked at it again, then said, "Well, it doesn't really hurt."

Daddy got off Lester, who was staring toward the retreating cattle. He said, "It will." He handed his reins to Mom and started looking around. After a moment, he trotted back up the hill and returned with a branch from one of the oaks along the ridge, half rotted. It had been there a long time, and the cows had stepped on it. It still had about three old blackened leaves. Daddy stripped the twigs off and broke it in half, then he took off his shirt, and used his pocketknife to cut off most of the left sleeve. Then he made me a splint—he put one of the pieces along the front of my wrist and one along the back, so that my hand and my wrist were straight again, and then he wrapped the pieces of his shirt around the whole thing and tied the two ends. Mom held my hand steady. Lester and Lincoln ground-tied, which they were trained to do—if you dropped the reins in front of their noses, they stood there. I held Happy with my right hand. She watched what they were doing to my left hand as if it were her business, and maybe she knew it was.

After Daddy was finished, I just sat there. The valley and the cows, who were now far enough away so that we could hardly hear their mooing, seemed to spin around a bit, and I also thought it might be a good idea to throw up. But still my wrist didn't actually hurt that much.

Mom said, "Honey, put your head between your knees and lean over." So I did that. Then I stretched out and lay back on the hillside. It seemed as though I could not resist doing that. The sun was off to the west, but there was brightness everywhere, even when I had my eyes closed, so I put my right hand over my face, and maybe I fell asleep. At any rate, there was the black kitten, staring at me. I was so startled that I woke up, and I must have cried out, because Mom said, "Oh, that must really hurt. I don't know what to do."

But it didn't hurt. I sat up. I felt better. Mom was sitting beside me, and Daddy was down the slope with all three of the horses. I said, "Did I fall asleep?"

"Honey, you passed out. You fainted."

"I did? For how long?"

"About five minutes."

I said, "Oh."

I sat there. Mom was holding my right hand. My left elbow was bent, and my left wrist, wrapped in Daddy's blue shirt, now throbbed. The hard hat was pressing against my right hip, so I moved it. But everything was okay. It was like I had taken a little nap, and now I was pretty relaxed. Daddy turned and looked toward us, then walked back up the hill, leading Happy and carrying his canteen, which he'd hooked to his saddle. When he got to me, he knelt down and gave me a drink. The water was warm, of course, but good, and it perked me up. Mom took a drink, then Daddy took a drink. Daddy wiped his mouth on his other sleeve, put the cap back on. He took a deep breath and said, "Thank you, Lord, for your mercy. Amen."

We said, "Amen."

"Now what?" said Mom.

Daddy sniffed. "Well, she can walk or ride. I don't see any alternative."

"They can't bring a—"

But no. We were far far back into the hills. A road ran to the other side of the ridge behind us, but no closer than that.

I said, "I'll ride."

"We'll have to follow the cattle, then. They're heading in that direction. Are you sure?"

"I feel okay. But I don't feel like walking."

"She can't ride Happy," said Mom.

"I can ride Happy," I said. "She didn't throw me. She just got excited about the calf. She took responsibility when she didn't really need to."

"She's a born cow horse," said Daddy.

I said, "You should give her to Danny."

It was like I hadn't said anything.

* * *

84

The question was how to mount. I knew I could ride, since it was my left wrist that was broken and when I rode western, I used my right hand to hold the reins. But when you mount from the ground, you have to grab the pommel of the saddle or the mane with your left hand and pull yourself up. Even with a leg up, you have to balance with your left hand. Mom thought they both should lift me onto the horse, but I didn't see how that would work. Daddy said, "I'll give you a leg up from the right side, and your mom can help. That way, you don't have to use your left hand. But, Abby." He stared at me.

I said, "What?"

"Remember not to use it! Habits are hard to break."

I nodded.

We positioned Happy sideways on the slope. It was weird to put my right foot in the stirrup, and weird to put my right hand on the mane, and weird to keep my left hand against my chest and have Mom put her hand on my rear and push me. It was weird to throw my left leg over the saddle. But Happy stood like a good girl, and I didn't touch anything with my left hand. Once I was in the saddle, I rested my hand and splint across my lap. Daddy handed me my hard hat. He said, "We forgot this." Happy stood there while I put it on, which was awkward with one hand. Daddy led her down the slope toward the other two horses, and we waited while Daddy gave Mom a leg up and then got on himself.

Mom said, "At least one person could have waited with us."

"Cattle come first," said Daddy.

"They don't even know if she's okay."

"They know they'll find out."

"That seems kind of hard-hearted to me," said Mom.

"We'll see," said Daddy.

But I was glad they hadn't waited. The last thing I wanted was for everyone to stand around staring while I fainted and had to be hoisted back on my horse. I knew that people didn't die from embarrassment, but I wondered right then if you could die in preference to embarrassment.

We walked down the valley, following the path that the cattle had trod. It wasn't very steep. At the bottom, that valley turned (really, it was sort of a box canyon), and then we went over a very gentle ridge, and down again. Pretty soon, we could see the cattle in the distance, and then we came to the fence.

Mom said, "I think she needs a sling."

I couldn't disagree with her, because it was funny the way I still wouldn't have said that my wrist hurt, but it did hurt. Every thought I had about it seemed a little slow, as if as soon as I had the thought, it was no longer true. I pressed my hand against my chest, as if I could get the pain to drain downward and run out my elbow somehow.

Mom said, "She's breathing a little hard. Abby, do you want to get off and lie down again?"

I shook my head, then thought that I would like to, then looked down at the ground. The cattle and the horses had come through here, and it was a muddy mess—not like the hillside where I'd been sitting and fainting before. I shook my head, but that was a bad idea. Every place where I might lie down seemed really far away. Now Daddy and Lester were right next to me, and Daddy was leaning toward me, putting his hand out and touching my forehead. Then he gave me another drink of water.

All of these things that were done and said jumped rather than flowed—one thing would be happening and then another, and I wouldn't understand how one thing became the other. But I didn't feel faint or weak. I said, "Let's keep going."

Mom said, a little more sharply, "Well, she needs a sling."

Daddy took off his neckerchief, but it was a small one. We looked at it. That's what it felt like—we just looked at it for a long time. Daddy said, "I could rip the other sleeve off this shirt, but I'm not sure that would be long enough, either."

And then there were hoofbeats. I lifted my eyes and looked in that direction, which took a long time, too. The next thing that was happening was that Danny had taken the bandanna he was wearing, which was strangely bigger than Daddy's and had been wrapped around his face against the dust of the cows, and I was bending down, and Danny was looping it over my neck, and then he helped me slip my arm into the fold. It rested there. It was okay.

Mom said, "Oh, honey. I think that did the trick. Thanks for—"

But Danny was like Daddy, and being thanked was not the sort of thing he liked, so he interrupted her and said, "Well, we got the cattle down to the water troughs, so we're done with that, and I just got to wondering about you guys."

He and Daddy coughed at the same time. Daddy said, "I was beginning to think this shirt was done for."

Mom and Danny smiled.

Danny said, "The ranch house isn't far from here, really. Just down along the lower fence line and around that stand of trees. There's a little crick to cross, but . . ."

He walked on one side of me and Mom walked on the other. Dad and Lester went ahead to check out the terrain. Right then, I started to cry, but I didn't know why. Mom and Danny pretended not to notice. I cried all the way down to the stand of trees, and then partway down to the house, just sniffling and dripping, and hiccupping every so often, and then I stopped crying. Happy was walking along nicely—I mean, she was pinned between Jefferson and Crockett, so what else could she do?—so I let go of the reins and wiped my face on my left sleeve and thought that I should probably have brought a bandanna myself.

When we got to the ranch house, Mr. Louis was happy to see us and kept saying, "What a girl! To ride all that way with a broken wrist! Good for you!" while all the time sorting out Happy and Lincoln and getting someone to bring a car around so he could drive me, Mom, and Daddy home. "Now, these horses can just stay in one of our corrals, by themselves, until you pick them up, or a couple of the boys can pony them home. We'll give them plenty of hay. You get this girl to the hospital."

It was dark by the time we were going through our own gate, and then Mom had to feed Spooky, and Daddy had to give Jack, Blue, Lincoln, Foxy, and Sprinkles their hay, and after that, we had to get to the hospital and wait in the emergency room and look at the X-ray ("Straight across the radius. Clean fracture, no displacement. Ulna's okay. That's a surprise, given how she fell, but you never know. Bones have their own opinions about things. We'll just cast this and she'll be right as rain in six weeks. No horseback riding, my girl; you just leave those equines alone. No baseball. No football. No jumping out of trees; that's what I always tell the boys.").

The cast ran from the first knuckle of my forefinger to just below my elbow, and it was sort of moist and cool. I had a sling, too—not Danny's red bandanna, but a hideous enormous white thing. And I was not to take my arm out of the sling— positioning was important; none of this throwing my arm around hi, ho Silver and away! The doctor laughed at all his own jokes. When we got home, there was a bag on the table with a note from Mr. Louis, and inside it, three steaks from the barbecue and some baked potatoes and some baked beans and salad. It was late, but we were hungry, and so we went inside to the kitchen table and sat down. Mom had to cut my meat. I think that was when I realized that the next six weeks were going to be an enormous pain in the neck.

The next day was Sunday, and though we had to go a little early to set up chairs, it was not our turn to cook, which was a good thing, because I was tired from not sleeping very well. The break hurt and did not hurt—every time I decided that it hurt, then I thought of other things that had hurt more, like an earache I had for three days when I was seven and something my mom called a "migraine" that I got once from not eating breakfast. Every time I decided that it didn't hurt, it would give me a throb or two. What with the sling and the throbs and the cast, one thing it did not let me do was forget about it.

All of the brothers and sisters were very nice, and, of all people, Brother Abner patted me on the head and said, "Little Abby, let me tell you a tale. When I was just your age, I was climbing on the roof of my house, the one we had back in Rochester, New York. Now, that house had a mansard roof. You know what that is?"

I shook my head.

"Well, that's a roof that is real straight up and down in the lower part, and then flattens out on the upper part. My brother Levi and I were holding on to the chimney, right at the peak of the roof. We'd climbed out the attic window. And Levi said, 'Ab, I dare you to go down to the gutter and come back up,' and shoot, if I didn't take that dare, just because it was Levi, and he was the older one and always making me remember that, and I slid off that roof, and I would have landed on my feet, maybe, but I tried to catch the gutter as I went past, so I landed upside down and broke my arm."

I said, "I'm surprised you ever did anything naughty, Brother Abner."

He leaned back in his seat and actually grinned, maybe the first time I had ever seen that, and he said, "Didn't you realize, girl, that it's the naughtiest ones who quest the most sincerely for redemption?"

I said, "No, sir, I didn't realize that."

He said, "Well, don't tell 'em I told you." He slapped his Bible on his knee and stood up.

Carlie Hollingsworth sat right next to me, in case I might need someone to turn the pages of my Bible. I could see by the way that she and her mom glanced at each other that her mom had put her up to this. I let it go on for a while, but finally I whispered, "I can do it. I'm fine," and she moved her chair back to the normal spot. Carlie should have been better friends with me—she was about my age and we had known each other for as long as we could remember—but we never saw each other outside of church, since her family had to drive an hour from one direction to get to church, and we had to drive twenty minutes from the opposite direction. So I never saw Carlie when she wasn't being a really good girl with great manners, and it was the same for her. I'm sure she wondered about me what I did about her—did she have any personality at all? And no, she would not have allowed Brad Greeley out of her sight.

The Greeleys were not there, either. At first I thought this was something of a relief. It wasn't until we had our plates and were eating our supper that I realized that it meant something. In fact, it was the Greeleys' second absence, since they hadn't come Wednesday night, but the Wednesday night meeting was short, and not everyone came every week. But it was rare for people not to come on Sunday—today even the Goods were there. The last time the Greeleys had missed a Sunday was when both boys had the flu (because so many of the brothers and sisters were pretty old, it was important not to come if you were sick).

Our supper was good, but not my favorite—beef stew, with cabbage as a vegetable, which the older brothers and sisters just loved. There was also carrot and raisin salad, a big circle of lime Jell-O, and only some cookies for dessert. I could eat everything without having someone cut it for me, though. I was sitting there picking at this and that when I heard Sister Nicks say, "Maybe it's just as well."

I didn't know what she was talking about until Sister Larkin said, "Quieter. I did notice the peace and quiet."

Then Sister Hazen said, "Too quiet, if you ask me. Bunch of old people sitting around a room is too quiet."

"Not everyone is old, sister," said Sister Larkin.

"Too many are. A one-year-old and a three-year-old and a five-year-old lower the average considerably."

The other two ladies chuckled and Sister Hazen said, "You think I'm joking, but it's a sad joke. Jesus and his disciples were young men. They had energy and strength." And then—I saw her—Sister Nicks pulled her two fingers across her lips, zipping them, and raised her eyebrows. Something about the Greeleys was not to be talked about.

Of course Carlie knew all about it—I asked her when we went around to the back of the mall to go to the girls' room. The very first thing she said was, "Nobody blames you."

"For what?"

"It was only a matter of time, my mom says."

"What?"

"One of those Greeleys getting lost."

"Oh."

"You saw me."

"What were you doing?"

"I was pretending not to see Brad throwing a fit. So you got stuck with him."

"I don't think he was throwing a fit."

"Well, he was about to. And I just didn't want to put up with it."

"I wanted to get out of there anyway."

I didn't say why, but as we walked back to the hall, I thought how relaxed and happy Danny had seemed all day the day before, from the moment he saw us until the moment he put us in Mr. Louis's car to go home. And that morning he had called and told Mom that he would be ponying Lester, Happy, and Jefferson home from Mr. Jordan's ranch, and Mom hadn't said a word about working on Sunday, or going to church, just, "Thanks, honey."

I finished my supper, and got up to take my plate to the bin—every Sunday, one of the families that didn't cook took the dishes and silverware home to wash it, and then brought it back the next Sunday.

Daddy and Mom talked about the Greeleys on the way home. I kept quiet in the backseat and listened to them. They didn't actually mention the Greeleys by name, but I could tell. Mom said, "I hope they're okay. It's been a week."

Daddy said, "I'm sure something came up. With little kids there's always a sore throat or pinkeye or something. Don't you remember when Abby was two and Danny was seven, and we all came down with the flu one right after the other? We didn't go anywhere for three weeks."

"Oh, goodness," said Mom. "If we hadn't been living near my parents, I don't know what I would have done! You were so grumpy I had to set your breakfast outside the bedroom door and run."

I smiled.

Daddy lowered his voice, but I heard him. "Abby just cried and cried. She must have had a terrible headache. I know I did."

They shook their heads. I, of course, didn't remember this, though I remembered other illnesses, like the measles.

We drove on.

Daddy said, "They should—"

"I know you think—"

93

"Well, maybe it was a wake-up call."

Mom didn't say anything.

Daddy said, "Too much yessing and don't-worry-about-it. I said to Joe Hollingsworth that maybe if we had taken them aside two years ago when—" He coughed. "Anyway, I don't see why everyone's so shy about—" He coughed again. "It's our responsibility to our flock to counsel them on important issues, and not every important issue is a question of doctrine."

We drove on. I wanted to hear what Mom had to say, but my eyes were closing.

Dad said, "I think I need to call an elders' meeting."

All Mom said was, "Mark, trying to tell other people how to rear their kids is very thin ice. You know, it is so thin I can see through it."

I smiled.

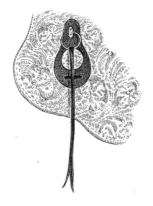

Saddle Strings

Tapaderos with Stirrups

Chapter 9

OF COURSE I COULDN'T RIDE. THAT DIDN'T HIT ME UNTIL I GOT home Monday afternoon, after a whole day of there being plenty of things that were hard, like carrying my books, taking notes in class, eating lunch, and sitting through tennis while they figured out what else I might do during physical education period, not to mention saying over and over, "Yes, I fell off a horse. Saturday afternoon, at a cattle drive. No, it doesn't hurt that badly, thanks. The doctor says six weeks." If the person I was talking to was an adult, I would have to add, "Yes, it could have been a lot worse." Most of the kids just stared, and I thought, Gee, it's a broken arm! Ed Harding broke his arm last fall! What's the big deal? I was not in a good mood by the time I'd dropped my books both getting on the bus and getting off, but then when I walked into the house, there was the worst thing—no riding. What was left, only homework?

Mom was upstairs when I came in, but Spooky was staring at me from his little box. I sat down on the floor and petted him with my forefinger on the top of his head. His eyes were wide open and very bright. After I'd petted him maybe three times, he grabbed my finger with his front paws and wrestled it to the ground, so I reached over and picked up a toy Mom had made him by putting a row of tight knots in an old rag. I snaked the toy around the box, and at first, Spooky bounced backward as though he'd never seen such a thing before, and then he leapt high in the air (maybe four inches) and landed on one of the knots. I let go, and he shook it until he was sure it was dead, then he looked at me and jumped back as if he'd never seen me, either. I laughed out loud, my first good laugh of the day. Mom came downstairs. She leaned down where I was sitting and kissed me on the top of the head and said, "I wanted to talk to you about six times today and see how you were doing."

I said, "It's more boring than painful."

She said, "Try to think of that as good. Want a snack? I made some brownies."

I knew she had made them for me. I got up, which was awkward (you don't realize what you use a particular hand for until it's not there to use), and went into the kitchen. Out the window, of course, I could see Jack and Jefferson and Lincoln in the gelding pasture, Happy, Foxy, Sprinkles, and Amazon in the mare pasture, and Blue looking out of his stall through the door of the barn. Everyone was doing something—Jack and Jefferson were having a bit of an argument, Lincoln was taking a drink,

Amazon was off in the corner of the mare pasture with Happy, Sprinkles was looking for strands of hay on the ground, and Foxy was playing with the gate chain. Some horses are very intent upon figuring out locks, and Foxy was one of those, but the chain was loose and had a snap, so she hadn't managed to understand it yet. Rusty was up the hill behind the gelding pasture, investigating something. She finished her business, whatever it was, then sat, facing down the hill, and surveyed her kingdom, or queendom. Only Blue was staring toward the house. If I hadn't known better, I would have said that he was looking at me through the window. But I knew better. I picked up a brownie. No nuts. I liked that. Mom poured me a glass of milk.

She said, "I rode Lincoln and Jefferson. Your dad rode the others." She looked out the window. "Except Blue. He'll ride Blue before supper. He wanted you to be there."

I nodded.

"We'll figure something out."

I nodded.

She said, "I just wish I could ride better and be more help. Maybe I can ride Foxy a bit."

"I could watch you. I used her for Barbie. She was okay."

"It's a short way to the ground."

I sighed. My problem was not that the horses would not get ridden. It was that I would die of boredom. I looked at the kitchen clock. Two and a half hours until supper. I had a second brownie and finished my milk, then changed, awkwardly, into my jeans and went to the barn. As soon as I got out among the horses, my wrist, which had been okay all day, began to throb. It was like it had a mind of its own. And it itched, too. I kept

99

wanting to stick something down the cast and scratch the itch, but I didn't have anything, and I was a little afraid to.

I went to the gelding pasture, and Jack and Jefferson came to the gate. Jack immediately looked into my hands, to see if I had anything, but he didn't push at me. He sniffed the sling and the cast, especially the cast, for at least a minute. His ears flopped a little in perplexity, but then he decided that it was not understandable, but also not worth any further investigation. While he was doing this, I stroked the side of his head. Jefferson looked at the cast, too, but he was not as naturally curious as Jack, so he only gave it one sniff before giving up on treats and wandering away.

I got up on the gate and leaned over it, anchoring myself with my left elbow and patting Jack down the side of his neck. He was fourteen months old now, and his mane and tail were those of a grown-up horse, at least in texture. His tail was thick and had grown out almost to his hocks. His mane actually needed to be thinned, but since it was still rainy season, we left it thick so he could use it to let the rain run off. Same with his forelock, which was so thick now that you couldn't always see the cowlick in the middle of it. There'd been a time I hated that cowlick, because I thought that it meant for sure that the real owners of the mare who was his dam (and had a similar cowlick) would take him away from us, but they didn't do that—every time we heard from them, they were very nice ("How's Jack? Send us a picture when you get a chance. Wish you could come for a visit and see the ranch in Texas. Maybe in the summer."). He still loved to run, especially when Jefferson would run with him. Just then, I thought maybe I would turn him out with Happy, which we'd never done because Daddy didn't believe in turning mares and geldings out together. But I thought she would be more likely to play with him and give him something to do.

I finished patting Jack and went into the barn. Blue was standing with his chest pressed against the door of his stall, the way he always did, and he gave me a throaty nicker when he saw me. I had had him a week, and today was going to have been when we got serious with him, and started working him every day and turning him out every night, as preparation for going in with the other geldings. But my stupid broken arm had gotten in the way of that.

Since Daddy was going to ride him, I found a brush and went into the stall. Grooming horses can be a full-time job, which was why Rodney Lemon, out at the stable on the coast, was a "groom." When Rodney groomed a horse, he started with the currycomb, which was for getting out the dirt and loose hair, but since it's made of metal, you can't use it on a horse's face or legs. Rodney then brushed away everything that the currycomb loosened with a brush that had bristles like a broom, stiff and blond-colored. You could use this on his legs, if you brushed downward in brisk strokes, but not on his face. Then he went all over the horse, including his face, with a soft brush. After the soft brush, the horse was supposed to be clean and smooth from his nose to the base of his tail, but Rodney polished him again with a cloth. I liked to use a chamois for this, which is a piece of leather that is very soft.

The next thing was to pick the horse's feet with a hoofpick—he lifts his foot and you pry out the dirt with the point, always pushing away, toward the toe of the hoof as it's resting in your hand. The important thing in picking hooves is to be sure that there's no dirt in the grooves between the frog and the sole. The frog is a wedge-shaped, sort of springy area from the middle of the hoof to the back, and the sole is around it. The sole is hard, like a fingernail. If you don't clean out the grooves, they can get something called "thrush," which is caused by germs and really stinks. A horse should be taught from foalhood to stand still and pick up his feet, but some are not, so when I was working on a new horse, I was always careful to run my hand down the outside of his leg from the elbow to the pastern, and then squeeze the area just above the pastern with my fingers. This makes those tendons go a little limp, and then the horse relaxes his foot and you can pick it up.

Some horses then promptly lean their weight on you, but you have to teach them not to do that by dropping the hoof as soon as you feel a shift. It can take a while to get a new horse to stand up properly while you pick his hooves, but you have to do it, because a horseshoer will not tolerate misbehavior, and Jake always charged us a dollar more per foot if the horse was bad. That was a lot of money. After I had tried for about five minutes to figure out a way to pick Blue's hooves with a broken arm, I gave up—Daddy would have to do that.

After the hooves, I picked the tangles out of Blue's tail and gently combed his mane—I could do that one-handed. Daddy didn't believe in combing tails, because he thought it made too much hair come out, and then the tails look too thin, but you also have to watch the tangles and not let them turn into knots, because then the tail also loses hair the next time you comb it.

In a parade, everyone likes their horses' tails to float just above the ground in a soft cloud. I was sure that Rodney had some English secret for tails, but we didn't, so we were careful. The fact is, I did not groom every horse the way Rodney would, because I was not a groom, and grooming was not my full-time job. I curried off the mud, used the stiff brush where needed, and concentrated on the soft brush. Some days, I didn't do the legs at all—I had discovered without being told that lots of times the mud falls off after a day or so, especially if a horse has plenty of opportunities to roll. And that's how a horse keeps himself clean in the wild—he rolls. If a horse in the wild cares about being clean.

Some horses hate to be groomed, but most don't mind. They stand there eating their hay and acting otherwise like a brick wall being scrubbed while you work around them. Blue was not like that. He acted as if the currycomb was torture, the stiff brush was ticklish, but the soft brush was heaven. He especially liked me to stroke the soft brush gently over his face—he closed his eyes, set his ears out of the way, and lifted his nose. I always brushed with the growth pattern, and so who wouldn't like it? The other thing about Blue was that he always knew where I was while I was grooming him. Some horses don't care where you are, and some horses pretend not to know where you are—they step into you, or even on you. Other horses push against you as you brush them, and you have to tell them to move over—if you push back, they only push harder. But Blue knew where I was, and always moved out of my way. I didn't know how he saw it, but to me it felt very polite, as if he were saying, "After you, miss." Even for the parts of the grooming that he didn't like, he never pinned his ears or gave me a look—he only twitched his skin. The result was that I paid more attention to what I was doing, too. I didn't want to make him more uncomfortable than I had to. I liked grooming him; it was not like brushing the living room couch all over every day with three different tools. It was like doing something with a friend. Or, at least, a nice person who would someday be a friend.

I could not say that he had completely relaxed in the week we'd had him. It was more like he had decided that certain places seemed safe enough—his stall, the aisle of the barn, the training pen, a patch of grass along the fence of the gelding pasture, and part of the arena (but only part). I could lead him in these places and he didn't seem tense, but when we went outside of them, his head went up, his ears went up, and he started staring again. He also started whinnying again, as if he were calling to someone, then listening for an answer that never came. Sometimes a mare or gelding answered him, but evidently, that answer was not what he was looking for, because he didn't answer back.

Once I finished taking bits of straw out of his tail and smoothing out the only really big tangle, I snapped the lead rope onto his halter and led him toward the arena. He hadn't been in there since our last ride, on Friday, and all the same things were in there that had worried him before, so I just led him around the arena and up to all of those things so that he could look at them and sniff them. He was willing to do that, but he still didn't like the poles on the ground and the chairs on the other side of the railing. He recognized the straw bales and didn't mind the cones. While we were doing this, Daddy drove up in the truck and parked beside the barn. He stood and looked at us for a moment, then went into the barn and came out with his saddle and the bridle I'd used before. He walked over and hung his saddle on the gate, then watched us until I went to him.

"How you feeling, Abby?" He nodded at my hideous white sling.

"Stupid."

He laughed.

"But Brother Abner told me he fell off a roof once on a dare and broke his arm. So I wasn't that stupid."

"Here's what I think. One of the evidences of God's grace is that people only sometimes suffer from the stupid things they do. He gives them another chance, and then another, and another."

I said, "I hope so."

"Well, I was there Saturday, honey, and you weren't stupid. She just zipped out from under you and there you were."

I nodded.

He said, "How is True Blue today?"

"He still doesn't like the chairs or the poles, but he's willing to consider that they MIGHT be harmless. The cones are fine and he would eat the straw if we let him."

Daddy opened the gate, closed it, and then lifted the saddle off the gate and onto Blue's back. Blue looked at him, then looked suddenly up the hill, as if something had appeared, but it hadn't—even Rusty was no longer up there; I could see her sitting on the back porch. But Blue kept looking up the hill with his ears pricked until Daddy distracted him by cinching up the saddle and then turning him around in a little circle.

I handed Daddy the bridle, and as he put the bit in Blue's mouth and lifted the browband over his ears, I said, "If I were you, I would work him a little on the ground first."

"You didn't take him in the pen?"

"I forgot." Then I added, "I was thinking about other things. Sorry."

"That's okay. But let's see what he wants to do in here. We'll just play it by ear."

Daddy's coiled rope was still tied to his saddle, and Blue cocked his head to look at it. When he moved, it flapped, and he jumped. I said, "I doubt he's ever had a western saddle on him before he came here."

"Maybe not."

We stood there. Then Daddy did the smart thing, and led Blue to the training pen, and had him trot around.

There was more than the rope—Daddy's saddle had strings hanging down and rear cinch billets flapping and the stirrups were surrounded by tapaderos, which were pieces of leather that surrounded each stirrup and hung down and also sort of flapped against them. As soon as Blue was in the pen, he skittered around, trying to get away from all of these things, but once he realized they were attached to him, he gave up and started trotting. His trot was nervous, though, fast, with short strides. Every time he kicked up, or trotted faster, the parts of the saddle flapped more.

Daddy said, "Give it time."

We did.

When Blue finally began to calm down, Daddy went into the pen with a flag and urged him to go faster. I knew this was the right thing to do—once a horse gets used to some flapping, you have to make him endure more flapping. Eventually, he won't care about flapping, and you let the flapping stop. I would have done the exact same thing with Jack automatically. But part of me wanted Blue to not have to do it—he was so pretty and so kind, it seemed a shame to ignore the fact that he didn't like the saddle. Why not just take the saddle off and try another one that he might like better?

But of course I didn't say anything. I glanced over at Jack, who was standing by the fence, watching. I thought, If it's good enough for Jack, it's good enough for Blue. But even though Jack was just a yearling, he already seemed to be made of tougher material than Blue. The thought crossed my mind of Blue coming in the house and curling up in a basket by the fireplace. Rusty would be very envious. I laughed.

Blue went both ways, and then when he was blowing and a little calmer, Daddy got on him and walked him around the pen. He went with his head down and his tail relaxed. Daddy tried a few neck-reining things with him, and even though he had probably not been trained that way, he turned as Daddy was asking him. I opened the gate of the pen and walked behind them toward the arena. They went in, and I closed the gate.

The amazing thing about the unexpected is that it's unexpected. I certainly thought that Blue was completely ready to walk around the arena on a long rein, breathing a little hard, maybe, but tired enough. Judging by the way he was riding, Daddy thought the same thing. Judging by the way he was walking, Blue thought the same thing. They went across the arena, toward the cones—not the chairs or the poles. We'd been in that part of the arena half a dozen times, no problem. But even so, Blue went from relaxed, head down, walking, to terrified, head up, running back toward me in the time it took for me to take a breath and jump out of the way. He missed me by two feet, and I looked into his eye as he passed. He didn't even realize I was standing there.

Daddy didn't fall off, but he came close—he was unseated and lost one stirrup. He had to grab the horn of the saddle, then the mane, and then shorten his reins to stop Blue. They ended up on the side of the arena next to the gate, with Blue snorting and shaking his head. It took the three of us about five minutes to get ourselves sorted out again. Daddy picked up the reins and kicked Blue to move on. Blue shook his head and trotted out. He was not resistant—he didn't try to buck or kick up or rear or anything. He tried to do what Daddy was asking of him. My wrist throbbed, but I hadn't hit it on anything. I put my right hand on the cast. It was as though the effort of jumping out of the way had made it hurt.

Finally, Daddy said, "What was that? Was something over there?"

I peered in that direction for a minute, but I couldn't see a thing besides the back of the barn, the side of Daddy's truck, and the pen. If he shied by the poles or the chairs, I would have understood it better—there were trees and shadows, and maybe something moved across the hill, but the place where he shied was well known to him. I said, "I don't see anything." Then I said, "He's a strange horse." I must have sounded glum, because Daddy said, "They're all strange at first." He walked Blue over to me, then looked down at me. He said, "I think you can look at this horse in one of two ways. He's a horse I would not have picked myself, but he did come into our lives, and maybe that's for a reason. The Lord will provide."

To myself, I thought, Maybe the Lord should provide a lesson with Jem Jarrow.

The rest of Daddy's ride on Blue was uneventful—mostly walking and trotting, with a bit of canter, some backing up, lots of turns. When he got off, he said, "How old did we say this horse is?"

"He's seven."

"Well, he's willing enough, but plenty ignorant. I don't see how someone can let a horse get this old without giving him a job to do."

We led Blue back to the barn and untacked him. After Daddy took the saddle into the tack room, and I put Blue in his stall, I brushed him off a little. I could hear Daddy whistling "The Yellow Rose of Texas" and moving things around—at the end of every day, he hung things up and straightened boxes. Blue's two trunks and his blankets and the other stuff were still across the aisle from his stall, mostly because we hadn't had time to put it away, but also because I still didn't know what to do with it. Take the blankets, for example. I guess at big stables, especially in the East, they blanket a horse inside and out, but we let them grow their coats, because Daddy said that their coats are actually warmer, and anyway, who's to say that Jack or one of the other geldings wouldn't go up to Blue and rip his blanket—horses love to do that sort of thing. His halter, too, was a beautiful brown leather with a brass nameplate, but you wouldn't want to hang it on the fence of the gelding pasture to get rained on. And then there was the other stuff. I put him in the pen with Jefferson for a couple of hours, along with their hay. I hated the idea of putting him right back in the stall after so much running around.

Just after supper, the phone rang, and it was Jane Slater asking about Blue. I told her about my broken arm. She did NOT say that it could have been worse; she said, "Well, at least you broke it falling off a horse. I always think it's such a waste when a horseman breaks something skiing or falling into a manhole, or something like that."

She was silent for a moment and then said, "Of course you can't ride. So, come work for me."

"Do I have to be a groom?"

"Not at all. You can give Melinda Anniston and Ellen Leinsdorf their riding lessons. Two a week, Tuesdays and Saturdays. I'll pay you two dollars a lesson."

"That's eight dollars a week."

"Yes, it is."

With Barbie, that was over ten dollars a week. That was a lot of money. Even Stella, who got a good allowance, only got three dollars a week.

I said, "I'll see if Mom will drive me out there." But I knew she would, because what else was I going to do with my time? And I could pay her for gas. That was a very grown-up thing to do.

She said, "Go ask your parents, then. Because you can start tomorrow."

I set down the phone and went into the living room, where Mom was knitting, Daddy was reading his Bible, and Spooky was standing on his hind legs, with his paws on the rim of his box, as if he were preparing to jump and looking for a landing spot. Mom was happy to drive me, and Daddy thought it was a great idea—ten percent tithe to the church, five dollars into my savings account, and the rest for me. I went back to the phone. I felt rich. I forgot to tell her how Blue was.

Daddy and I didn't talk about the way Blue spooked. For Daddy, a spook was just a spook. Some horses are more nervous than others. Some spook, some buck, some rear, and you've got to deal with it, whatever it is. But it still gave me a funny feeling.

I went out and put the horses away—first Jefferson to the gelding pasture, then Blue to his stall. I carried what was left of the hay in the pen to him and threw it over the door, then I went in. In the dark, I shivered. Yes, I knew that the "ghost" I'd seen sitting on the trunk was just Daddy's shirt hanging on a hook, but as the days passed, she'd gone from being a vague, light shape in the gloom to being a slender woman in dark breeches and black boots, sitting on the blue trunk with her legs crossed. Her shirt was pale and she had a long neck, and her dark hair was pulled back. She was looking at me, and she was about to say something.

See? She was practically living with me. It was all I could do not to imagine her following me into the house. I thought, What if that was her, walking around the barn, between the barn and the arena, and Blue saw her?

He was standing right next to me, head down, eating his hay. I stood with my hand on his withers, watching him bite off hunks of the flake, then root for more while he chewed. He blew out. He stepped forward and flipped the flake over with his nose. I wondered, Does Blue know she's dead? What does Blue think happened to him? The woman he knew disappeared and new people appeared and took him to a new place. And no one ever thought to tell him what was going on. And then I thought, Does a horse know what "dead" is?

For the moment, though, it seemed as though all he cared about was the hay. I left the stall, hanging his beautiful halter there on a hook, and headed for the house. When I stepped up onto the back porch, as I was giving Rusty a pat on the head, I turned and looked back. Blue was pressing his chest against his stall door and staring at me.

Saddle with Strings

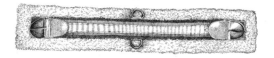

Western Fleece Cinch

Chapter 10

MOM BROUGHT MY JEANS AND BOOTS WITH HER WHEN SHE picked me up at school the next day, and also a jacket because if it was misty around the school, then it was certainly rainy at the stable. But she hadn't gotten any calls from Jane saying not to come. She said, "They don't care about the weather out there. They just put on their raincoats and ride, like in England. How does your arm feel?"

I shrugged. Fortunately, my jacket had a pretty wide sleeve, so I could get it on, and then put the sling around that. When we got there, it was the same weather as at school. It was just after three-thirty, and the sun would be going down around six, so we had enough time. Especially since Rodney Lemon put his head out of Gallant Man's stall as soon as he heard my voice and said, "Ah, there ya are, lass. Here's the pony." He opened the stall door and led him out.

Only a year before, I'd ridden Gallant Man in a show—my first at the stable—but it would have been hard for me to ride him now, he had gotten so small. Or I had gotten so tall. While I was staring at him, Jane came over with Melinda. Melinda was now maybe ten, but the only thing different about her was that her hair was longer. She ran up to me and gave me a hug. She said, "Oh, Abby, I missed you! What happened to your arm? Jane said you broke it! I hate Los Angeles! I'm so glad we've moved up here. We have a new house, did you know that? And I have a new school where there are NUNS and it's much better." She put her arms up and pulled my head down and whispered in my ear, "I have to do fourth grade again, but I don't care! I didn't listen to a word they said at my school in Los Angeles."

I said, "I'm glad to see you, too, Melinda." She kissed me on the cheek.

And all of a sudden I was glad to see her. Rodney lifted her onto the pony and I started walking toward the ring. Melinda on Gallant Man walked beside me, and Jane walked behind them. We went to the smallest ring, which was empty. I opened the gate. Melinda said, "I want to hear all about how you broke your arm. I do so hope it wasn't falling off a horse, because I don't want to think about that." I didn't tell her, and she kept talking. "My mom had to stay in LA, but May and Martin came along, and she takes care of me and he drives me to school." She stopped Gallant Man in the center of the ring and took her feet out of the stirrups. I bent down and checked to see how long they were. I decided that they were too short and began to adjust the left one, which was awkward and slow with one hand. She said, "May lets me do whatever I want, but I never want to do anything bad."

I said, "I'm sure you don't, Melinda."

I went around and adjusted the right stirrup, then had her stand up in them. Maybe she had grown. I said, "Walk him out on the rail, Melinda, and let me see how you've gotten better."

I wouldn't have said that Melinda had improved much, but she'd always been more skillful than confident. Now she picked up her reins and gave Gallant Man a kick. When they were out on the rail, I could see that her heels were down, her thumbs were up, and her back was straight without being arched. I called, "Don't stick your chin out, Melinda. Just let it float along like a flower." Her head turned on her neck a bit, and then she did it.

Even when they are lazy, most ponies don't look lazy—they look perky and bright, as if somewhere, there is a horse who needs to be told what to do, and if the pony is lucky, that horse will appear any minute. That's how Gallant Man looked just then. I called out to Melinda, "Shorten your reins about an inch, so that he brings his chin in a tiny bit, but squeeze your legs while you're doing it, so that he knows that you don't mean to stop him." She did all these things.

Jane was standing beside me with her hands on her hips. She said, "Such a custody battle! It's like nuclear war! Now she's with her dad, but I don't know—"

"Who's May?"

"May is the housekeeper, and in my opinion, she's the only

one who actually cares about the child. She's married to the chauffeur. He brings her out here."

"What's a chauffeur?"

"Someone who drives the car."

I tried to imagine Daddy allowing some stranger to drive either the car or the truck. It could not be done. Jane said, "Well, good luck. I'll come back in a little while to see how you're doing, but I'm sure you'll be fine," and she walked away.

I called out, "Okay, Melinda. I want you to do three things in a row. I want you to turn the pony in a small circle, then I want you to trot for fifteen steps, then I want you to halt." As she did this, I realized that this was what she needed. When she had halted, I went over to her, and I said, "Okay. We're going to play a game."

"I love that," said Melinda.

"Here's the game. You are going to count to ten—fairly slowly, like this." I counted to ten. "At the beginning of each count, you are going to do something, like walk out or trot, and when you get to ten, you are going to change what you're doing to something else. You can do anything you want, walk, trot, canter, halt, back up, trot faster, walk slower, but it has to be different enough from the last thing so that I can see that it's different. Okay?"

She said, "Can I have points?"

"Sure. One point for making a change, one point for making the change right on ten."

"What about two points?"

I thought for a second, then said, "Next round, I'll give you something to do for two points."

She said, "Okay, tell me when I get to fifteen points."

I hadn't thought of that. I said, "Okay."

She gathered the reins and trotted away. I could hear her saying, "One, two, three . . ." I went back to the center of the arena.

I could see Melinda's lips moving, so I tried to count along with her, which I hadn't thought of when I was making up the game. She was pretty good—she walked, then trotted, then turned in another circle, then trotted more quickly, then walked, then halted, then trotted, then cantered, then walked and turned to go the other way. Every so often, I called out "Heels down!" or "Sit up!" or "Don't forget to look where you're going!" She was a little slow on a couple of the changes, but she got to fifteen points, and I called out, "Okay! Fifteen points."

She laughed and came trotting over to me. She said, "Can I do it again, but jump something?"

"Do you really want to jump something, Melinda? You used to be afraid of jumping."

She nodded. "I've been jumping with Jane for the last few weeks."

I saw a little crossbar in the middle of the ring, not more than a foot high, and pointed to it—I was glad I didn't have to build a jump myself with only one hand. Before she started again, I said, "If you make a good jump, you get two points, but if you make a bad jump, like if you're left behind or you get ahead, then you lose two points. That means that your score can go way down for bad jumps."

She grinned and nodded even more enthusiastically. I said, "Melinda!"

"What?"

"Don't forget to pat your pony!"

She put her hand down and patted Gallant Man on the neck. I said, "If you pat him right after he's done something good, you get an extra point."

This game worked out even better—we went to twenty-five points, and Melinda jumped the crossbar four times, but only when she wanted to. She stayed right with the motion, too, neither leaning ahead of the pony nor getting left. The rest of the time, she did sharp transitions—even one from the walk to the canter, which is a little harder than from the trot to the canter. When we got to twenty-five points, Gallant Man was puffing a little bit, so I made her walk him around on a loose rein for a while. All told, she remembered to pat him five times. I said, "Melinda, you are pretty brave these days."

She said, "I like to do what I want."

"Isn't that the truth," said Jane Slater, who was coming into the ring.

I said, "This is pretty fun. Do we have time to do it again?"

Jane shook her head. "We have to get her out of here in some way before you know who arrives."

I said, "Really?"

"Really."

"When does she arrive?"

"Ten minutes."

I walked over to the pony and said, "I know a back way to the barn. We can go on the trail."

"I don't like to go on the trail."

"I'll go with you. You can keep playing your game. We'll

start down the trail, and I'll go behind you, and everything you do, I'll do, too." I figured I could keep up with Gallant Man.

"No, you go in front."

I said, "Okay," and I ran out the gate. Melinda laughed as she trotted after me. By the time we got back to the barn, I knew she'd been right not to go ahead of me—I had to sit down on a tack trunk, I was breathing so hard. And my wrist was throbbing. Gallant Man could easily keep up with me, but I would not have been able to keep up with him. Melinda came over to me and gave me a hug and said, "Thank you," and then Rodney handed me the pony's reins and spirited her away to the Coke machine.

Of course, now I figured I knew everything about teaching horseback riding. Ellen Leinsdorf wasn't so sure. The first thing she said when she saw me was, "Why isn't Jane teaching me?"

"She said I—"

"What's wrong with your arm?"

"I broke it."

"I bet you fell off a horse. Were you jumping?"

"No, I—"

"I've never fallen off a horse."

"Everybody falls off eventu—"

"I never have. I'm not going to."

I looked down at her. Her two braids were like sticks, they were so stiff. I said, "You know what my daddy always says?"

"What?"

"You aren't good until you've hit the ground three times."

"I don't believe that."

Even though she was shorter than Melinda, she walked up

to Gallant Man, gathered the reins, put her hand way up on the cantle of his saddle, and mounted from the ground. Then she checked and shortened her own stirrups, and even leaned down and checked to see if her girth was tight. I was impressed. She shook her shoulders, settled into the saddle, and said, "Let's go to the ring. I only have forty-five minutes. I want to jump."

She walked away from me, and I trotted after her to catch up. When we got to the ring where I had been teaching Melinda, I opened the gate and said, "Do you jump with Jane?"

"Sure."

"Show me jumps you've jumped."

Without hesitating, she pointed to a brush and a coop, both of which were maybe two foot six, and a somewhat larger panel that was leaning against the fence. I said, "That's pretty big."

"That's why I like it best."

As I closed the gate, she trotted away from me. I went to the center of the arena and watched her for a minute. She did have her heels down, but they were way down, so far down that I couldn't believe that her ankles had that much stretch in them. But everything about her riding was exaggerated—she held the reins too tight, kicked the pony too hard, arched her back, held her chin too high. I called out, "Turn and go the other direction!" Her turn was abrupt, and the pony tossed his head. She trotted the other way. I watched for another minute, until she shouted, "Tell me to do something!"

"Halt!"

Not a good idea. I almost had to hide my eyes as the pony lurched to a halt. Ellen's braids didn't move, though. I looked around for Jane, but she was nowhere to be seen. I walked over to Ellen.

With her on the pony, we were eye to eye, and she stared at me. I said, "Ellen—"

"What?"

"I want you to practice being nicer to the pony. He's trying to be good."

"I am nice to the pony."

"Well, loosen your reins a little."

She loosened them about a quarter of an inch.

"No, really. More than that."

Another quarter of an inch.

"Look at his head. You're making him stick his neck up in the air. It's like if I had to walk around like this." I bent my head back and walked around looking at the sky for a couple of seconds.

She loosened another quarter of an inch. I took hold of the left rein down by the bit and said, "Let go of the reins completely for a second."

"He'll run away."

"No, he won't. I've got him."

"I wish I had a grown-up teaching me."

I thought, The grown-up doesn't want to teach you, and I knew this was true.

"We can have plenty of fun."

Her lower lip pushed out.

"Can you let go of the reins for a minute?"

She waited, and then dropped the reins. I positioned myself next to her leg, facing toward the front, and then I picked up the reins so that I was making contact with the pony's mouth, but not pulling on it. The reins were nice—old and well used. I said, "Can I have the ribbons from your braids?"

She said, "Yes! I hate these ribbons. I hate pink."

I thought, I bet you do. I untied the ribbons, then tied one to each rein where I thought her hands should go. Then I said, "Okay, you put your hands on the ribbons, and make sure they're always covered up. I don't want to see them coming out behind your hands or in front of your hands." I set her hands on the reins the way I thought they should be, with the ribbons inside her hands, and said, "Okay, now walk." She walked away. The pony looked much more comfortable. It was a good thing the ribbons were pink, because I could see them every time she moved her hands. After a moment, I told her to trot. That seemed to be harder, because she wanted to shorten the reins and hold on. I called out, "I see pink!"

Ellen scowled.

I said, "Keep trotting!"

And again, "Keep trotting."

But she was determined, I have to say that. It took her about twice around the small arena with a real scowl on her face and her shoulders hunched before she realized that she was doing fine, and it was easier than she thought. I called out, "Make a nice turn and go the other direction!"

She made sort of a nice turn, but she did go the other direction, and after about half a circuit, she relaxed going that direction, too. I let her go one more circuit, then I called out, "Okay, walk! But just sit down in the saddle, don't pull on the reins!" She managed to do this. I went over to where she was walking the pony and said, "Now pat your pony." She put both her reins in one hand and reached around with the other one and patted Gallant Man behind the saddle once.

I said, "Pat him on the neck."

She patted him on the neck.

I said, "Pat him on the shoulder."

She bent forward just a little bit and patted him on the shoulder.

I said, "Pat him on the underside of his neck with your other hand."

She switched hands on the reins and reached under his neck.

I said, "Pat him on the cheek."

She did the right thing—she halted him, then turned his head toward her slightly with one rein, and patted him on the cheek.

"Now the other side."

She did the same thing on the other side.

I said, "He's a good pony."

"I love him."

"Did you really jump that brush and that panel?"

She shook her head.

"Did you jump anything?"

She shook her head again.

"Well, let's do it."

"Really?" Now she grinned for the first time the whole lesson.

"Yes, but I'm going to move your ribbons." I moved the pink ribbons forward about an inch and a half and said, "I'm going to lead you over the crossbar, there, and the pony's going to trot.

You stand up in your stirrups and put your hands with the reins right here on this place on the mane"—I made a little braid—"and just hold on right there the whole time, okay?"

She nodded. I took the pony by the bridle and trotted toward the crossbar. It was a good thing my right wrist was the unbroken one. As we were trotting, I turned and looked at Ellen. Her lips were pursed and she was trying hard to keep her balance. I said, "Hold on."

She tightened her grip. When I jumped over the crossbar and the pony jumped right next to me, her mouth opened in an O.

We slowed to a halt. Ellen sat down. I said, "Want to do it again?"

She nodded.

"Are you holding on?"

"Yeah!"

I almost laughed. "Heels down!"

We jumped the crossbar again and came down to a halt.

Ellen said, "You go right there, by the standard. I want to do it."

"Let me take you once more, but not holding the bridle."

We did this.

Then she did it once in each direction on her own. The pony was perfect. After the second time, Ellen rode the pony back to me and said, "I was really good, wasn't I?"

I said, "Yes, you were really good."

She grinned.

Then I heard, "Oh, my goodness! Oh, dear!" I turned. Mrs. Leinsdorf was hurrying in the gate. She said, "Ellen! You were jumping! Who is this child?"

"It's Abby. She's my new—"

"Well, Abby, I don't know who you are, but Ellen does not have permission to jump!"

I looked around for Jane, then opened my mouth to say something, though I wasn't sure what that was going to be. Ellen's scowl deepened. She said, "Abby owned Onyx when he was Black George. She trained him. She lives on a ranch and she's a great rider." I would have been flattered by what she said, but she said it in such a threatening voice that I was more amazed such a small person would talk like that to her mother than I was pleased by the compliments.

Mrs. Leinsdorf said, "Well, that's all very well, but I told you that if you were going to have riding lessons, there would be no—"

"I want to jump! I can jump! I'm good at jumping! It's not fair that everyone else can jump and I can't!" She was still sitting on Gallant Man, and the pony's ears flicked as her voice rose. I put my hand on his rein. I looked at Mrs. Leinsdorf.

She said, "I've told you time and time again—"

Ellen turned to me and said, "Is the pony a safe jumper?"

"Yes, but if your—"

"See? See?" shouted Ellen to her mother.

Mrs. Leinsdorf gave me a look. Embarrassment. I looked away, back toward the barn, to see if Jane was coming.

That's how I missed what next happened, which was that Ellen fell off the pony. The next thing I saw was Ellen lying on the ground, and the pony cocking his head to look down at her, then stepping away from her.

Mrs. Leinsdorf exclaimed, "Ellen!"

Ellen sat up, then stood up. She lifted her chin and said, "I fell off, and I'm fine!" She stomped away.

Mrs. Leinsdorf took a deep breath, and then did the thing I didn't want her to do, which was apologize to me. I shrugged, then began to say, "It's okay. I think—"

But by that time, she was running after Ellen.

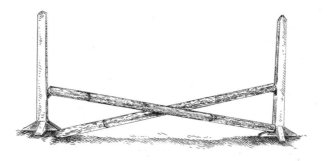

Crossbar Jump

Hay Bale

Chapter 11

THE ONLY THING I TOLD MOM WHEN SHE PICKED ME UP WAS THAT it was harder than I thought it would be. She said that she was sure everything would be fine in the way that grown-ups do when they are thinking about other things, but that was okay with me. I would tell her that I was finished teaching Ellen after Jane called me and told me. At home, all the horses were standing in their pastures, Rusty was sitting on the porch, Mom's flowers were blooming in their pots, and even the breeze and the mist were quiet. It was a relief.

Mom went in to start supper. I headed straight for the barn to give the horses their hay. Now that I had had some practice, it was a little easier, and my wrist stayed quiet. Jack whinnied and trotted to the gate, and then Happy whinnied, and then

Foxy. Truly, they were like kids in a classroom. Jack and Foxy and Happy were the ones in the front row who always raised their hands, Jefferson and Lincoln didn't even realize that the teacher was talking, and Amazon and Sprinkles had their own ideas that they discussed when the others weren't looking. Only Blue, in the barn, was left out. I went over and took him a flake of hay. When I looked into the stall, I saw that there was a lot of manure in there. That was the thing Daddy hated the most about keeping a horse in a stall—the time you spent cleaning up after him was time you were not riding.

I gave him a pat as he dove into his hay and then headed toward the house. Just then, Daddy pulled up in the truck. He got out and slammed the door. As I followed him into the house, he said, "I don't see how we are going to do this. I just don't." Mom was reaching a fork into the oven to test the potatoes. She closed the oven door, set the fork on the top of the stove, and picked up a wooden spoon. She took the lid off a pot. Broccoli.

He went on. "I expected the truck to take at most two hours, and it took six, so there I was. Could not ride a single horse all day."

Mom said, "I rode Jefferson and Lincoln."

Daddy said, "That's good. I don't mean to—"

Mom said, "Danny rode Happy and Foxy. That was all he had time for." Her face was blank. She wasn't smiling or frowning.

Daddy said, "Happy and Foxy need—"

Then he stopped and said, "What? Sarah?"

"I said, 'Danny rode Happy and Foxy. That was all he had

time for.'" She lifted the lid of the frying pan and flipped the minute steaks. Then she said, easy as you please, "Do we want gravy?"

I said, "I do. I would like gravy."

Mom said, "Good." And then she said, "He said he would ride Blue tomorrow, after Abby gets home from school."

I said, "I think he's ready to go out with the other geldings. He seems lonely to me."

Daddy left the kitchen. After a moment, we could hear him pounding up the stairs, and then we could hear him walking around in their bedroom. Mom looked at me and smiled.

When we sat down for supper, Daddy had his Bible next to his plate. He wasn't saying anything, though. Mom asked me about my day at school and the lessons, and I told her about Melinda and May and the chauffeur and about Ellen falling off her horse on purpose when her mother wouldn't let her jump. I said, "I mean maybe it was my fault in a way, because she saw my cast and was bragging about never having fallen off, and I told her that thing about how you have to fall off three times—" I expected Daddy to say something, but he just kept eating.

Mom said, "I hope you can handle those girls."

"I hope so, too. But they were nice to the pony. Melinda can ride and Ellen really wants to."

"And it was only the first lesson. That's the second-hardest one."

I looked at her. "What's the hardest one?"

She said, "The second." We laughed, but I wasn't sure why. Daddy kept eating until he had cleaned his plate, then he pushed his chair back a little, lifted his eyes to the Lord, and opened the Bible. He stared at the page for a moment before saying, in a little bit of a weird voice, "'Therefore all things whatsoever ye would that men should do to you, do ye even so to them: for this is the law and the prophets.'"

Now it was our turn to stare, because he had landed right on the Golden Rule. The first thing I thought was that the Lord had answered Mom's prayer and not Daddy's, but then I made myself not think that thought, because it seemed like a bad one. Daddy pulled his bandanna out of his back pocket and blew his nose. He read the Golden Rule again and said, "Well, we have our answer."

Mom said, "I guess we do." When she got up to clear her plate, she patted him on the head. I said I would do the dishes, and they went into the living room. I heard her say hi to Spooky, and then I heard the sofa squeak as someone sat down on it.

It was time-consuming and thought-consuming to do the dishes with one hand, making sure not to get my cast wet. By the time I was finished, I couldn't believe how happy I was that when I got home from school tomorrow, Danny would be there, and he would ride Blue.

The only other thing that happened was that Spooky jumped onto my bed in the middle of the night and snuggled down under the covers. He was gone by morning. I know he was—I saw him curled up in his box when I left the house for the school bus. He didn't even wake up and meow. Nor did I stop and say anything about it to Mom—I was late for the bus, and could see it almost at our gate. I had to run.

By Wednesday, I was used to walking from class to class,

dropping my stuff every so often, and clumsily opening my books and notebook with one hand in class while everyone stared at me. I was used to the fact that my wrist was like a second brain—it didn't think, but it did throb every time I worried about anything. During lunch, Alexis and Barbara brought out a bunch of markers and drew on it—Alexis drew six different types of flowers, and Barbara drew the face of a horse looking over them, a tiny horse, smaller than the tulips. After that, everyone wanted to see the drawing, including the painting teacher, Miss Rowan. The horse was on the palm of my hand, so I could close my fingers over it if I wanted to.

When I got home, Danny was already there, dumping the wheelbarrow full of horse manure into the manure pile at the far end of the mare pasture. Rusty was sitting in the aisle of the barn, looking out the door, and Blue was in the pen, trotting around. He looked at me, but he didn't stop—he stretched his nose down and kept trotting along with big strides, then he squealed and kicked up, and broke into a canter. Halfway around the pen, he slid to a halt, reared up, and turned back the other way. Danny came up to me. I saw that he had some new boots—black ones with fancy yellow stitching. He poked me in the ribs with his elbow. Then he noticed my cast and said, "Hey. Nice. Who did that?"

"Alexis and Barbara." I showed him the horse.

"Mmm. You friends with them?"

"Yes. Do you know them?"

"I know their cousin."

I said, "She's way too smart for you."

"We'll see."

It was my turn to poke him.

Blue kicked up again, and ran for about three steps, then trotted forward. Then he stopped where we were standing and snorted.

Danny said, "Where's the flag?"

When Danny had his back to me, it was so much like watching Daddy that it didn't even seem strange for him to be here, though he'd been away for eighteen months now. His shoulders were Daddy's shoulders, the back of his neck was the back of Daddy's neck, his cowboy hat was tilted the way Daddy's was, and his hips sat to one side, like Daddy's did. He had been riding horses all his life, so maybe that's why he had Daddy's bowed legs (mine weren't bowed at all, and I had been riding all my life, too). He was a tall drink of water, and it was only when he turned to follow Blue's movement around the pen that he looked like Danny to me—he had Mom's blue eyes and his own nose, long and straight with a little tiny cleft in the tip. When Blue slowed down, he lifted the flag, and Blue sped up. Danny nodded. He said, "Go on. Go on now, Blue horse."

The way he was not like Daddy was that he seemed to have all the time in the world. He told Blue to do a few things, and then he stood there and watched him before telling him to do something else. There was plenty that Blue didn't know how to do, even though I had started getting him to step under, which was a very important exercise for getting him to relax and pay attention to you. Now Danny let Blue come to him, and then he did what I had done. He stood beside Blue's head, facing his back end, with the lead rope in the hand closest to Blue. Then he lifted his hand upward and away from Blue, so that Blue turned his head and lifted his nose. This was meant to throw him off balance, and in order to regain his balance, Blue lifted the back foot on the side Danny was standing next to, and stepped it across in front of the other back foot. Then he stepped the other hind foot over. Eventually. Danny asked him again and then again. Blue turned a little circle around Danny. The idea was that as he made these steps, he was using his spine and back muscles, and when he was using them, they were soft rather than stiff. When he was stiff, he was using his strength against Danny, and when he was soft, he wasn't.

Horses stiffen for all sorts of reasons—one of them is laziness, another is stubbornness, another is fear, and another is simply not knowing what the rider wants. But you don't want your horse to be stiff for any reason, so this stepping under is a good exercise for getting a horse ready for anything. Danny asked for lots of repetitions on the left, lots of repetitions on the right, then back to the left, first dismounted, then mounted. When a horse knows this exercise and understands what you want, all you have to do at any gait, even going down to a jump, is tweak the rein, usually on the inside, and he will lift his shoulder, soften his back, and relax. His front legs will get more rhythmic and his back legs will start making bigger strides. It is almost a miracle.

They never did canter. But Blue had a little bit of a sweat when they were done—he had used muscles that maybe he had never used before. When Danny dismounted and began to uncinch the saddle, I said, "Aren't you going to take him in the arena?"

"I think he needs to get through kindergarten first."

"That's where he was scared before."

"Well, turn him out in there for a while. But if you're riding him, he needs some tools to work with."

"What do you mean?"

"He's never been taught anything. If he's been a pretty good horse, then he's doing it out of the kindness of his heart. But you can't rely on that in every situation. Especially new situations."

That made me glum. I said, "Daddy said that he's untrained, too."

"I wish I could come every day." He pushed his hat back on his head.

"How often can you come?"

"We'll see."

"Now you sound like a grown-up."

"Uh-oh." Then he said, "But I guess I will be a grown-up in a couple of months."

I said, "Yeah." I knew he would be eighteen in May.

He took the bridle off Blue and put the halter on. I am telling you, until you've tried to halter a horse with one hand, you don't know what impossible is, so I was glad of that. Then he handed me the lead rope. He said, "Let him run around in the arena before Dad gets home, and then teach him something."

"Like what?" I held up my arm.

"Like a trick." He gave me a little kiss on the top of the head.

I stood there thinking about this, watching Danny from the back walk toward his car just like Daddy. Just like someone, as

Mom said, who couldn't be told what to do, but could be asked, if you were the type of person who didn't mind asking. The trouble was, Daddy always told, he never asked. But that's where the Golden Rule came in. I shook my head. Danny drove away and I took Blue to the arena.

He did run around, and seemed to enjoy it, though unlike Jack and some of the other horses, he didn't investigate things. There are some horses, and Happy was the best example, who see something and want to know all about it. They might startle or even spook a little bit, but then they want to go right over and sniff it and get a good look at it. Those kinds of horses learn quickly and are always pretty trustworthy. Most other horses will tolerate something they don't like the look of if you ask them to and if they trust you. Then they get used to it and don't worry about it anymore. But some horses avoid things, and that's what Blue did—he remembered the spots where he had been worried before, and he stayed away from them. I watched him, thinking about tricks, but not coming up with anything.

After Danny left, Daddy and Mom and I did what we always did, just as if he had never been there, and it wasn't until later, when I was half asleep, that I remembered that Spooky had jumped onto my bed and slipped down under the covers the night before. When I remembered that, I sat right up, wide awake.

Really, it was hard to imagine that little kitten, who was now maybe six weeks old, doing anything of the kind. When Mom took him out of the box, he ran around, especially if we dragged a button or a ball of yarn across the floor. When Daddy laid an old towel on the rug and then snaked his hand under it until his finger poked out, Spooky was all over that monster. And though he stood with his paws on the edge of the box, looking and looking, he hadn't jumped out yet. If I put him at the bottom of the stairs, he would put his paws on the first step and stare up to the second floor as if he knew his mice were up there, but he didn't try to leap onto the step. I knew all this.

But when I lay back and closed my eyes and thought, Got to get up early in the morning, I could hear him coming, a sort of almost-inaudible popping and skittering, as if those stairs were really fun, and then there was the race down the hall and the leap into my bed. Just thinking about it made me start and open my eyes again. I knew it wasn't true, but try as I might, I couldn't not believe it.

Finally, I lay on my back with the covers tucked down around my shoulders and across my neck. No kitten had any way to slide in there. I took ten deep breaths, and maybe I went to sleep, but maybe I didn't. What came to me was not a kitten jumping up the steps in a plump, kittenish way, but another kind of kitten, the kind who rose a little in the air and floated up the stairs and then along the floor of the hallway and through the door (I had, I am embarrassed to say, closed the door of my room). Then it rose like a shadow and hovered over me, staring down with those round black eyes, making no sounds, but twitching its whiskers. My eyelids popped open. It! Spooky was not an it! He was a he, a little black kitten who was downstairs, full of his last feeding of the night, and sound asleep.

There was one window in my room—at the end of my bed. It was closed because of the winter weather. In the summer,

140

I could hear the sounds of the horses outside, moving around and snorting or whinnying or grunting. Sometimes, when I was listening to them, I could picture just what the horses were doing, and that put me to sleep, but now the room was very quiet. There wasn't even the faint noise of Daddy snoring or the heater coming on. It was very very quiet. There was enough light from the window to see the shapes in my room, but not enough to make anything out—not my championship ribbon from the show in the fall or the books on my desk or the picture of my two sets of grandparents back in Oklahoma. So when a shape seemed to float across the ceiling, I could not tell what it was. That was my first thought.

My second thought was that the shape was that of a slender woman with dark hair, carrying a black cat in her arms. She looked sad, and then they floated out the window. I sat up. My whole body was tingling, and then hot, and then cold. There was only one thing to do. I got up and went to the window in my pajamas and looked out. Nothing. The geldings were quiet. Jefferson was lying down, stretched out in profile against the paleness of the pasture. Lincoln looked like maybe he was doz-ing on his feet, and Jack, ever active, was investigating some-thing, maybe some small animal, by the water trough. None of them were spooking or nervous-looking. If there was a ghost, they hadn't noticed her. The trouble was that as soon as I decided that, a whinny came from the barn—Blue—long and sad. And it made the skin on the back of my neck crinkle and my wrist throb. I could not keep myself from thinking that it was a hello. Or a good-bye.

I went to my closet and got my robe. Then I tiptoed down the stairs and looked at Spooky in his box. He was sleeping.

There was nothing wrong or different about him. He was a black kitten curled up in an old sweater. I leaned my back against the corner of the hallway and watched him. That seemed the safer thing to do.

The good thing was that I woke up before Mom, so I didn't have to tell her anything about why I was hunched against the wall by the front door. I went upstairs very quietly, found my clothes, and looked out the window. The horses, of course, were wide awake, looking for their hay. Not a thing was happening in the entire world that was more important to them than that.

Tack Trunk

Brush

Chapter 12

At lunch on Friday, Barbie asked me if I wanted to spend the night that night—I could borrow some pajamas from them, then her mom would drive us to my house, and she would "continue with her equestrian career."

I said, "You still want to take lessons?"

"Mom said I could take ten lessons, and if I wasn't bored with it by then, I could take ten more." I couldn't see how she would get bored with it, but I nodded. Then I remembered. I asked, "You know your cousin Leah, the one I met last fall?"

"The quiet one who needs to sign up for the Famous Writers' School?"

"What does that mean?"

"It's an ad. If you're one of the quiet ones, you send them

your book, and they get it published. Mom says that Alexis and I don't qualify."

"Yes, her."

"The one who is going out with your brother, Danny?"

I stared. Then I said, "That one."

"They've gone to the movies three times and for a walk once."

"For a walk?"

Barbie shrugged. "That's all I know. Maybe Alexis will know more. We'll ask her tonight."

It was a strange thought, Danny going for a walk. I mean, yes, I had seen Danny walking around our ranch, out to the barn, over to the pasture, up the hill. But when I thought of him, he was always on a horse, galloping, most likely, or in his car, or coming through the gate in Jake Morrisson's shoeing truck. One of my earliest memories of Danny—I was maybe four and he was maybe eight—was of him standing still, absolutely still, perched on the haunches of a horse, as the horse walked and then trotted around the arena Daddy and his brothers had back in Oklahoma. Danny held his arms out, to keep his balance, for a minute or two, then he crossed them over his chest and the horse just kept trotting. It was in those days that he learned to do a backflip off a horse, landing on his feet. He did that trick for a couple of years, but when he started getting tall, he stopped. Maybe standing still on the back of that trotting horse was the closest I ever saw to Danny just plain walking.

As for spending the night at the Goldmans' house, what a wonderful invitation. I had slept the night before, but only because I was exhausted from sitting next to Spooky's box the night before that. A vacation from Blue, Spooky, and any floating slender ladies in black boots with black cats in their arms was just what I needed. When I called Mom from the principal's office after school to ask if I could go, she said, "Oh, that's a good idea."

I didn't quite understand her tone, though I was happy to get permission. I said, "Why?"

"Well, someone was still here when someone else got home from the feed store, and then the first someone helped the second someone unload the feed sacks and put them in the feed room, and everything was going fine, but then the second someone forgot to say thank you, and so the first someone got a little chip on his shoulder and said, 'Thank you, too, Dad!' But it will all blow over by morning, I'm sure."

"Barbie is coming for another riding lesson."

"That will be fun."

Of course, I had to be prepared for strange food at the Goldmans'. In this case, the new food was called a "keesh." I said, "That rhymes with 'sheesh,'" which was an expression our principal, Mr. Canning, always used, as in "Sheesh! You kids are out of control this morning!"

Barbie and Alexis laughed as if this were the joke of the century, so we got off the bus in a good mood.

"Quiche" turned out to be a custard pie, but not sweet, with cheese and bacon. There were also some artichokes with garlic butter, a salad, and homemade chocolate ice cream for dessert. Alexis and Barbie did not act as if this were a special thing, and Mrs. Goldman, who had made it that day, said, "Now, Abby, this batch has lots of crème de menthe in it. I hope you won't mind that."

I didn't know what crème de menthe was, so I did the polite thing and ate my portion. It was very minty and very chocolaty, so minty that it made my nose tickle until I had to sneeze. As we were going up to their room, Barbie said, "At least I'm not staggering. Are you?"

Alexis said, "No. Sober enough."

I said, "Why would you be staggering?"

Barbie said, "You too. She put a lot of crème de menthe in, more than last time. Crème de menthe is seventy proof."

"What does that mean?"

"That means it's thirty-five percent alcohol."

Alexis said, "The more alcohol she puts in, the easier it is to scoop out. She *says*."

We continued up the stairs. I didn't answer, but maybe I made a noise. Barbie turned to look at me when we got to the second floor. She said, "We're joking. I bet there was a table-spoon of booze in your bowl of ice cream at the most."

I didn't say that that was the first tablespoon of "booze" I had ever had. I said, "Maybe that's why I sneezed."

"Maybe," said Barbie.

For the next two hours, we played games. I know it was two hours, because for the first hour, Alexis and I played Concentra-tion while Barbie practiced her violin, and for the second hour, Barbie and I played a word-guessing game called Jotto while Alexis practiced the piano. When it wasn't my turn, I some-times looked over at whoever was practicing. It wasn't like they had to do it, though they did have to do it. Each one was intent—staring at the music, practicing short parts over and over until they sounded right, then fitting the parts together, practicing slowly but evenly, then speeding up the tempo, putting as much together as sounded right, and then starting somewhere else, and fitting that in. It was like training a horse, but it was training your own fingers. I liked it.

When they were both finished, we played a round of Spaghetti, which is Concentration, except you use two packs of cards, and you spread them around the whole room. You have to move around, and the mess of the cards seems more difficult at first, but actually it's a little easier, even though there are so many cards. What you do is think, Jack of hearts/piano leg or Four of clubs/end of bookshelf. Even after you've forgotten it, somehow it stays in your mind, so that when you see the jack of hearts or the four of clubs, "piano leg" or "end of bookshelf" comes into your mind. Though Alexis had beaten me at Concentration and I had never guessed, or even heard of, one of Barbie's Jotto words, *avert*, I won the Spaghetti game. I *averted* embarrassment.

Then we started Monopoly, but before we were halfway to Connecticut Avenue, we were yawning. Alexis said, "We used to go to Atlantic City."

I said, "Where is Atlantic City?"

"It's in New Jersey. All the streets on this game are in Atlantic City. We used to ride the Reading Railroad between Atlantic City and Philadephia, then to New York. It was weird to come out here to California, and drive to the ocean, and have it be on the other side. It took Dad a year not to get lost every time he made a right turn when he came to the water." Alexis yawned.

Barbie said, "Who's riding the gray horse now?"

"Danny rode him this week."

"I want to ride him."

I thought about this, then said, "For now, I want you to be closer to the ground."

"Just in case," said Alexis.

"Just in case," I repeated.

"I think he likes me."

"Do tell," said Alexis.

"He was staring deep into my eyes."

"He stares," I said. "He stares at everything."

"What does that mean?" said Alexis.

I said, "I don't know. I can't tell. Sometimes I think he's just interested, but other times I think he's looking for something, or looking at something that we can't see." I didn't mean to say this. Barbie and Alexis both turned toward me.

Barbie said, "Like what?"

"Oh, well, like this, I was standing next to him, petting him, and he was staring, and a couple of moments later, our dog, Rusty, came trotting into the barn and set a kitten on the ground. He saw them coming before I did."

"She brought you a kitten?"

I nodded.

"Where was the mother cat?"

"No idea. It was almost dark by that time, and when my mom went out to have a look the next day, there was no sign of a black cat or any other kittens. But did Blue just see them coming, because horses have good night vision, or did he hear them, or did he know they were coming in some other way?"

"What else has he seen?" said Barbie.

But I couldn't say it, so I said, "It's a cute kitten. Our one female barn cat is tabby, and Mom said a tabby cat can't produce a black kitten. But it was all right. Not hurt or anything. So, it's a mystery."

"I love that word," said Alexis.

"What word?"

"MMMMMYSSSStery."

We laughed.

"Last year I read about twenty-five Agatha Christies. My favorite two were *Death on the Nile* and *Murder in Mesopotamia*, but there was another one, too. It was called *The Mirror Crack'd*." She deepened her voice. "Out flew the web and floated wide; the mirror crack'd from side to side; 'The curse is come upon me,' cried the Lady of Shalott."

I said, "Who's the Lady of Shalott?"

"Oh, she's this girl who kills herself and comes floating down the river toward Camelot. No one knows her, so she's scary, and they all wonder about her. I didn't like the book that much, but I said the poem to myself a lot. 'The mirror crack'd from side to side.'" She shook her shoulders. "It was so creepy!" She grinned.

Barbie said, "Yes, but I like Poe better." She turned to me. "Did you ever read 'The Black Cat'?"

I shook my head.

"Talk about creepy! I was in Mrs. Lawson's class in sixth grade when she read a story aloud called 'The Tell-Tale Heart,' where this guy puts a body inside a wall, and then the heart of the body beats louder and louder and you don't know whether he's really hearing it, or whether he's just going crazy from guilt."

"I had Mr. Jacobs."

"I thought they all read that one."

I shook my head.

"Well, 'The Black Cat' is sort of like that, but instead of the murdered person's heart making the noise, it's a cat. I mean, it's the second cat—he hanged the first cat just because he felt like it, after putting its eye out with a knife—"

I said, "You read that?"

"Well, it's Poe. For some reason, you are allowed to read Poe even if you aren't allowed to stay up and watch *Night of the Living Dead*." Barbie and Alexis exchanged a glance.

I said, "What's *Night of the Living Dead*?"

"Oh, you know," said Barbie. "The graves open and all the dead people appear with lots of makeup and walk around like this." She paused for a moment, then stood up and did a kind of stiff, hunched, sideways stagger across the room, with her mouth half open. It was a joke, but it was sort of scary even so.

Alexis said, "I hated that 'Black Cat' story. I like the dog in 'The Hound of the Baskervilles.' It's not a bad dog or an evil dog—they've just put something around its mouth to make it glow in the dark as it runs across the moor. You feel like you could bring that dog home and get him up on the couch and make friends with him."

"The MOOOOOR!" exclaimed Barbie. "What do you think a MOOOOOr is?"

"A moor is an open plain," said Alexis. "They have them in England. A MOOOR is where the MYSSSTERY begins." She spoke in such a deep gasping voice that we shivered and then laughed.

Then I said, "Do you guys believe in ghosts?"

"Why?" said Alexis.

"I just wondered."

Neither of them answered, and then Alexis got up and came back with two fat candles. She set them down on the floor in front of us and lit them with a match. She set the book of matches on the floor beside the shorter of the two candles. They were both white, and in the darkness of the room, the glow of the flame traveled down the column of each candle, drawing our gaze and making the room seem very black.

"Listen to this," she said.

Bridle

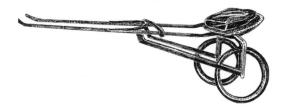

Racing Cart/Sulky

Chapter 13

"Mmm," said Barbie. She grabbed my hand.

Alexis said, "You know our cousin Leah?"

I nodded.

"She has this friend in her class at the high school, and he has two cousins who are brothers down in Los Angeles. The older brother is a junior and the younger brother is a freshman. They started going to school together this year for the first time since elementary school. Anyway, the older brother is one of the popular kids, and the younger brother is not—he wears glasses and keeps to himself and stuff, but the older brother has always been nice to him. Anyway, the older brother is always in a group of friends, and the younger brother sees them around the school, and one day he says, 'You've introduced me to all your friends but that girl.' And the older brother—I think his name is Larry—says, 'What girl?' and the young brother, who I think is named Freddie, says, 'The girl with the red hair, who's always right behind you.'

"So Larry says, 'We don't know any girls with red hair,' and Freddie drops it because he's one of those guys who's used to thinking he must be wrong. And then he doesn't see the girl anymore for three or four days. The next time he sees her, he's a little surprised, because she's sitting next to Larry in the school library, and while Larry is studying, Freddie sees the girl put a note in Larry's biology book and then get up and walk away. That afternoon, when Larry is taking Freddie home in his car, Freddie asks him what the note said, and of course it turns out there is no note, and Larry never saw any redhead—he was alone at the library table the whole time. So Freddie doesn't say anything more because he doesn't want to get teased—he's always getting teased.

"After that, Freddie sees the red-haired girl all the time. Sometimes she's by herself; sometimes she's with Larry's group. Sometimes she's RIGHT NEXT TO LARRY, putting notes in his pockets or writing things in his books. It's like she really wants him to like her, and he's just ignoring her and she can't get through to him. Every time Freddie sees her, she looks sad, but he's afraid to go up to her. In the lunchroom, he sees the girl do things like move Larry's glass of milk, or, once, knock it off the table, and Larry just acts like she doesn't exist."

"She DOESN'T exist!" said Barbie.

"Remember, it's the beginning of freshman year and Freddie doesn't have many friends, or any friends, so he doesn't have anyone to tell the story to, but one day Larry can't take him

156

home, so he's waiting for the bus outside of the school, and he hears two girls talking about this girl named Mary Lynne, who would have graduated three years before, but one day she disappeared, and she never came back to school and she was never found. The FBI has been looking for her, or her body, for the whole time, but it's like she vanished into thin air. So Freddie, who usually doesn't talk to anyone, says, 'What color was her hair?' and one of the girls says, 'Red. She had long red hair.'" She looked at Barbie and me. She said, "I swear this happened. Leah told me."

"Oh, please," said Barbie. "But do go on." She squeezed my hand again.

"Okay. So the next day, Freddie sees her. She's sitting in the bleachers after school, watching the swim team. Larry is a diver on the swim team, and she is watching him. Freddie has missed the bus, and has to wait for Larry to be finished with practice, so he's waiting. When he sees her, he decides to talk to her. She's sitting by herself and staring at the diving board. Larry is doing jackknifes and stuff.

"So Freddie climbs up the bleachers, and as he gets closer to her, she moves away, just sliding down the bleachers, not running or anything, but he just can't get close to her, and he also can't say whether she sees him—she makes it seem as though she's just moving, not running away. That night, Freddie says, 'Did you ever hear that a girl disappeared once?' And Larry says, 'Yeah. That happened when I was in eighth grade. You must have been in sixth grade.'

"'What was her name?'

"'I don't know. Something like Mary Louise, Mary Ellen. Oh—Mary Lynne Murphy.'

"So, a couple of days later, he sees her again in the hall when he's late to class. She's standing by Larry's locker. And he says her name, and she turns to look at him, but not like a person—her face doesn't change expression. It's just that her head turns and then she looks through him, and that's when he realizes that she's a ghost. That's when he realizes that being a ghost is the reason her clothes look old-fashioned. But now he can't figure out what this has to do with Larry."

Barbie said, "You mean like she's wearing round-collared blouses and circle pins instead of button-downs?" To me, she said, "Don't listen to her. It's just a story."

I said, "Do ghosts have to die violently to get to be ghosts?"

Alexis nodded.

She said, "Leah said it was true. It was in the *LA Times*." She tossed her head. "That night before bed, he goes into Larry's room and tells him what he thinks about the girl and the ghost. But Larry just tells him he's crazy, and if he doesn't shut up about it, he's going to have to tell their parents that Freddie is acting weird again."

I said, "Did he act weird before?"

"I guess he had nightmares that were so bad he had to go to a psychoanalyst."

I didn't know what this was, but it sounded scary.

"There," said Barbie. But she still had my hand. The candles flickered, and one of them seemed to go out, then flared up again.

"Freddie was now convinced that the ghost of Mary Lynne had something to tell and that she had chosen Larry to tell it to. And really, deep down, he was afraid that maybe Larry was chosen because he knew something about the disappearance,

158

but Freddie couldn't imagine what that would be, since in eighth grade, Larry was just a kid. So Freddie goes into Larry's room again, and Larry is listening to records, not doing homework or anything."

"Oh, please tell us what he was listening to," said Barbie.

"He was listening to 'Paint It Black,' by the Rolling Stones, okay? Freddie sits down on the bed, and he says, 'Larry, I want you to do me a favor without asking why. Without asking anything about it.' So Larry stares at him, and, you know, he really does love his little brother, and besides that, he knows that Freddie knows that he is sneaking out at night by climbing out his bedroom window and shinnying down the roof of the family room and not coming home until five in the morning some nights, so he says, 'Okay,' and he doesn't ask.

"The next day, first thing, Larry is standing by his locker, and Freddie is watching him. And sure enough, the red-haired girl comes up in the crowd and stands behind Larry and stares at him. Larry happens to look over at Freddie, and Freddie holds his hand up like a stop signal, and the bell rings, and all the kids run off to class, but Larry and Freddie keep standing there, Larry looking at Freddie, and Freddie watching the red-haired girl. She is in the middle of the hallway, looking at Larry, and then she goes up to him and kisses him on the cheek. Then she walks over to the drinking fountain and takes a drink. Then she turns her back and starts walking down the hall and disappears."

I knew this was coming, but I gasped anyway. I couldn't help myself.

"Freddie says, 'She kissed you on the cheek. Did you feel anything?'

"Larry shakes his head, and for a moment, they don't know

159

what to do. Freddie says, 'She took a drink from the drinking fountain.' They go over to look at the drinking fountain, and the drinking fountain is wet. Larry is now a believer, and he says, 'The next time you see her, we'll follow her.' They go to their classes, and every time Freddie sees Larry all day, he looks for the girl, but she never appears."

Barbie said, "Are you almost finished?" But she was still holding my hand. Of course, in my mind, the red-haired girl looked like the slender lady—she was a cross between Eileen Corcoran, who was in the ninth grade and was the only girl in our school with red hair, and the slender floating lady. I shook my head, trying to get the picture out of my mind. Barbie said, "Abby is bored."

I said, "No, I'm not."

Alexis smiled at me. The two candles flickered. She went on, "Two days later was Friday. By this time, both Larry and Freddie were nervous wrecks, because they hadn't seen the ghost. You would have thought they would be relieved, but the longer the ghost stayed away, the more mysterious it was, and the more they thought about her. They couldn't decide where to wait—in places where lots of people were or places where no one was. And they couldn't decide whether to look for her or to not look for her, although at this point Freddie couldn't not look for her. By that afternoon after practice, they hadn't seen her in three whole school days, not since the morning when she kissed Larry on the cheek. After practice, they lingered a little bit and looked one last time around the school, but nothing—

"So they were already a little scared when they walked to the car, and there, sitting in the front seat, was Mary Lynne.

She had turned on the radio, even though the key was not in the ignition. Freddie said, 'She's sitting in the passenger's side,' and he got in the backseat. Larry didn't say anything; he just got into the driver's seat, turned on the car, and drove away. Freddie saw her put her hand on the wheel, and he saw the wheel turn this way and that. They drove down some streets, and pretty soon they were going along Mulholland Drive."

"You saw that in a movie," said Barbie.

Alexis ignored her and turned to me. "Mulholland Drive goes along the top of a ridge. It's really windy. Freddie just sat there, watching the backs of the two heads, and feeling this weird feeling of not in fact being scared. Larry didn't say anything the whole time and the road was too dangerous for him to turn around and look at Freddie or anything. They crossed under a big highway, and then went into a secluded, parklike place where there was a lake and a dam. They drove along there for a while, and then they had to stop and turn around, but when they stopped, the door on the passenger side opened— Freddie said she opened it, and Larry just saw it get open—and Mary Lynne Murphy got out, ran across the grass, then got onto the dam and ran about halfway down it, and jumped into the lake. Freddie watched her. She did not make a splash."

"And that's *right where they found the body*," said Barbie in a deep voice.

Alexis stuck her tongue out at her sister and said, "Yes, Miss Know-it-all, it is."

"And they'd never thought to look there before?"

"Not in that exact spot."

I said, "Who killed her?"

Alexis turned to me. "Well, it turned out to be the boyfriend, but he was dead by that time, too."

I said, "Why?"

"He had gotten drafted into the army and was hit by a truck one night when he was standing in the middle of a road and didn't get out of the way. He didn't want to get out of the way."

"How did they know he was the one who killed her?" said Barbie.

Alexis looked first at me and then at Barbie. She said, "When they sent his duffle bag home, and they opened it, it was filled with little rolled-up notes and scraps of paper in her handwriting, and they all said, 'Meet me by the dam. I have something to tell you, Love you always, Mary Lynne.' There were hundreds of them, every one dated up in the right-hand corner, one for each day, starting with the date when she disappeared, and ending with the day the police found her by the dam."

I said, "What did she have to tell him?"

"Well, that she was pregnant," said Alexis. "Or that's what Leah's friend told her."

"Okay, then," said Barbie. "Why Larry and Freddie?"

This seemed like a hard question. I expected her to say that Larry looked like the old boyfriend, or had his locker or something, but she said, "I don't know. My guess is that she had been roaming around the school, trying to get someone to pay attention to her for years, maybe the whole time, and it was only Freddie who bothered to wonder about her. Or maybe it was only Freddie who could see her." She shrugged. Then she leaned toward Barbie and said, "That part wasn't in the paper." They laughed.

By this time, Barbie had let go of my hand, but she turned

to me. "It's only a story. One time over Christmas vacation, I woke up late and she told me that the whole downstairs was flooded from the rainstorm we'd had and Mom said we had to jump out the windows. I believed her for about ten seconds."

"At least a minute," said Alexis. "Maybe two. Anyway, Leah swore that this happened."

I said, "I don't believe in ghosts."

"But do they believe in you?" said Alexis.

I swallowed, thinking all the time how glad I was to be sleeping that night at Barbie and Alexis's house, nowhere near Spooky the kitten or the floating lady, or True Blue.

In the end, we stayed up late, got up late, and had to scramble to get home in time for me to give Barbie her lesson and then go to the stable for Melinda. And Ellen. According to Mom, the phone call from Jane never came, so she expected to leave me there for two and a half hours while she shopped for food. It was our turn to cook for the brothers and sisters, which meant an afternoon of work, but included, she decided, two lemon meringue pies.

Even though I was glad for the break, I felt as though I hadn't seen the horses, especially Jack, in weeks. And maybe I hadn't, in a way. I'd been thinking about so many other things that even when I was with them, I wasn't paying much atten-tion to them—I would wrestle with the hay the way you have to with one arm, just glad that you've managed to get it to the gate and then annoyed when you can't throw it the way you are used to doing. The horses themselves sort of disappear into the job you are doing, and then you walk away, already thinking about the next thing.

But with Barbie along to help me bring in Foxy, and groom her, and tack her up, there was time to take some carrots to the geldings, put Blue into the pen with Jefferson, and have her help me brush Jack—not a full grooming, but just some brushing with the soft brush to get the dust off. First I held him, keeping the rope in my left hand and stroking his face and neck with my right, just the fingertips, while she brushed his neck and sides, then she held him while I brushed his haunches and took a few tangles out of his tail. He stood nicely as he was trained to do, but not dully—he looked at her and sniffed her and even put his nose up to her face. I said, "Blow gently into his nostril. He's wondering about you."

She did it, then petted his neck again. I said, "You're a natural." She smiled a real smile, then said, "Well, I always wanted to ride. When I first heard that you ride all the time and live with horses, I was so impressed that I was afraid to talk to you."

I stood up from brushing his belly and stared at her. "You're kidding."

"No! That's why we invited you to do *Julius Caesar* with us. We'd been trying to figure out a way to get to know you for a year." Then she laughed out loud and said, "Don't you know how shy we are?"

I said, "No. I don't think anyone knows that."

She grinned. "Well, don't tell."

"How can you be shy when you'll do almost anything?"

She shrugged, then looked at me. "Okay, here's something. Alexis is six minutes younger than I am. She just can't get over that six minutes, so she's always wanting to do things that she knows I'm a little afraid of doing, but she knows if she wants to do it, it's like a dare, and I will do it. And most of the time I do, then it is fun, and we laugh about it. But she is exhausting. Did you notice that?"

"She's fun."

"Did you like her story last night?"

"It was a good story."

Barbie nodded. "Well, maybe it's true. About half the time what she tells is true, but the other half, it's made up. She doesn't care. But I try to make sure I know the difference."

I said, "Do you know the difference this time?"

She shook her head.

It didn't take us long to catch Foxy—she was standing at the gate, wondering why all the others were getting carrots and not her, so she got a carrot and got caught, too. Barbie was the kind of person who only needed one lesson to learn something— she groomed Foxy and put on the saddle and led her toward the arena while I carried the bridle and a lunge line—I thought I would have her trot around on the lunge until she felt the rhythm and learned to post. That was the way I learned when I was a kid—up down up down, holding on to the horn of the saddle and trying to feel the steps of the horse. But first I slipped the clasp through the right ring of the bit, passed it under Foxy's chin, and attached it to the left one.

Then I had Barbie stand in the middle with me while Foxy trotted around us. Foxy had a good trot—maybe her ancestors had been Morgans, which were famous carriage horses. She picked up her front feet and bent her knees, which a lot of horses do, but she also bent her hocks, which meant that you could notice how her hind legs were moving in sync with the front ones. She went around like a horse who was born to cover ground at the trot. I let Barbie watch her for a minute, then I said, "Do you see how the outside hind moves with the inside fore, and vice versa?"

"Yes."

"Boom boom boom. It's easy for her. That's why lots of driving horses, who used to pull wagons and stuff, were bred to be really good trotters."

"Like that kind of racing with carts?"

"Yes, but they're called sulkies. Some of those trotters go almost as fast as galloping racehorses."

Foxy lifted her head a bit and blew out her nose. Then she slowed down just a hair, but I shook the line to speed her up.

"Why'd you do that?" said Barbie.

"Because she can't do what she wants to do, or she'll start doing what she wants to do more and more."

"One time, oh, I guess we were eight, maybe, we went on a horse ride, and all my horse wanted to do was eat the grass."

"Yes," I said. "Because there was no one to remind him every day that he had a job."

Now I called out, "Whoa," and pulled a little on the lunge line. Foxy turned toward me and halted. I went over and switched the clip to the other side, which took a while, but she was patient. I sent her off to the left. I said, "You have to learn to ride the trot, because you get bounced around. There are other horses who race with sulkies called pacers. The two legs on each side move together. No one can ride those, but sometimes they're faster than trotters. They're also more likely to start galloping, so they wear these things that hang down that loop around the two legs on each side to keep them pacing."

"Is she going to pace?"

"No. Never. I never saw a horse pace myself. They are born to do that, and most horses don't do it."

I pulled on the line, and Foxy slowed, then halted, and turned and stared at me. I said, "Okay. Riders up."

Barbie walked over to Foxy and put her hands on the horn and the cantle of her saddle, then lifted her foot. I said, "Wait a minute."

She froze in place, which made me laugh, but I said, "Did you check your cinch?"

Still frozen in place, she shook her head.

"Well, you better, because the saddle could just slide right down."

"That would be funny."

"Not to Foxy."

She tightened the girth two holes, then started over. I still had Foxy on the lunge line, and she stood quietly.

The lesson went well. Barbie settled herself in the saddle and sat up, the way she was used to doing when she was playing music. As she walked along, I saw that her back was strong but loose, and she had no trouble following the movements of the horse's body. I let her go around me for about a minute, one time flicking the lunge line to get Foxy to speed up a little. Then I said, "Close your eyes."

She closed her eyes. They walked along for another minute. I said, "Do you feel things more with your eyes closed?"

"You mean, my legs hanging down and my hips kind of going side to side?"

"Yeah."

"I do. It's a little scary."

"I've got her. All she can do is go in a circle. And anyway, when we were watching her trot, she was tiring herself out a little. She wants to walk. Take your feet out of the stirrups."

She did. She looked a little nervous, but she was so used to sitting up straight that she kept sitting up straight and didn't hunch forward. I called, "Keep your eyes closed until you are really enjoying walking along. Until you're not nervous about it at all anymore. Whistle something."

She started whistling, and it was not "Mary Had a Little Lamb" or even "In My Life," which was a Beatles song she liked. I don't know what she was whistling, but it lasted a long time, and even Foxy seemed to enjoy it. When she was finished, I said, "Okay, you can open your eyes." I went over to her and switched the lunge line so that they could go the other direction. I thought she should practice doing everything both ways, because it is a good habit to get into for the sake of the horse.

I went back to the middle, and sent them walking to the right. I said, "This time, keep your eyes open, but put your hands on top of your head for ten steps, then behind your back for ten steps, then stretch your arms out in front of you for ten steps." She did this. When Foxy showed signs of getting bored—switching her tail, looking off toward the mares—I rattled the lunge line to keep her going. Then I said, "Close your eyes and whistle something short this time." She closed her eyes. I said, "And look up, even with your eyes closed." She tilted her head back. I think she was whistling "The Sound of Silence." When she was done, I halted Foxy and went out to her. I said, "I bet you are really bored."

"I'm not, though. I'm relaxed."

"Okay, well, that part is over. Now you're going to trot. I want you to hold the horn of the saddle with one hand and I'm going to get Foxy to trot. As you feel the steps, you count aloud, like you're playing music or something, and then try going up on one, down on two, up on one, down on two, like that. Push off the balls of your feet, and then sink down again." I demonstrated as best I could by bending my knees and straightening them, but keeping my shoulders even.

"Okaaaay."

Foxy didn't have a terribly bouncy trot, but even I preferred posting to it to sitting it. I went back to the middle of the circle and shook the end of the lunge line with my broken wrist, which wasn't hurting much. Foxy picked up a nice trot and Barbie bounced for about twenty seconds, counting out loud, and then she figured it out, and got the rhythm. I called out, "You have to go around and around. You have to post a thousand times before you really know what it feels like." I made this up. But I had her circle me four times, twice in each direction, with a rest between the times. If she got out of rhythm, I let her figure out how to get back in rhythm. Rhythm was no problem for her. When she was finished with her lesson and we had untacked Foxy and put her away, I said, "What did you whistle? What was that long piece?"

She said, "It was the singing part to Beethoven's 'Choral Fantasy.' I love that." She whistled for a few seconds, and then Mrs. Goldman showed up outside the gate to pick her up. I have to say I wished I were through for the day. Barbie and Alexis were about as much fun as anyone I had ever known, but Barbie was right, they were exhausting.

Chamois

Currycombs

Chapter 14

IT WAS ONLY WHEN WE WERE DRIVING TOWARD THE STABLE that Mom asked me how my night had been. We were both a little bundled up, because the morning, which had started out fairly bright, was now foggy, and getting foggier with every mile. But there had been enough rain (sixteen inches since December, according to Daddy, who checked the rain gauge on one of the fence posts of the arena every time it rained, and wrote it down), so that the hills were a bright, appley green and the oaks looked dark and wet. I was just beginning to tell Mom about the ghost story and ask her what she thought when we started to see more and more wildflowers. The shooting stars were out, and as we got toward the coast, there were lupines. Mom kept saying, "Oh, look at that. So beautiful coming straight up out of the green of the grass. I love the fields of lupines so much! Remember last year when we rode around the mountainside, when was that, maybe the second week in April, and there were so many lupines and they smelled so good it seemed like we were going to pass out from the fragrance?"

I did remember that. Mom just sat on the horse she was riding at the time and took deep breaths and smiled. It seems like every year, someone says, "Oh, the lupines are better this year than ever!"

I said, "What do you think about ghosts? I know Daddy says they can't be, but—"

"Oh, some people can't help but believe in ghosts." She was still in a good mood from the flowers. "My grandmother swore that the ghost of her father came to her at sunset the day after he died, and said he was fine, and she shouldn't worry about him. I think she was thirty at the time."

"Did you believe her?"

"Heavens, I don't know. She always swore it happened, but she also said she was napping, and the ghost woke her up, so your grandma Lillian and my aunt Claire said she was dreaming. But it was a vivid dream. At any rate, whatever it was, it seemed to reconcile her to her father's passing."

We turned left, onto the main road toward the stable. She said, "Why?"

"Alexis told a ghost story. But it wasn't about castles in Scotland or *Julius Caesar* or anything. It was about LA."

"A ghost in LA? There might be a few in those movie mansions." She chuckled, and I was going to ask another question, but then we drove into the stable, and there was the actual nightmare—the groom, Rodney Lemon, holding Gallant Man, and on one side of the pony was Melinda Anniston and on the other was Ellen Leinsdorf. Ellen was standing with her arms crossed over her chest, and Melinda looked like she'd been crying. When Mom pulled up and I got out of the car, Rodney said, "Ah, here's the lass that will solve all our problems. Mornin', miss. Welcome!" And he patted me on the head (and since he wasn't much taller than I was, he had to reach up to do it) and he handed me Gallant Man's reins. He sang out, "Good luck to ya, lass!" and turned and walked away.

Ellen spoke up. "We called and said that we had to be first, because we have to drive to San Francisco to see my aunt, but then she was here already."

"He's my pony," said Melinda. "I get to—"

I looked at Gallant Man. He was watching the other pony who lived at the barn, a pinto. His ears flicked, then he put his head down and scratched his nose on his knee. He was being like the horse I had ridden in the fall, the one we called Black George. One of the ways that he was a good horse was that however big a deal I thought some of the jumps were, for Black George they were just a fun way to pass the time. The more I paid attention to his mood, the easier it was. So, Ellen was mad, and Melinda was upset, but Gallant Man was just waiting to see what was going on over in the arenas. I patted him and said, "So, girls, what was the main thing we practiced last week?"

Melinda said, "Jumping?" She sniffed.

"Nope." I patted the pony again.

"Heels down!" asserted Ellen.

"Nope." I patted the pony again. Then I said, "Don't you see the clue?"

Both of them looked around. I patted the pony again.

173

Melinda said, "What clue?"

Now I held up my hand, and then I patted the pony.

Ellen said, "Patting the pony!"

I demonstrated a long stroke down the pony's neck and said, "We aren't going to do anything until you've each patted the pony ten times—ten nice times, like you're really glad to see him. I'll hold the pony, and, Melinda, you stand on this side and, Ellen, you stand on this side, and you pat and count, and then we'll decide what to do." They counted to ten, and I made them count to twenty. Melinda said, "He's really soft."

Ellen nodded.

Well, at least they could agree on something.

I looked around for Jane Slater and didn't see her anywhere. I figured she must be hiding. Ellen had stopped patting Gallant Man and was staring at me. I said, "Do you know how to pick up his feet?"

She shook her head.

"I do," said Melinda.

I said, "Then show Ellen."

Melinda did so, standing next to the pony's left shoulder and facing backward, running her left hand down his leg and then picking up his hoof. Her whole body was saying, "Nyah nyah nyah," but she smiled a little bit as Ellen came around and she showed her how to hold the pony's hoof, her left hand cupping its horny exterior. Ellen said, "I want to hold it," and Melinda placed Ellen's hand around it. When Ellen had had it for a few seconds, I said, "Now let it drop," and she did. We went all around the pony, four legs, four feet. I guessed we were now about six minutes into the lesson.

They stood up. Now they were both looking at me. Ellen said, a little orneriness creeping into her voice, "Who's first?"

Melinda's face fell.

I said, "Both of you." I bent down and unbuckled Gallant Man's girth and lifted off the saddle. There was a fence nearby. I gave the reins to Melinda, hung the saddle on the fence with the saddle pad. When I came back, I said, "Ever ridden bareback?"

They both shook their heads.

I said, "Now's the time to start."

I walked the pony over to a mounting block. Melinda climbed the two steps. She looked at the pony for a moment, then grabbed his mane and threw her leg over his back. She was a little scared, but she picked up the reins in one hand and a clump of mane in the other. I would have lifted Ellen on, but I couldn't with my broken wrist. It didn't matter, though—if Melinda was going to be on the pony, then Ellen was, too. She took my right hand, walked up the steps, and grabbed Melinda around the waist, then slithered her leg over the pony. In about two seconds, she had her cheek pressed up against Melinda's back. I said, "It's not all that different from riding in a saddle. You just have to make sure you're in the center. Ellen, if you pull Melinda off, then you're going to go off, too. You understand?"

She nodded. Then I thought maybe I shouldn't have said that, because of the way she'd thrown herself off Gallant Man the time before, but, of course, her mother wasn't around, so there wasn't anyone to impress, was there?

Gallant Man snorted away a fly, and both girls started, but

when he didn't do anything, they sighed. I said, "I'm going to lead him to the little arena. Just relax and feel his back underneath you. I think it's easier to ride some horses without a saddle, if you sit up and stay in the middle. Don't try to keep your heels down, but don't point your toes, either. Just relax your legs from your toes to your hips."

I grasped the left rein, gave the pony a pat, and started walking. After I was sure they were both sitting up, I didn't look back. Maybe that was a bad idea, but I wanted them to feel it out on their own without me telling them what to do. If worse came to worst, it wasn't very far to the ground, even for Melinda. Gallant Man, of course, walked along beside me as if nothing in the world was going on.

I did hear Ellen say, "Hey, I—" but then she fell silent. Melinda said, "Ouch." I didn't turn around. We came to the gate of the arena, and I led them through. Only when I turned to close the gate did I look at them. Ellen was no longer pressed against Melinda—she had a hand on each side of her waist, but she was holding herself up. Melinda was staring straight ahead, as if Ellen weren't even there, which was the best thing, I thought. I said, "Now I'm going to let you girls ride around the arena. Melinda, I want you to steer in a loop around every jump, like you were weaving something. Ellen, your job is to feel how the pony's back feet are moving and say 'one two' as you feel them."

She hesitated for a moment, then started saying, "One two one two one two."

I shouted, "Don't stop saying that no matter what happens."

She said, "Okay."

"You stopped saying it."

She laughed, and started again. "One two one two." I thought a laugh was a good sign. Melinda was sitting up straight, and steered in a very responsible manner. I hadn't told her she was the boss, but she knew she was, which meant that when the pony slowed down or felt like he might wander off, she gave him a little kick and straightened him out.

Four poles were set in a grid in the middle of the arena. I walked over them and saw that probably the pony could walk through them without stumbling, so when Melinda had looped around the brush fence and was heading toward a chicken coop, I pointed toward the grid. She turned the pony and walked straight toward it. I didn't even have to tell her. I wasn't far away from them, so I heard Ellen say, "Are we going to jump?" and Melinda say, "Sort of," and Ellen say, "Good!" They walked through the grid. The pony picked up his feet very nicely. Of their own accord, they did it again, and I didn't stop them.

They walked toward the railing. I went up to them. "Do you want to trot?"

Melinda shook her head, and Ellen nodded. I said, "You sure?" Both were sure, so I helped Melinda slide off. There was a lunge line hanging over a jump standard. I picked it up and snapped it onto the pony's bit ring. Melinda stood with me in the middle. Ellen sat on Gallant Man with an eager tenseness that indicated that she was about to start in the Kentucky Derby. I clucked to the pony, and he began to trot.

Well, she bounced and she started to slide, and Melinda said, "Ohh!" but Ellen grabbed the pony's mane and pulled herself back into the center, and the pony just kept trotting. I called out, "Relax your leg and make yourself really heavy!" She trotted around the circle without bouncing too much. Fortunately, the pony had a firm back, not bony, but not slippery. Melinda said, "I want to try it."

I thought that I would see if she would say that to me three times. I would not say, "Do you really?" or, "Are you sure?" which was what I was certain people always said to her. Ellen kept trotting, and pretty soon she looked happy, and not long after that, she looked triumphant, and then I went over to her and switched the clip to the other bit ring, and they went the other way. Finally, Melinda said, "I want to try it. Please, Abby, can I try it?"

I let Ellen go two or three more steps, then said, "Melinda wants to try it."

Ellen's eyebrows begin to lower and a pout started to form, so I said, "Do you have any advice for her?"

Ellen pulled a little bit on the pony's reins, and he stopped. Ellen stared at Melinda. Then she said, "It's easier if you make him go a little."

They took turns until Jane showed up at the gate, looking as though she'd been watching the whole time. She was smiling, but walking a little fast. Ellen had just gotten back on Gallant Man, and Melinda was standing by his head, holding the reins. "Very good," exclaimed Jane. "Ellen, your mother just pulled in," and Ellen understood perfectly. She leaned forward, brought her right leg over the pony, and slid to the ground. Jane said, "Melinda and Abby can walk the pony back, okay?"

Once again, Ellen understood—some things were better done in private, and one of them was riding bareback.

Instead of getting on the pony, Melinda brought the reins over his head, and when I went up to her, she took my hand. My bad wrist was throbbing a little from the various bits of work—not lifting the two girls, but supporting them now and then. In the course of giving the lesson, I had done more than I realized. I pressed it against my chest, wishing that I hadn't left my sling at home.

Melinda said, "She thinks she's really good, but she's not."

"Well, she hasn't ridden as much as you have, that's true."

"She pinched me once."

"She did?" I hadn't seen that.

"Right at first, when I was walking past her. She pinched me on the arm."

Melinda looked up at me, then she said, thoughtfully, "But she was okay at the end. She isn't a BAD child."

This made me grin and I looked away. We walked along, then stopped. She let go of my hand and gave me the reins. Then she started stroking the pony's neck and said, "I learned my lesson."

"I think you've learned lots of lessons today, Melinda. Riding bareback is an important lesson, and you trotted. That's hard."

"Ellen is braver than I am."

I said, "Why do you think that is?"

Melinda said, "Because I don't think she knows what might happen."

I took Melinda's hand again, and we walked back to the barn.

After Rodney took Gallant Man and Melinda went home in

the backseat of the black car, I sat on a hay bale waiting for Mom. I was worn out. I was hungry, too, and I was wondering what Mom would have to eat. Oranges, probably. She loved oranges. Crackers. Jane sat down next to me. As always, she looked extra neat, with her hair in a bun on her neck and the bun in a hairnet. Her boots were polished. Looking at them made me think of those boots in the trunk in our barn. Jane held out her hand. There was a ten-dollar bill in it.

I said, "You paid me for last time."

"I did. This is all for this time. There's five dollars for giving them their lessons, and there's five dollars as a thank-you gift because I didn't go crazy."

"It wasn't that bad." I thought for a second. "Though Melinda did get pinched on the arm."

"I'm sure if she'd fallen down, she would have gotten kicked in the head. Ellen is a street fighter if ever there was one. But you did a good job. As much as I hate to seek the approval of a headstrong child, I did ask Ellen how her lesson was, and she said it was, and I quote, 'Excellent.'"

"It was sort of fun."

"And how is True Blue?"

I sat up. I said, "I wish I knew."

"He's not working out?"

"Well, he's hardly been ridden, though Danny did fine on him. He's spooky. He seems like he's—he's always looking for—something."

"Or someone."

I nodded.

"He was like that here, after she—"

"How long did she have him?"

"No one knows. No one knows anything about her or him. They just appeared out of nowhere one day."

I thought just then about Freddie and Larry and Mary Lynne. I knew that was a story, didn't I?

"Did I tell you I went to her apartment?"

I shook my head.

"The landlord called us. This was the number she put as her reference, you know, when you need someone to say you're good about paying or something like that. It was me who told him what happened to her, so he said would I come over and get her stuff. I could have said no, and he would have had it picked up by the Goodwill, but I was curious."

After a moment, I said, "What was there?" but I really didn't want to know.

"Nothing. Nothing in the refrigerator, some clothes in one of the drawers. Some sheets on the bed and on top of those a couple of surplus army blankets. A toothbrush and a hairbrush. A couple of books and an old easy chair that looked like it had come from the Goodwill in the first place."

"What were the books?"

"Let's see. One was called *We Have Always Lived in the Castle* and the other one was *Wuthering Heights*. Have you read that one? We read that one in eighth grade at the Linden Hall School in Lititz, Pennsylvania."

"Is it a ghost story?"

"Kind of. It's a mysterious stranger story. A ghost appears."

"Is it a real ghost?"

She looked at me. "Is any ghost in a story a real ghost?"

181

I said, "I don't know. I hope not." I saw Mom's car pull into the parking lot and then start to turn around. We stood up. I said, "What did you do with her stuff?"

"I took it to the Goodwill. There weren't even any pictures. I guess she spent all her money on Blue."

"But Daddy and Danny say he doesn't know anything."

"Abby, sweetheart, what other people think a horse needs to know is always always always a conundrum to me."

Mom pulled up not far from us. I could see her lean forward and look at me with a big smile. I said, "What's a conundrum?"

"A riddle."

I stood up, put my ten dollars in my pocket, and said goodbye to Jane. In the car, Mom had oranges and saltines and a bag of licorice. That was fine with me.

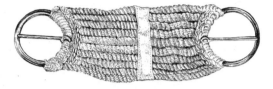

Western Cinch

Lunge Line

Chapter 15

At home, the Golden Rule was working, in a way. Danny was ignoring Daddy as he would have had Daddy ignore him, and vice versa. When I got out of the car to open the gate for Mom, I saw that Daddy had Amazon up on the hillside, riding along the fence between our place and Mr. Jordan's place. Rusty was galloping ahead of them, ranging up and down the slope, and sometimes, where the grass was especially tall, disappearing altogether. Daddy and Amazon were walking, and every so often, he stopped and leaned out of the saddle and pushed on a fence post to see if it was still secure. The Brahmas had broken through the fence in the fall, and because the ground got so hard in the summer, you had to do fence-mending in the spring. And there had been plenty of rain. A fence post can always rot in the winter.

Danny was in the arena, on Blue. He waved as Mom drove through, and after I latched the gate, I ran over. My arm was still throbbing and I knew I had to go up to my room to find my sling, but I wanted to see Danny and Blue more than I wanted my sling. I sort of hooked my fingers over my shoulder. That helped a little.

Danny was doing an exercise that involved asking Blue to spiral inward at the trot until he was in the center of the circle, at which point, Danny would shift his weight and ask Blue to trot the other direction, spiraling outward. Blue was a little awkward—his spiral wasn't completely smooth—and his ears were cocked to either side, as if he were perplexed. When he got all the way to the center and Danny asked for the slight turn, he got a look on his face that said, "Oh, I get it," and he moved off in the new direction with extra energy. They spiraled outward until they were going along the railing of the arena again, then they spiraled inward and did the whole thing going the opposite direction to the way I'd first seen them. I realized that this would be a good exercise for Barbie, and wondered if I would remember it for a whole week. By the time Danny and Blue had done the inward spiral three times in both directions, Blue was much smoother, and his hind legs were working perfectly—he stepped very precisely, curving his body more and more as the spiral got tighter, then when he crossed to the other direction, he seemed to unwind—instead of his left hind foot stepping in front of his right, now his right hind foot stepped strongly across in front of his left and pushed him off. At the end of the third spiral, Danny kicked him just a little, and he took off loping down the side of the arena, and it was that floating lope I had seen him do on his own, so graceful and soft that it reminded you of flowing water.

They came to the end of the arena and went past the oak tree there, and just then, Rusty leapt out of the grass, and Blue reared, turned, and bolted in my direction. Danny grabbed the horn of the saddle and his hat flew off. He lost a stirrup, but he didn't fall off. But even when he had the reins and was with the horse again, he didn't make him stop, as I would have done. He turned him back into his spiral, this time at a gallop, then at a canter, and when they got to the center, he trotted him for two steps and went off on the other lead. They did the spiral at the canter twice, not as smoothly as they had done it at the trot, but pretty well, considering that Danny directed the spiral so that its outer rings got closer and closer to where Rusty had scared Blue.

I shouted, "Rusty!" but Danny waved his hand at me. I realized that he wanted Rusty to be there—he wanted Blue to see what had scared him and understand it. I crossed the arena, avoided Danny and Blue, and picked up Danny's hat. Finally, they came over to me, and Danny let Blue halt. Blue was heaving. Danny was breathing pretty hard, too.

I said, "That was good riding."

Danny said, "Yup. It was." He took his hat and straightened the brim, then put it on. He glanced up the hill. Daddy was still inspecting the fence posts—he was practically to the end of the fence and out of sight by this time. I could just see Amazon's tail and the roundness of her haunch.

We didn't say anything for a moment, and then I said, "He did that with Daddy, just ran. Almost ran over me, too."

"What did he see?"

"A ghost."

"Oh, you mean the ghost of a big brown dog jumping out of the grass?"

"No. I don't mean that."

Danny blew out a little air and said, "Well, this one I have to give him, because he was concentrating on what I was asking him to do, and then there was the dog, who I think was chasing a rabbit, so sometimes there is a reason."

"But it seems like he's always got a reason, or at least an excuse."

"What did he do before?"

"No one knows. He went on trail rides. Everything about him and his owner is a mystery." I thought of Alexis saying, "Mmysstery!" as if mysteries were fun, and smiled. Then I said, "Who did you ride today?"

"This one. Happy. Just the two."

"How did you like Happy?" I said this innocently, as if I didn't know the answer, which was that Danny and Happy were made for each other.

Danny said, "She's a pretty nice horse."

At school, when someone really loves something, it's great, or it's really cool, big smile, wow! When Mom really loves something, she just says, "I love that." I think maybe one time I heard Daddy say that so-and-so was "a pretty nice horse" and that horse was Lester, his favorite ever. From someone like Danny or Daddy, "a pretty nice horse" was the best compliment of all. But I didn't say anything. I nodded, and then changed the subject. "So, what are you doing tonight?"

He pushed his hat back. "I don't know. Why?"

"I don't believe you."

"I might go to a movie."

"Danny, the cat is out of the bag."

"Which cat?"

"You know!"

He pulled on the lobe of his ear, then turned Blue away from me. Yes, they were sweaty and had to walk. I shouted, "Just tell me what movie!"

Danny shouted, *"Lord Love a Duck!"*

This was a movie no one had talked about in school, not even Alexis and Barbie, so I figured it was a strange one. Probably Leah's choice.

By the time I was finished helping Mom as best I could with the cooking, Danny was gone. Mom seemed in a good mood, though. Daddy came down from the fence line and rode Jefferson before feeding the horses and coming in for dinner. No one said anything about Danny, and the rain started again while we were eating. Before bedtime, I made myself read *Le Petit Prince* in French until I fell asleep. It worked.

Mounting Block

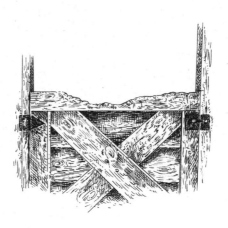

Stall Door

Chapter 16

Getting a lot of food to church was always time-consuming, and getting it there in the rain was really hard—you did not want a lemon meringue pie to be rained on. We started out the door about ten minutes before we usually did, but still we were heading through our gate about five minutes later. This was why, as Mom and Daddy were sitting in the car and I was closing the gate while trying to keep my cast dry, we happened to see Danny going past in his car, on his way to the Jordan ranch. He waved. I waved. I couldn't see whether Daddy, who was driving, or Mom, who was sitting in the back-seat guarding the pies, waved. I opened the door and got in, not forgetting to pick up the two dishes I had to carry in my lap, the salad and the beets. I hated beets—I could smell them through the waxed paper that Mom had rubber-banded around the bowl.

As we pulled away, Mom said, "I was so silly to make these pies. I just—"

Daddy said, "They're fine, Sarah," in a way that suggested that *seeing* Danny drive away from church, even though we knew he didn't go to church, was especially bad. I glanced at her. Her lips said, "Shh," but she made no noise. We drove to the church in silence, which was fine with me, because those beets and that salad occupied all my attention. When we got to church, Brother Abner and Sister Larkin and Carlie and Erica Hollingsworth were waiting by the curb to take the dishes. The rain was even worse in town, but Brother Abner walked next to each pie, holding his umbrella over it until it got through the door. Once all the food was taken in, Mom and I got out, and Daddy went to park the car.

Mom said, "Wooo. Ice cold in there."

"You mean in the car?"

She nodded. "Danny working on Sunday."

"Maybe he's not working."

"Wouldn't that be worse?"

I said, "I don't know what would be worse, Mom."

She nodded.

Daddy was the last person in the door, and he had to take off his raincoat and stomp the water out of his boots. By the time he sat down, it was clear that the five empty chairs in the second row that had been empty for two weeks now, the Greeleys' chairs, were not going to be filled. I could hear the sisters all around clucking, and there was some head-shaking, too, but no one said anything, and we sang a few songs. Carlie's dad started these, and they were good ones: "How Can I Keep from Singing?" and "Gather Them In" and "Rock of Ages." After we sang all the verses to these, then we did our favorite, which was "Amazing Grace," all the way through, seven verses. And after that, all the brothers and sisters sighed and smiled, and Brother Abner got up and read his text, which was, "'Then the cup-bearer and the baker for the king of Egypt, who were confined in jail, both had a dream the same night, each man with his own dream and each dream with its own interpretation.'" This led Brother Abner to talk about a dream that he had had, that he was walking down the road, and a girl came up to him, and he realized that the girl was his own mother. The girl said that she was lost, and Brother Abner took her hand and walked with her down the road, the whole time asking himself whether he should tell her that he, an old man, was her son. He didn't know if this would make her sad or happy, and at this point the dream ended.

Everyone was quiet, and then Carlie's dad stood up and read a selection about Jesus and the loaves and the fishes, which we had heard many times. He finished talking, and then Brother Ezra Brooks, who had never said anything that I could remember, jumped to his feet and said, "'And it shall come to pass in the last days, saith God, I will pour out of my Spirit upon all flesh: and your sons and your daughters shall prophesy, and your young men shall see visions, and your old men shall dream dreams!'" Sister Brooks turned and stared at him, then took his hand and got him to sit down again. Everyone else acted like he hadn't spoken. Carlie's dad stood up and looked around, then started another hymn, which was "Balm in Gilead." Then we separated, and the kids went to study the Bible with Sister Larkin, and the parents studied the Bible, too. Sister Brooks quietly slipped out with Brother Ezra.

Maybe it was a Sunday like any other, but it didn't seem to be. As I passed slowly around the table where Mom and Mrs. Larkin had set out the food, putting down my plate and steadying it with the fingers of my left hand, while dishing some stew and rice onto it with my right, and then salad and bread and the other things, I heard everyone talking in low voices about Brother Abner's dream. "Just the saddest thing," said Sister Larkin, and Mom asked why, and Sister Lodge said, "To come to your own mother as an old man? I had tears." And Sister Ethelyn Larrabee, who had never married, said, "I imagined that he was talking about meeting her in heaven, and he only thought he was an old man. Really, he appeared to her as she appeared to him, a golden youth."

But Sister Marian Larrabee, who had also never married, said, "The first thing I thought was that she was going to forgive his sins and ask him to forgive hers."

Sister Lodge shook her head. "She was lost. That was the saddest part for me."

And Mom said, "Who isn't, really?"

But no one answered her.

I wondered if any particular sins committed by Brother Abner were known to the ladies, or if they were just talking in general. Daddy already had his food, and Mom was walking toward where he was sitting. I had set my plate next to the creamed corn and picked up the spoon when I heard his voice rise. He said, "It is the sins of the fathers that are visited on the sons, and this is how it happens."

Mom stopped in her tracks.

Carlie's dad exclaimed, "I told you Thursday that it's not our business, and I still think that."

Brother Abner said, "Each man with his own dream and each dream with its own interpretation."

Daddy snapped, "We're not talking about dreams!"

Brother Abner pursed his lips, but said no more.

Brother Brooks, who had not left with Sister Brooks and Ezra, said, "Maybe we should say what we are talking about, then."

Daddy said, in his firm voice, "We are talking about rules, and more than that, we are talking about sparing the rod and spoiling the child. When you are young, these things seem much more difficult than they are, but it's quite simple, really. The children are wild and disruptive. If we don't speak up, if we just stand back and let it happen, then we are implicated. We owe it to the children more than anyone else." I realized he was talking about the Greeleys.

Brother Abner said, "To make sure they get whipped, you mean?"

"If that's what they need," said Daddy. But then he looked around and saw that everyone was staring. He said, "Everyone in this room's been whipped and more than once."

"That's right," said Brother Abner. "I was whipped at home and I was whipped at school. What I think now is that those whippings raised the spirit of rebellion in me. Made salvation take longer, you ask me."

Now Sister Brooks came back in with Ezra, and they went to their places and sat down. Ezra put his hands between his knees and looked at the floor.

Sister Larkin began thumbing through her Bible.

Daddy said, "If the devil is in there, then the devil has to be driven out."

Sister Marian and Sister Ethelyn muttered that this was true, though regrettable. I looked at Mom. She was sitting near Daddy, holding her plate on her knees. She was looking at the floor.

Brother Brooks said, "I'm not sure it's as simple as all that—"

I thought they could have asked me. Over the past couple of years, Carlie and I had spent more time alone with the Greeley kids than any of them had. I looked over at Carlie, but once again, she had her nose in a book. I watched her. She didn't turn the page, but she wouldn't look at me. Erica, who was ten, was hiding her face in her mother's side. Mrs. Hollingsworth was patting her on the leg. I saw that no one but Daddy wanted to have this argument. Finally, Mr. Hollingsworth said, "Brother Lovitt, we may all have our opinions about each other, but unless we maintain a spirit of forgiveness, the congregation will split."

"What's right is right," said Daddy. "I cannot sit here in good conscience and allow wrong to persist."

At last, Sister Larkin spoke up. She said, "The fact is, they've been driven off already. Rhoda Greeley told me last week that they don't expect to return to the fold."

"They were not 'driven off,'" said Daddy. "No one spoke a word of blame the day that child ran away. Not one word of blame."

Except, of course, they had blamed me—not angrily, but sorrowfully.

"Looks were enough," said Sister Larkin. "They knew."

Sister Ethelyn said, "It was understandable that some of us felt that our patience had been tested. But if we cannot welcome the testing of our patience, then we are weak vessels indeed. That's what I think."

Sister Brooks said, "The poor child might have been killed."

"Exactly," said Daddy. "Exactly."

I couldn't tell what he felt Sister Brooks was agreeing with. I thought she was carefully reminding everyone that if I had been paying attention, none of this would have happened. I felt my face get hot and I set my fork on my plate. My feeling got stronger when I saw her glance flick toward me, just for the briefest second. I wasn't even sure that she realized that she looked at me. Mr. and Mrs. Brooks both took deep breaths at the same time, and then Brother Hazen, who usually had a lot to say but hadn't said anything so far, turned to Daddy and said, "We've spoken of this over and over, Brother Lovitt, most recently Thursday afternoon. Every congregation has to welcome younger members. You, yourself, don't see this, because you are young, but we see it."

Mom set her plate on the floor and put her hands on her knees.

Daddy said, "What happens if the children don't learn to submit? What happens if the children are never taught to submit? 'God is opposed to the proud, but gives grace to the humble. Submit therefore to God. Resist the devil and he will flee from you.' That verse seems clear to me." Now he looked around. Then he said, "Tell me I'm wrong. Instruct me and I will listen."

Everyone went quiet. Carlie closed her book, but she didn't look up, and I had the feeling you have when you walk into study hall at school, and you know they've been talking about you. You might be wearing the wrong shirt, or there's something on the hem of your skirt. One time, Kyle Gonzalez walked all around school for three periods before Richie Russo told him that there was a piece of paper on his back with the words SO SUE ME printed on it. "So sue me" was something Kyle had said to Johnnie Rogers by the lockers one morning. I never knew why.

Mr. Hazen spoke up and did the thing we always did. He said, "I suggest we turn this situation over to the Lord, asking for guidance on how we proceed with this matter."

Sister Larkin then said, "I don't see what good guidance for us is. They aren't coming back."

But Brother Hazen bent his head and said, "Lord, in this situation concerning the Greeleys, we seek your divine inspiration. In Jesus's name we ask, amen."

In about another minute, we all picked up our forks and started eating again.

It didn't take as long to put the dishes in the car when we were ready to go home. Some of the older sisters and Brother Abner had divvied up the leftovers, so the dishes were empty and we put them in the trunk. This time I got in the backseat, and Mom got in the passenger seat. As we pulled away from the curb and headed toward the place where the parking lot exited onto the street, it was as if the hours between dinner and the end of the second service hadn't even happened, because Daddy said, "I know you agree with me, Sarah."

Mom said, "About what?"

"About sparing the rod."

We drove. The windshield wipers swished and the rain, which was still pretty heavy, flew to either side. I wished Daddy would talk about the rain—would there be an inch in the rain gauge at home, or two?

Finally, Mom said, "You know I wasn't whipped and was hardly spanked when I was growing up. If my mom slapped me once on my bottom with an open hand, I'd be surprised. And I never saw her spank my sisters, either."

Daddy turned and smiled at her. "Because you girls were always good and never prideful."

Mom ducked her head.

I said, "You never spanked me, did you?"

Daddy glanced around, then looked back at the street. He said, "I smacked you on your diaper when you were two and a half once. You were running into the road. I wanted you to remember never to go there. But you were like your mom."

And who wasn't, I thought.

After a minute, Daddy said, in that voice parents use when they are telling you about when they were kids, "Your grandpa whipped us boys every week, whether we needed it or not. That's what he always said. But he knew we needed it. If he didn't know everything we'd done, well, he knew we'd done something."

Neither Mom nor I said anything, so he smiled and said, "One time when your grandpa was gone out of town, your grandma just lined us boys up outside her room, and we went in one by one and got our whipping. Your uncle Luke was first, and he came out bawling and crying and then winked at us, so we knew it was nothing—wouldn't hurt at all. But we wanted her to think we felt it, so we all made a big fuss." He laughed.

Mom smiled. Then stopped smiling.

What I couldn't figure out was why she was saying nothing at all. Daddy said, "You do agree with me, Sarah, don't you?"

She coughed. Finally, she said, "What does it matter, Mark? Our kids are grown."

"It's a principle. It's about what it takes to understand God's word and embrace it. Sometimes it takes submission and humility. If the devil is in there, you have to drive him out."

Finally, I could hold it in no longer. I said, and I really was wondering, "Do you think the devil is in Brad Greeley? He's only three."

Before Daddy could answer, Mom turned around, put her arm over the seat, and said, "What do you think, Abby? You've been minding him for a year, off and on."

Daddy said, "I think—"

But Mom interrupted him. "I want to know what Abby thinks. I really do."

I said the first thing that came into my mind, which was, "I don't think whipping him is going to make him stay still. I think it's only going to make him run away."

Daddy said, "Those children don't know how to mind."

I said, "I don't think they even think about minding. They think about running."

I had another thought.

"I think they're like Jack, not like Jefferson. If we whipped

Jack, it wouldn't make him stop running. It would make him run faster. If we whipped Jefferson, he might not run at all. He might just stop and buck."

Mom reached over and smoothed my hair. Daddy didn't say anything, and we drove the rest of the way home. When we got there, we discovered a couple of interesting things. The first of these was that it hadn't rained nearly as much at home as it had in town—there was only half an inch in the rain gauge and you could see some sky to the east and south by the last bit of sunlight. The second of these was a note tacked beside the barn door, which read, *I rode Happy, Foxy, and Blue. I put out all the hay, and I left Blue in the pasture with the other geldings. When I left, he was getting along fine, but you might check them. Love, Danny.* Sure enough, Blue was out in the pasture. He was standing by the fence, hidden by the barn from the gate, which was why we hadn't seen him as we drove in. He looked beautiful— his gray coat shone a little in the twilight. His ears were pricked and his neck was arched. As I was watching him, Jack and Lincoln trotted across the pasture together, and Blue turned and trotted after them. They squealed and kicked up, and all three took off at a gallop, bucking a few times, but mostly running. They looked like they were having fun—that was one thing (no kicking or pinned ears). And Jack won. That was the other thing.

Inside, Mom was sitting with Spooky, petting him a little with one finger while the kitten gobbled down his supper, oatmeal and milk mixed with some cat food. This was the first day we'd left him for this long, and he was hungry. Mom said, "Oh, he was crying when we came in. I should have come home at noon and fed him, but it seemed like such a long drive in the rain."

"We could take him with us."

"Maybe next weekend we will."

Then she said, "You understand what Daddy's talking about when he talks about the Greeley kids, don't you?"

"Mom, I know I should have been more careful that day. It was a nightmare. I was looking at him, and then I looked at something else, and then I looked back at him, and he was gone. We ran all over the store. It was like he had disappeared into thin air. I thought I was going to die when that lady came in with him. I mean, it was like everywhere we looked was exactly the wrong place, and then because of that he went to the very place that was the worst place for him to go."

Spooky finished his food and burped. Mom picked him up and took him over to the cat box, where she set him down and kept petting him with her finger. I went on, "But if I had paid attention, he wouldn't have run off, and none of this would have happened!"

"None of what?"

"With Daddy and the elders."

"We all know it was a difficult situation, Abby. Rhoda Greeley never blamed you for a second, because once last fall, she found him down in the basement at her mother's house, standing on a box, looking into that washing machine her mother has, just a big old-fashioned tub without a lid. It was full of clothes soaking in bleach. She told me she nearly fainted. The only reason she'd gone to look in the basement was that the cellar door was pushed slightly open. She said to me, 'It was so dark and damp, I can't imagine why any child would go down there, but he did.'"

"Did she spank him?"

Spooky scratched sand over the tiny little pile he had made, and Mom picked him up and set him on the living room rug. He raced out to the middle of the floor and leapt into the air. Mom said, "No, she put a latch on the door."

After we'd watched Spooky for another minute (he hopped over to the couch and reached under the flap, and then fought with the flap for a few seconds before running away), Mom said, "Your dad has been upset about Brad and Bart for a long time. Long before the drugstore thing. He's thought they were disruptive and distracting ever since Brad could walk and Bart could crawl. It was the drugstore thing that made him feel like he could say something. He thought everyone would agree with him, so he's a little surprised that so few do."

"Do you?"

She leaned toward me and whispered in my ear. "I agree with *you*." She sat up. "But your dad isn't really talking about Brad and Bart. He's talking about Danny. You understand that, don't you?"

I nodded.

Mom picked Spooky up and held him in her lap. I could hear Rusty come onto the porch, and then she looked through the window at us. She sat down as if to say, "Oh, there you are. I've found you."

"You know, your dad and Luke and Matthew have been talking for years about those weekly beatings they got from your grandfather, and not just because the girls didn't get them. They can never decide whether they needed them or they didn't need them. You could say they got used to them, but you could also say that those beatings made those boys mad, and they misbehaved in spite of them, or even, I think, *because* of them. There was a 'try and stop me' sort of thing, or even 'okay, if you're going to beat me anyway, then I'll do whatever I want to.' And the beatings stopped. Do you know why?"

I shook my head.

"They stopped one day when your uncle Luke was fourteen, and he just grabbed the belt out of your grandfather's hand and he went after your grandfather, and he said, 'If you ever lay a hand on me or my brothers again, I will kill you.' Your grandfather backed off after that. And then when Luke and Hannah and Ruth and your dad had kids of their own, they did not whip them. I think he spanked Danny once and switched him once, and he did spank you that time about running into the road, but his heart wasn't in it."

Now Spooky climbed onto Mom's knee, and then stepped very carefully over to my knee. He fell into my lap. We laughed. Mom sighed. She said, "I think he wonders if maybe he had spanked Danny more, Danny would be less prideful."

I picked Spooky up and held him next to my chest with my good hand, and then petted him with my casted hand. It wasn't very easy. But my wrist didn't hurt at all. It hadn't hurt all day, I realized. I said, "Danny is Danny."

"That's what I tell him."

I said, "I don't think the devil is in Danny."

"I don't, either."

"Does Daddy?"

She shrugged.

I said, "Really?"

She said, "Really."

"Why would he think that?"

"Well, it's not exactly that the devil is *in* Danny, it's that Danny is doing lots of things that are temptations—movies, dances, listening to all kinds of music, having his own car and driving wherever and whenever he wants. Consorting with all sorts of people who might not have Danny's best interests at heart."

"But has he gotten into trouble?"

"Not that we've heard. Jake would tell us if the police didn't, I'm sure. But your dad would say that you don't have to break the law to be lost."

I set Spooky on the rug and then moved my finger. He pounced on it. I made my finger absolutely quiet, and Spooky turned away, then I moved it again, and he pounced again. I said, "I think he's having fun. I think his girlfriend is Leah Marx, and she reads books and makes animals out of napkins and goes for walks. I don't think the devil is tempting him with those sorts of things."

Mom said, "Maybe not. But your dad didn't get to have that sort of fun. For one thing, that sort of fun really didn't exist in Oklahoma when we were kids—no kid had his own car. There was no rock and roll, we weren't allowed to go to the movies, and there wasn't a nearby movie theater anyway. If we went to a dance, it was a square dance, with about six adults there for every kid. If you danced too close to your partner, a grown-up walked by and gave you a poke on the arm, and you backed away. I mean, I don't know what your dad thought Danny was going to get from Jake for working for him, but Jake actually pays him a pretty good wage, and he also works as a ranch hand, so he has some money. We didn't have any money, so fun was a pretty abstract idea."

"And you were married by the time you were eighteen."

"Well, your dad was nineteen, but yes. That was pretty normal then and there, but I would be shocked if Danny did the same thing."

"Leah Marx is going to college and has lots of plans."

"I'm sure she does. Anyway, what I mean is, lots of times the devil is in the things you don't know about, or that's the way it seems—"

Daddy appeared at the top of the stairs in his robe. I could see that he had been taking a shower. He said, "What are you two talking about?"

Mom looked up at him. She said, "This and that."

"Well, I feel a little, I don't know, like I'm coming down with something. Can you check the horses before bed? I'm turning in right now."

"Oh, dear," said Mom. She stood up and handed Spooky to me; she went up the stairs and put her hand on Daddy's forehead, then the back of her hand on his cheeks. "Did you take an aspirin? You go to bed and I'll get you a couple." Daddy went into their room. Normally, he would have argued with her, but since he didn't, I thought maybe he was feeling pretty sick.

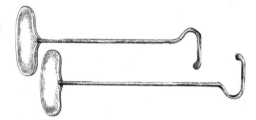

Boot Hooks

Braided Rope Reins

Chapter 17

I SET SPOOKY IN HIS BOX AND FOUND A COUPLE OF TOYS FOR HIM to play with—a ball of yarn and a wooden spool. What I did was, I nested the ball of yarn in his old sweater bed, and then perched the spool on top of it so that it would fall and roll as soon as he touched it. Then I went into the kitchen. Mom or Daddy had brought the dishes in from the car, and they were sitting by the sink. I knew that I could wash them, but instead I went over and looked out the window.

Except for footsteps, probably Mom's because they were quick and light, walking from one room to another upstairs, the house was quiet. The rain had completely stopped. I thought it was amazing in a way that Uncle Luke had threatened my grandfather, who always seemed to me to be pretty much fun, full of jokes and things, but he did have a temper, and so did Uncle Luke, so if someone was going to threaten him, it would be Uncle Luke.

But what I wondered about more was the idea of the devil being in Danny. I would have thought that the devil was in a person who would be mean for no reason, like some of the kids at school. When I was in fourth grade, we had a boy with some sort of heart problem. He was little and pale, and one day, two of the bigger boys walked up to him in the hall and took his pants down. That was the sort of thing I would think that the devil would do. I had also noticed that some kids got in trouble at school, and they were sorry about it, but other kids, a few at least, truly didn't care—they didn't care about hurting others and they didn't care about being punished because the punishment didn't seem to hurt. I would have thought that there was the devil in that, because it was superhuman, and the devil was superhuman. And we all knew people who liked to hurt others. When those boys pulled down Marty Gorman's pants, not everyone laughed, but some kids did—at Marty.

It did not seem to me that the devil was in things that were just fun, like going to dances or listening to music. What I decided that Mom had been trying to tell me was that Daddy didn't actually know what the devil was in, given all the things that Danny was doing that he himself had never done, but better safe than sorry. However, I thought that if the devil was in Danny, Danny would not think to write a note to us that had *Love, Danny* at the end. The devil wouldn't think of that sort of thing.

When Mom came down and saw the dishes on the kitchen

counter, she said, "Why don't you go check on the horses while I clean this up, and then maybe we all need to go to bed a little early, if there's something going around."

My jacket was hanging by the back door. I put it on. Rusty was there to accompany me as soon as I stepped out onto the porch. She sat down and watched me as I slipped into my boots.

Sometimes the rain we get is from Hawaii—in that case, there is plenty of it, but it is warm, and the air after it is warm, too. You hardly need a sweater, even though your boots are sinking into the mud. Other times the rain is from Alaska. In that case, the wind that comes after it is dry and cold and the temperature drops almost to freezing, even when it's March, not December. Daddy always says that where we live, it can be "four seasons a day." When I stepped off the porch, I knew we were back in winter, even though the day before I had given Barbie her lesson in shirtsleeves.

The clouds were completely gone now—the winds had blown them off, and I could just barely see the moon, which was not even a crescent, but a tiny bright sliver. Stars were everywhere. In the fall, the hillsides all around our house were pale, so that the valley seemed full of light even at night, but now they were so thick with grass that everything was dark—the fence lines and the trees against the hillsides, the coats of the horses, the wet side of the barn, the dark water in the dark troughs, the mud in the areas of the pasture where the horses spent most of their time. Damp yellowness poured out of Daddy's bedroom window, and also from the porch light, which I left on, but it didn't get far. Within a few steps, I was making my way more by scent and sound than by sight.

I had my head down because of the chill, and mostly I was watching Rusty, who was just ahead of me, her nose lifted and her ears pricked. After cold rains, I didn't think there would be many fragrances on the wind, but Rusty seemed to think otherwise. I would have gone into the barn and turned on the light, but I decided instead to let my eyes adjust. I stood by the gate, and pretty soon I could see Blue, pale against the trees, and then I saw Jefferson by his white front feet, and then Lincoln turned his head and I saw his blaze. After that, it was as if the horses' bodies formed around their white markings, and I could see them standing under the trees. Only Jack was missing, and then there he was, on the far side of the pasture by the slope, rubbing his shoulder against a fence post, either scratching an itch or simply making trouble—a yearling is like one of the Greeley kids. He spent a lot of time exploring, and if there was something strange, say, a wobbly fence post, he would play with it until he did something to it. I whistled, to see if I could distract him from the fence post, and he looked up. When he saw me, he turned around.

In the meantime, closer at hand, Blue also was staring at me, and I suddenly remembered that thing Jane Slater had done, so I called out, "Blue, Blue, how are you?" and he at once answered back with a loud whinny. And this whinny was in turn answered by Jack as he trotted over from that fence post to see what was going on. The two of them met me at the gate. Fortunately, I had exactly two little pieces of carrot in my jacket pocket, and they were good enough even though they were at least a day old. Blue wasn't even all that pushy about getting his before Jack. As they chomped their morsels, I smoothed their forelocks and petted their faces. When their carrots were gone, they twisted their noses toward one another and started sniffing. I think each one wanted to see whether the other one had gotten anything that he himself had not gotten. But they were easygoing about it. I wished I had more carrots, but then I started walking along the fence line and picking handfuls of long green grass with my good hand. I would pick a good thick bunch, which was no problem because the ground was soft from the rain, and then give Blue half and Jack half. Rusty found this boring and wandered away into the dark. I could hear her for a moment, and then not—for a big dog, she was very quiet.

Jefferson and Lincoln allowed this to go on for a few minutes before they decided that something was happening that required their attention. They came over and chased Jack and Blue away from the gate, and stuck their own noses over for the grass. I gave them each a little bit, then walked over to the mare pasture.

Amazon, Foxy, Happy, and Sprinkles were already at the gate when I got there. No doubt they thought something better than grass was coming their way, too. But they were pleased with the shocks of grass. Happy got hers first, then Amazon, then Foxy, then Sprinkles. We had had Sprinkles for a long time, a year, and it now looked like Daddy had found a buyer for her—a local hotel that did trail rides had lost one of their string, and she would go there to fill the spot. I thought she was a little grumpy for a trail horse, because she didn't like other horses to come up behind her. But I supposed that they would put a red ribbon on her tail and put her in the back of the line, then teach her not to try to get to the front of the line. I hoped she would work out, since she had no talent for ranch work and she wasn't pretty enough to go in parades. Not every horse is a star, but Daddy always said that a horse has to eat and so a horse has to work. Trail rides at a hotel were not hard work. I patted Sprinkles down her neck.

I was now used to the darkness and the cold, and I was rather enjoying being outside by myself after all the "discussions" of the day. I wasn't sleepy. That was not what happened. I was on my feet and I was walking and I had just finished checking the water troughs (which were fine) and making sure the gates were locked (they were). I turned back toward the house. Daddy's light went out as I did so, but the porch light was still on, now rainbowed in mist. My next job was to close the barn door for the night so skunks and raccoons didn't get in. I was walking toward the barn.

Here is what the ghost did—she whispered in my ear. And then she touched my shoulder, my left shoulder. The only way I knew it was the ghost right then, since I wasn't thinking of her, was that a shiver ran down my spine, and when that happened, a picture of her came into my mind. I knew it was her.

I whipped around. I didn't see her.

But the horses did. Jack and Blue, and even Jefferson and Lincoln, were standing in a group, staring toward me and snorting. Jack's tail was up and so was Blue's. Blue suddenly gave a sharp whinny, which made me jump and go, "Ahh!" This wasn't a scream or anything, just a breath—I must have been holding it.

My first actual thought was to wonder what she had whispered in my ear. It was as if I could almost hear the words, but not quite—I could only hear that they *were* words, three or four of them, no more than that, "Go into the house," or, "He's still my horse." As I thought this phrase, it seemed to me that that was what she had said. Now the shivers that had run down my back ran down the front of my legs, and I felt cold and scared all over. I ran toward the house. As I lifted my foot onto the first step of the porch, Rusty came up behind me and leapt up all three steps and ran to the door and stood there, staring. She gave a whine. I opened the door, and even though she had never been in the house, I let her in, and then I let her come through the kitchen with me. The living room was empty. I turned out the light by Daddy's chair. Rusty and I went into the hall by the stairs, where Spooky was sitting up in his box. I turned out the light in the hall so I wouldn't have to look at him, and then Rusty and I went up the staircase, me with my hand on her collar so she wouldn't run ahead and wake Mom and Daddy. We were quiet, though. She stuck right with me up every step, and when I took her into my room, she went straight over to the side of my bed and curled up on the rug. All through the night, I knew she was there, and lots of times, I reached out from under the covers and scratched her ears.

Boots with Boot Tree

Boot Tree

Chapter 18

Usually, when you wake up and the day is already sunny, especially after a big rainstorm, you can't help feeling fresh and happy, and it is true that when I opened my eyes the next morning, the first thing I saw was Rusty sleeping on her back with all four legs in the air, and I laughed, which woke her. She rolled onto her chest and wagged her tail, as if to say, "How did this happen?"

I didn't dare let her be found in my room, so I immediately threw off the covers, but just then the door to my room opened, and Mom said, "Honey, Daddy is really feeling—" She certainly saw Rusty, since Rusty turned her head and looked at Mom and brushed her tail against the floor again, but she hardly paused before continuing, "Like he's got a bad cold or something, so I'll help you feed the horses, and then if you miss the bus, I can drive you." Not a word about Rusty, but she smiled as she closed the door. I looked at my clock. It was twenty minutes since the alarm should have gone off, which was why it was so light. I yawned and got up, petting Rusty several times as I pulled on my jeans.

We went down the front stairs and right out the front door. As soon as we were outside, while I was slipping on my shoes, Rusty went bounding away down toward the road as if plenty of things might have happened in the night, and she needed to sniff out what they were.

The horses were lined up by their respective gates, waiting for their hay, looking entirely as if they had not seen any ghosts. I had gotten pretty good at pushing the wheelbarrow with one and a half arms and tossing flakes of hay over and not into the fence. In the bright sunlight, I saw nothing at all weird, only that the grass was sparkling green and the lupines that we had seen driving toward the coast Saturday had now begun to spread over our own hillsides in a lavender wave.

The back door opened, and Mom came out, waving to me and saying, "Oh, what a beautiful morning! We deserve this!" She trotted over to me, and took the handles of the wheelbarrow and said, "I'll push and you throw, or whatever you want." As it turned out, she pushed and we both threw. I said, "How's Daddy?"

"Stuffed up and headachy. Not much fever, so I may have to tie him to the bed. He's already saying he's got too much to do to lie around all day."

I got a flake way past the fence, behind Jack. He turned and started to nose it apart.

218

"I'll give him breakfast in bed. That will keep him there for a while."

"What time is it?"

"I already put yours on the table. If you eat it now, you can make the bus." She picked up the next flake and threw it past Jefferson. That was the fifth flake, so he went to it, which meant that the other three horses all had to switch places, too. She started pushing the wheelbarrow toward the mares.

On the table, she had set out a bowl of Cheerios, a banana, a hard-boiled egg, and my lunch, which was always a peanut butter sandwich with strawberry jam, an orange, and some carrot sticks. This reminded me that Gloria had opened her lunch on Friday, and it smelled so strange that Stella and I asked her what it was, and she said, "Tongue." We could not believe that, but it was. Her dad had bought it in San Francisco, and the whole family actually liked it.

I knew the ghost had been out there, and I knew she had tapped me on the shoulder, I knew she had said to me, "He's still my horse," and I knew that the horses, or at least the geldings, had seen her. Maybe Rusty had seen her, too, since she was so eager to get into the house. But I also knew that if I kept myself thinking about other things—anything, even peanut butter or the boys on the bus who were sitting down every time the driver looked in his mirror, but jumping up every time he looked out at the road—I would not have to think about the ghost, and I didn't really, all the way until French class, which was so boring that the ghost came right into my head and sat down.

My earlier sightings of the ghost—sitting on her trunk, floating around the corner of the barn, even passing through my room and out the window, holding a black cat in her arms—were not so frightening in comparison to what had happened the night before. Those earlier times, she was just a misty thing, like a cloud, and even though she had a face and seemed to be wearing things—clothes, those black boots—it was still like seeing something that in fact had nothing to do with you. A bobcat crossing the hillside might be dangerous to moles or ground squirrels, but really, it had nothing to do with you—you could watch it, be interested in it, even take a picture of it if there were film in the camera, and it still had nothing to do with you. It could look at you (and bobcats often did turn their heads and lock your gaze) and it still had nothing to do with you. It would soon get up and walk away, disappear into the grass or the trees.

It now seemed as though I had been afraid of the ghost just because it was strange and I'd never seen one before. It now seemed as though I could have gotten used to the ghost if she had just kept to herself and pretended I wasn't there. What you didn't want a ghost to do was to decide that you were its enemy. As I sat there in French class with my book open on my desk, repeating the French words (sort of) along with everyone else (it was a long chapter of dialogue, and we were going around the room, reading and translating each line), I said, "*Oui. Même les fleurs qui ont des épines,*" but I wondered if the ghost's tapping me on the shoulder and whispering in my ear might be just the beginning. This made me shiver. Leslie said something about "the flowers" and "the thorns."

Madame said, "*Bon.*"

Then everyone read, " '*Alors les épines, à quoi servent-elles?*' "

And Madame said, "Mademoiselle Lovitt, *votre traduction, s'il vous plaît.*" She gave me that very courteous smile that she always used when she knew that you weren't paying *attention.*

I said, "'So, the thorns, which they serve to them? The sheep?'" I knew we were talking about sheep. Madame's courteous smile got larger, and she dipped her head. That's what she did to trick you into thinking that you had gotten lucky. Then Madame turned to Kyle Gonzalez and said, "Monsieur Gonzalez, *avez-vous une autre traduction de cette passage?*"

Kyle, of course, said, "*Oui,* Madame. 'Then the thorns, what are they?'" He paused. Madame nodded, and he went on, "'I do not know. I was very busy trying to unscrew a very tight bolt in my engine. I was very worried, because my failure was beginning to seem very serious.'" And even though the ghost was in my mind, I did pause long enough to reflect that Kyle's proper translation didn't make much more sense than my bad one.

A moment later, we mumbled on, "'*Le petit prince ne renonçait jamais à une question, une fois qu'il l'avait posée. J'étais irrité par mon boulon et je répondis n'importe quoi—*'"

I understood that the prince didn't understand the question and was irritated with his bolt, and I went back to thinking about the ghost. The important thing about the whole incident was Rusty. Rusty wasn't afraid of anything. Before we got her, she lived for who knew how long in the wild, by herself. She was a big dog and fast. Before we got her (or, before we knew we had already gotten her), she had chased Jack and one of the adult horses, and on the night the Brahmas broke through the fence, she herded a cow and a calf up the hill back onto the Jordan ranch. I had actually seen her take down a bobcat—a small bobcat, maybe a year old, but nonetheless a bobcat. For Rusty to run onto the porch and act like she had to get into the house was far more strange than the horses spooking, but the four geldings spooking was strange, too. Maybe the mares were also spooking, but when I saw Rusty, I got too scared to turn and check.

I heard Maria say, "Um, let's see. 'Flowers have thorns just because. Because of just naughtiness.'"

Kyle raised his hand and said, "Madame, *je ne crois pas que les fleurs ont les intentions.*" I understood that—flowers don't have intentions.

Madame smiled and said, "Monsieur Kyle, *ceci est seulement dans un roman, une fable.*" I understood that, too—it's only a story. Grown-ups were always telling you that.

But of course that was not enough for Kyle, who began drumming the desk with his fingers. The thing about Kyle was that though he didn't like to argue, he did like a straight answer. I wondered if he believed in ghosts. If he did, then he would have all sorts of good reasons, and if he didn't, he would have good reasons for that, too. Madame looked at him for a long second, then said, *"Peut-être que ça suffit pour l'instant. Nous avançons!* Mademoiselle Linda, *s'il vous plaît."* (Enough of you, Kyle; let's get moving, Linda.)

Linda A. read, "'Oh! *Mais après un silence il me lança, avec une sorte de rancune.'"* I stopped listening, and then about five minutes later, we all heard the bell. Madame looked a little relieved. As we rushed out, I saw Kyle go up to her.

When I got off the bus and went in the house that afternoon, Daddy was still sick—even sicker, in fact. He had tried to get up before lunch, gotten as far as the barn, and then come staggering back in the kitchen door and gone upstairs to sleep. Mom had ridden Lincoln and Jefferson, and also gotten on Foxy, but only after letting her run around with Blue in the pen for half an hour. Mom didn't look unhappy or upset, I have to say. She said, "Oh, I like Foxy. I should've ridden her before this. I think she's my new favorite."

I sat down at the table and she poured me a glass of milk. I picked a banana out of the fruit bowl. "Barbie likes her, too."

Mom laughed. "Those girls are so interesting. They do everything, it seems like."

"They have their own bathroom, and their mom let them paint it themselves, so the wall is covered with pictures. One looks just like Spooky."

"They have cats, right?"

"Two black and one orange. The orange one is huge."

Mom went into the living room and came back with Spooky on her arm. He was yawning. She said, "If you have three, I don't know that you notice a fourth one."

"I thought he was going to be a barn cat."

"And I thought Rusty was an outside dog."

We smiled at each other. Then I had a bad thought. "Is that what's making Daddy sick?"

"Oh, goodness, no. Dogs make him sneeze and clog his sinuses. He's got a fever and is throwing up. This is surely the flu."

"Are we going to get it?"

"Well, you stay away from him. I am washing my hands a lot."

I drank the rest of my milk and ate another piece of banana. Mom had set Spooky on the floor, and then wrapped him very loosely in a dish towel. He was jumping around trying to get out of it. When he did, she dragged it across the floor, and let him pounce on it and kill it. I thought about telling Mom about the ghost Rusty and I had seen the night before. I looked at her. She was laughing and bending down to toss the towel over Spooky, and I wondered why I didn't. Normally, I had no trouble talking to Mom. She didn't like complaining, but if you phrased your complaint as a question, she never minded that. I had told her about lots of things over the years, and when I had gotten in big trouble in seventh grade for maybe stealing an add-a-pearl necklace (which I didn't do, but it looked like I did until Kyle Gonzalez spoke up), Mom had only been mad for a few minutes. Afterward, I thought maybe she wasn't mad at me as much as she was mad at the school, though she didn't say anything about that. I kept looking at her.

The thing was, I didn't know whether Mom believed in ghosts. If she did, maybe I didn't want to be the one to tell her that we now had one, because if it scared her, then it would scare me more. And if she didn't, well, sometimes it's harder to tell your mom that you are stupid than it is to tell her that you've been naughty. I didn't even know if I myself believed in ghosts. At times during the day, I had been completely sure that ghost had tapped me on the shoulder and told me Blue was her horse and then chased Rusty into the house, and other times I thought I was crazy. But another thing was true, too—it's not so embarrassing to think crazy thoughts as it is to express them. So I didn't say anything, except, "I wish I could ride."

"How is it feeling?"

"Boring. It doesn't hurt anymore."

"It will when you take the cast off and start using it. Just don't do one thing that Nancy Hazen's nephew did when he broke his arm and had a cast up past his elbow."

I said, "What was that?"

"Stick a penny down there, so far that he couldn't get it out. It kind of ate into the skin."

I said, "Oh, yuck."

"Yup," said Mom.

After that, all there was to do was homework, so I got some carrots out of the refrigerator and cut them into pieces, then I put them in a bag. This way, I figured I could put off *Le Petit Prince* and the Mexican War for at least a half hour.

Because of all the rain, there was slop everywhere, so I paused to put on my rubber boots, which were sitting outside the back door. In California, you have to always look into your boots in case a spider has taken up residence since you last wore them, so I did that—I knocked each one against the step, turned it over, and shook it. Nothing came out. I stepped into them. And then there was a whinny—it was Blue, standing by the gelding gate and calling to me. I called back, "Blue, Blue, how are you?" And he whinnied again. I guess it was right then that I remembered that I had paid for him, yes, but the way that you make a horse your own is by doing something with him.

I ran to the gate and unbuckled one of the four halters that were buckled to it. Since Blue was already paying attention to me (in fact, he was hanging his head over the gate), I didn't open the bag of carrots, and so the other geldings didn't come over, even Jack (which would have bothered me, but just this once I didn't want to deal with anyone else). I got the halter on Blue (I was getting better at it, but it was still hard to do this one-and-a-half-handed), opened the gate, and led him out. He stood there while I closed the gate and did the lock. I had set down the bag of carrots, but even when I picked it up, he didn't nose it, or act as though it was his business.

I took him to the pen. He walked along politely, and when my boot got stuck in the mud for a moment, and sort of slid off, so that I had to stop and pull it back on, he stopped. Then we walked on. It was at that point that I remembered how nice he was to groom—always staying out of your space, but responding to the brush as if he actually felt it—and I realized that in spite of his worries, he was a very attentive horse. It was probably true, as Daddy and Danny both said, that he didn't know much because he hadn't been asked to do much, but he did know something that many horses did not—how to be with his person in a courteous way, except that was not really it, either. Horses are often praised for having good manners—just the way a person is supposed to know to say please and thank you and to knock before entering, a horse is supposed to know to stand still while he is being mounted and to trot when he is asked to trot and to halt when he is asked to halt. But Blue had something more than that. He had a way of paying attention to me rather than to everything else. It was as if he was wondering about me, and waiting to see what I was going to do, but not making suggestions or demands. When we got through the gate of the pen, I unsnapped the lead rope, but before I waved him into a trot, I opened the bag and gave him a piece of carrot. It was then I thought of the trick.

It was a silly trick, and one that most people wouldn't notice, but it seemed like a trick that was suited to Blue and his kind nature—I wanted to show him a carrot, and then have him look away from it in order to get it.

When I first started with this trick, I did it partly because it was the only one I could think of. Horses we had seen did lots of tricks—they reared on command, they bowed, they lay down, or they jumped up on pedestals. That horse on TV, Mr. Ed, moved his lips as if he was talking. Once when I was pretty small, Daddy and Mom took me to a rodeo where Roy Rogers made six or seven palominos do a bunch of tricks. But now I had a broken arm and the ground was muddy and somehow something quieter seemed better. I let Blue trot around the pen for a minute—the footing in here was less slippery than in the pasture, and he looked like he needed to loosen up. I took the bag to the middle of the pen and set it at my feet. I had one piece of carrot in my right hand. I was no longer wearing the sling, so I kept my left hand down at my side, but I didn't have anything in it. While Blue trotted and then walked around, I wondered how I was going to do this.

Blue came over. I stood there. He sniffed my shoulder first, and then my waist, and finally he sniffed my hand, and of course he knew the carrot was in there, but I didn't move. He nosed my hand once, then stretched his head and neck and checked my other hand. I waited. He waited, not doing much, and then one of the mares snorted, and he looked in that direction. Right then, I said, "Good Blue," and I slipped the carrot between his lips. He started chewing it, and I picked up the bag and walked away. I went to another corner of the pen and stood. After a moment, Blue followed me.

Now he was interested in the carrots—he knew I had them

and that he could get one—so the first thing he tried was to be a little pushier than he had been before, but I didn't do anything; I just stood there with the carrot in my hand without making any moves while he nudged my hand and then my other hand, and then my shoulder. However, being Blue, he didn't push too hard—a horse like Jack or a horse like Amazon might be more aggressive, but not Blue. Finally, he dropped his head and flopped his ears. I waited. This time, what attracted his attention was Rusty—she came around the house. As soon as he looked in her direction, I said, "Good Blue," again, and slipped the carrot between his lips. As soon as he was chewing, I walked away to another part of the pen. I knew Daddy would say, "How in the world is this useful?" and I couldn't have answered. But it was starting to be fun. Blue followed me.

We did exactly this same thing four more times—he looked for the carrot and didn't get it, and then as soon as he looked at something else, I said, "Good Blue," gave him the carrot, and walked away. The last time, I only walked two steps, so all he had to do was pivot on his haunches to be with me. Six times in all, and I was ready to do it lots of times—I had no idea how long it would take Blue to make the connection between looking away and getting a carrot. I was having fun. It was still two hours until it got dark, and what else was there to do? I wanted to pet him, but I didn't want to confuse him, so I made myself not pet him, but just stand there.

On the seventh time, he did it. He was a smart horse. He looked at me, then he looked at my hand, and then he looked away. There was nothing out there to look at—no noises, no movements, and his ears didn't prick in that direction. I said,

"Good Blue," and slipped him the carrot. This time his lips took it. That's how I knew he understood. After that first time, it was easy. I walked a few steps, stood quietly, Blue looked at me and then looked away and waited for me to give him the carrot. I got to where I made him wait a few seconds, just to see if he understood what he was supposed to do. He did—he kept looking away until I gave him the carrot.

It is hard to describe how it felt to teach Blue this trick. It was like having him read my mind, but also like reading his mind. For me, he was the only horse in the world at that moment, and I felt like I was the only being in his world, too. The other horses were unimportant, Rusty was nothing, we didn't hear Daddy come out on the back porch, there was no ghost, or even the memory of a ghost. There was just this beautiful gray horse who seemed like he was about to say something, who seemed like he could do anything, if only you knew how to ask him.

I walked over to the gate, where I had draped the lead rope over the fence, and I snapped the lead rope on his halter. Then I opened the gate and walked out and over to the barn. It was only there that I began to pet him and groom him and make a big fuss. I wanted that thing we did in the pen, even if it was a little thing, or because it was a little thing, to stay pure in his mind—or maybe in my mind.

Lead Rope

Flannel Bandages and Cotton Sheets

Chapter 19

AT SUPPER, DADDY WAS FEELING MUCH BETTER, AND IN FACT, HE said that he was fine. He ate plenty and was in a good mood, though he was still wearing his robe. He said, "So what were you doing out there with your horse?"

"Teaching him a trick."

"What trick?"

"To look away in order to get a treat."

"You get him to do it?"

I nodded.

"That's cute."

"Did you ever teach a horse a trick?"

"Not since we were kids. When I was eleven and Luke was thirteen, we taught Luke's horse to add and subtract."

Mom said, "How'd you do that?"

"Well, we taught him to paw the ground until Luke pushed his hat up. Then we would stop. It was a harder trick than it looked like, though."

Mom said, "Why was that?"

Daddy was already smiling. "Well, especially in the subtraction, Luke and I would come up with the wrong answers. So the horse looked like he hadn't properly learned his tables."

We all laughed.

So, I thought when I was lying in bed that night, a trick isn't a big deal in lots of ways. But that moment when Blue understood what he was supposed to do, that felt like a big deal. And I fell asleep without thinking about the ghost at all.

On Tuesday, it was raining again, and Mom called the school at lunchtime to tell me to come home on the bus, because Jane had canceled the lessons. That was fine with me, since I wanted to see if Blue remembered his trick from the day before. But as the afternoon went by, I got to feeling worse and worse, and when I got off the bus, it was all I could do to drag myself through the gate and up the front steps. I opened the door, walked inside, and sat down on the bottom step. It took me a long time even to close the door. I just slumped there with my eyes half closed, only partly aware of Spooky sitting in his box, staring at me. I think I might have said, "Go ahead and stare, Spooky. I'm too tired to care."

Mom must have been at the store, because when she came in, she had bags in her arms. She said, "Uh-oh," and walked past me, but then she came back and sat me up on the step and took my jacket off. I felt about three years old. But that wasn't bad. She said, "Did you throw up yet?"

I shook my head.

She felt my forehead with the palm of her hand and then my cheeks with the back of her hand. She said, "Not much." But I didn't feel feverish, or even sick to my stomach. I felt like Rip Van Winkle, and ready to sleep for a hundred years.

Here are the things I remember from that night and the next day:

Me lying on my back in my bed, with the room half dark, and Mom sticking the thermometer in my mouth.

Me opening my eyes and seeing that the light was on next to my bed, but not being able to reach it.

The sound of rain.

Mom putting a cool washcloth on my forehead, with Daddy standing behind her looking at me.

Spooky sitting on my chest.

Blue turning his head away from me, then toward me, then away from me again.

Daddy opening the window in my room, and the Lady floating in.

Me sitting up, and then lying down again because I didn't care about the Lady, I was so tired.

The door opening, and the light being on in the hall.

Kyle Gonzalez talking French, but not saying anything I could understand.

Barbie Goldman saying, "You're kidding!" then laughing and throwing a tennis ball at the wall of the gym.

My room being completely dark, so dark that I couldn't see anything, and me yelling something.

Mom feeling my head and saying, "Her hair is really damp."

Blue walking around me, once to the left and once to the right.

Spooky sitting on Blue's back in a green field.

Mom putting another cool washcloth on my forehead, then, sometime later, making me sit up and put my hands in a pot of cold water.

The room full of sunlight.

A glass of lupine sitting on the table next to my bed.

The fragrance of the lupine.

Feeling hungry, but falling asleep about halfway through a bowl of chicken rice soup.

Nothing.

And then I woke up.

It was almost dark, and I had no idea what day it was, or how long I had been in my room. I felt totally fine, and sat up, and put my feet on the floor. The rug next to my bed had been moved, and the floor was cool against the soles of my feet. It felt good. I reached over and turned on the light by my bed. My hand had a cast around it, so I twisted and reached with my right hand. That hand worked fine. The light came on and I saw that my room was very neat. I got up and opened the door. The hallway of our house looked bright, and all the corners were very sharp, almost sparkling. I was unbelievably hungry. I went to the bathroom, and then ran down the stairs. Spooky sprang up when he saw me, and gave me a sassy hiss, then jumped on his knotted rope and killed it.

In the kitchen, Mom was reading a knitting pattern. She looked up at me as soon as I walked through the door and said, "She is ris'n."

I said, "I am so hungry!"

Mom closed her knitting book. "No wonder."

"What day is it?"

"Wednesday."

I said, "Is that all?"

"You sound disappointed."

"It feels like it should be next year."

"That's what your dad said when he revived."

"How many times did I wake up in the night, though?"

"Only once after I took off your clothes."

"Did you give me chicken rice soup?"

She shook her head. "But I can give you some now."

I decided that Spooky, Blue, Barbie, and Kyle hadn't been in my room, either. But the glass of lupine was there.

I could see the horse pastures out the kitchen windows and Rusty, too, coming out of the barn. She sat and looked first to the left and then to the right. I said, "Where's Daddy?"

"He's out riding Amazon. But the ground is so wet, he was just going to ride her down the road a ways and back. That's what we did with Foxy and Jefferson."

"Did you ride Foxy?"

Mom nodded. She said, "I was good." Then she said, "And that's what Daddy and Danny did when they took Lincoln and Happy out, too."

I couldn't believe it. I said, "When was that?"

"First thing this morning."

"Did they come back—"

"With any bruises or black eyes?"

I nodded.

Now she grinned. "Not a one. Let me make that soup."

She also made me toast. I ate two bowls of soup and three pieces of toast and two hours later, I was ready for supper, which was a baked chicken and some rice.

But it wasn't as easy as that. After I had called Gloria, who was in some of my classes, and Stella, who was in another one, and gotten our assignments, I got a headache in the midst of working on the new book we were reading, *Ethan Frome*, and went right over to my bed and fell asleep.

But not for the whole night. I woke up again, just as I had before, bright and happy. The room sparkled the way the hallway had—I could see the edges of the window as if they were carved out of light. My shelves in the corner across from the bed were dim and bright at the same time—I felt as though I could read the titles on the spines of the books even though I could barely see the books. It was as if my eyes had grown bigger, and for a moment I thought, This is how horses see in the dark, and it's true that their eyes are so big that they probably make things out better than we do, especially at a distance.

It was twenty after two by my bedside clock. Not good. I turned on my side and closed my eyes, but every part of my body was saying time to get up and go; sleep was over.

Mom has always said that one of the great things about me is that I've been a good sleeper since I was four months old. "Put her down, pat her on the back, and she didn't make a peep until morning." This was in contrast to Danny, who was up every two or three hours until he was almost two. And he was

an early riser. There was a story about him from when he was three—Daddy heard something that woke him up, and as he opened his eyes, he saw Danny running past his bedroom door. He decided he'd better get up and see what was going on, and as soon as he sat up, he put his foot on a broken egg. When he went, "Ahh! Ugh!" Mom turned over in bed and put her hand in another broken egg right in the middle of the blanket. There were twelve eggs cracked all over the house they had then, and, as Mom always says, "It was only five-thirty in the morning."

Another time, Danny had climbed a fence and fallen, biting his tongue when he hit. They took him to the doctor and got stitches, and the next morning, he woke Mom and showed her the thread he had pulled out of his tongue. That time, the sun wasn't even up yet.

But me, I was perfect. I was such a good sleeper that I went down at eight like a tree falling in the forest and hardly moved all night. But after my twenty-four-hour virus, my body said, "Those days are gone."

I sat up and went to the window. I didn't feel that the room was cold. There was no moon, so I couldn't see the horses very well. The dark grass and the dark trees hid them, and since the window was closed, I couldn't hear them, either. I could see the angled bulk of the barn and the curve of the arena fence next to that. I could see the dark hillside, the way it rose and undulated, but mostly I could see stars and stars and stars. Usually, the sky looks flat and the stars look scattered across it, small, smaller, and smallest, but tonight, the sky looked deep, and the multitude of stars looked far, farther, and farthest. I really could see what they told us in science, that the sky bent around and enveloped the earth. The more I stared, the more I could imagine those light-years Mr. Ramirez was always talking about.

When I looked back at the clock, it was a little after two-thirty. I saw that it was going to be a long night. But I didn't want to turn on the light for some reason. If you are going to be wide awake in the middle of the night for what felt like the first time ever (but not really the first, of course—there were times that I woke up to worry about something and then went back to sleep, but this was not about worrying), then you could not do homework or read a book you had already read six times. You had to do something special. It was just that I couldn't think what to do. I lay back in my bed and stared at the ceiling.

Then I remembered that moment when we came home Sunday night, when we pulled through the gate and saw Blue in the pasture, where Danny had left him. Just like tonight, it was very dark outside because of the weather and the time of year, but there was Blue, glowing gray in the gloom, his neck arched and his tail switching, his ears pricked, and his nostrils flared, my horse, looking as beautiful as maybe it was possible for a horse to look. I lay there. My ceiling was so dark that I couldn't see the water stain that Daddy kept saying we had to fix, but in my mind I could see Blue, dapply and shining. I decided to go find out what the horses were doing.

I had sense enough to be sneaky and quiet. At the very least, if Mom heard me moving around, she would get up and ask me how I felt, but I felt great, and I didn't feel like talking. I slid on my jeans and put a sweatshirt over my pajama top. I picked up some socks—whether they matched, I didn't know. I opened my bedroom door veeerrrrry slowly and peeked into the hallway. Mom and Daddy's door was open, but I tiptoed past it and down the stairs, one step at a time. No creaking. I even got past Spooky, who was sound asleep in his sweater with his paw over his face. I thought I got past Rusty, since I heard no movements on the front porch, but I was wrong. She startled me when I opened the back door—she was standing there with her ears up and her tail wagging. But she didn't make a sound and neither did I.

I stepped into my rubber boots. Only after I was in them did I think about spiders, but nothing bit me. I tiptoed across the porch and down the steps. Rusty was right in front of me. I had never been out of the house at this time of night before. It was darker than I thought it was going to be, but I had that same feeling, that I could see every edge and corner, even that I could see every single hair along Rusty's back, distinct from every other hair. Or every dark, wet blade of grass. I looked up. The stars were even deeper than they had been through the window, layers and layers of stars beyond stars. I took a breath and then another one. The air was wet, but I could smell the grass and the lupine.

My boots made a noise in the mud. I tried to go more quietly.

The halters were buckled along the second bar of the gate. There was no one at the water troughs, no one scrounging for bits of hay. The horses were under the trees. It was too dark even to see Blue. And then he walked out into the open, his head stretched down and his tail swishing. He was walking carefully, because of the mud, and the dark-haired lady was lying across his back, her head and chest resting along his neck, and her legs in their black boots hanging down. Her arms were hanging, too, but her elbows were bent, and her hands were resting under her chin. He had no saddle, of course, but also no bridle—he was just walking along free. Her hair was so thick that it hid her face. I stared at the two of them, walking here and there. His coat was brighter than she was—she was wearing dark gray or black. Sometimes I could see her and sometimes I couldn't. The other geldings, even Jack, were lost under the trees. I turned and looked at the mare pasture. The mares had gone down to the crick. I said, in a low voice, "Rusty! Rusty! Where are you?" but she was nowhere nearby. I realized that I was alone with Blue and the ghost. For the first time in days, my broken wrist began to throb.

Blue was walking slowly, but I counted his steps—one, two, three, four, pause, snuffle the ground, five, six, seven, shake his head, snort away a bug of some sort, eight, nine, turn toward me and prick his ears. I said nothing. He stared at me as if wondering who or what I was, and I thought of calling "Blue, Blue, how are you?" but the lady was still lying on him, her face hidden in his mane, and I was afraid if I did call out, she would sit up and do something strange and ghostly, like rise into the air. I tightened my lips and held back the greeting.

Blue and I stared through the darkness at each other.

Just then, from off to my right, came a series of yips and then a long howl, *owooo!* There was a pause, followed by another. It was only for a moment that I wondered what it was—I knew it was a coyote, or more than one. And then, from my left, so loud it made me jump, came the answering howl—Rusty. "*Owooo!*" I could see her now, maybe ten or fifteen feet from me, standing with her nose pointing into the air and her mouth partly open. She sat. She howled again. Her howl was deeper and more eerie than the coyotes' howl, longer, too. It seemed like it went into my head and made my scalp prickle even though I could see her and understand what was going on—the coyotes were shouting, "Anyone here?" and Rusty was answering, "I am, go away!" Then she bounded past me to the corner of the pasture, where she stood staring off into the distance.

I turned back to Blue and the ghost.

Maybe it was the howling, or maybe it was my movement in the dimness, but Blue reared and ran, and the dark-haired lady seemed to slide—she held on around his neck, and then she seemed to drop as he took off. I was staring. He kicked up and galloped away, and in a second or two, Jack had come out of the trees and was scampering along beside him, rearing and bucking. The two of them galloped out of sight, into the darkness. I stepped over to the gate and climbed it, leaning into the pasture, still staring.

That feeling I'd been having, of being able to see everything, was still with me, but at the same time, I could see nothing— no horses, just the dim landscape and the bright stars. My skin under my sweatshirt was freezing cold, my mouth was open, my wrist was throbbing, my hair was damp and flopping around me in the breeze, my hand on the rail of the gate seemed locked shut. And then I made myself call out, not very loudly, "Blue, Blue, how are you?" and the two horses appeared out of the gloom, and Blue gave a big whinny, and then Jack whinnied, and they trotted over to the gate.

It was Jack who made me feel normal again. He snuffled my hands and his warmth was just his warmth, and his winter coat was just his puffy winter coat, and his ears were just his ears, long and inquisitive, and his nostrils and the curve of his neck, and he snorted the way he always did, not frightened, only interested. He smelled like he always did, too, only damper and chillier, as he would have, staying outside on a damp and chilly night. I petted him the way he liked it, down the curve of his neck, and then Blue pressed in (though not chasing Jack away) and I petted him, too, and tickled him along the base of his mane, alternating my good hand between one and the other, and sort of hooking myself onto the gate with the elbow of my broken arm. I could see that Blue was nice to Jack—he had become his friend the way Black George had been his friend before we sold him. While I petted them, I said, "Was she here, you guys? Was she riding you, Blue? Does she come very often? Does she come every night? Do I want to know?" But they didn't have any answers, and didn't act as though I had asked any questions. Pretty soon, Rusty appeared again, having, I suppose, seen those coyotes on their way.

Western Stirrups

Whip

Chapter 20

THE NEXT SURPRISE WAS THAT IT WAS DADDY WHO FIXED MY breakfast when I got up in the morning. Mom was sleeping. He handed me two pieces of buttered toast and said, "I'm not sure she's got it, because she didn't seem sick in the night, but she's sleeping, and it's best to let her sleep."

I said, "Did you hear anything in the night?"

"Nothing special. Coyotes now and then, but I hear that lots of nights."

I peeled my banana. "You do?"

"Sure. Don't you?"

I shook my head.

He said, "Honey, you're lucky to be such a sound sleeper."

I just nodded.

He said, "What about school?"

This may have been the first time in my life that he asked me whether I wanted to go to school. I shrugged. Even though after coming in (sneaking up the stairs the way I sneaked down them, step by step), I had only gotten maybe two hours' sleep, I wasn't very tired.

"If you're shrugging, then you'd better hurry, because the bus will be here in ten minutes."

I stopped shrugging. Shrugging is a little like rolling your eyes, in Daddy's opinion. I said, "I could stay home another day. I could help you if Mom's sick."

Daddy smiled, then said, "That's better. Okay, let's do a few things and get organized, then I'll take you to the school and drop you, because I have to go into town anyway, but I want to wait until your mom wakes up to see how she is."

"Did you feel better after you were sick than before?"

"In some ways. But it's false, too. I think I felt better than I actually was, so I wouldn't push it, if I were you. And eat all your breakfast." One thing he had done that Mom never did during the week was fry some bacon. I liked bacon. For the rest of breakfast, we talked about how good bacon was; I had two slices and Daddy had four.

Mom slept for a while, but when she woke up, she said she felt fine. By the time I got to school, I had missed science, French, and home economics. During study hall, I went around to my teachers and got my assignments from the day before. Before lunch, we had history, and all we did was watch parts of the second half of a movie called *The Alamo*. I had heard of the Alamo, of course—there was a section about it in our history textbook. It was a battle in Texas, where all the men inside the Alamo were killed. That was sad enough, and some of the men were very famous, like Davy Crockett and Jim Bowie, but what I didn't like the most was when the bombs exploded among the horses and the horses fell down. There was lots of whinnying, too, as if the horses were hurt. I don't know if the other kids enjoyed the movie, or even watched it. I saw Stella and Debbie passing notes, and I saw Brian Connelly with his head on his desk, maybe sleeping. Larry Schnuck kept kicking Randy Jellinek under the desk. Finally, Mr. Harrison had to come over and smack Larry on the head with his ruler. Even though he didn't hit him very hard, Larry put his hand on his head and said, "Ow! That HURT!" In the end, given how sad the movie was, I was glad of the distractions.

As usual, I was able to put the slender lady ghost in the back of my mind for most of the day. Every time she occurred to me, I made myself think of something else, and during that movie of the Alamo, that was pretty easy. But the bad thing was that she had attached herself to some of my favorite things to think about. I had been riding for such a long time—as long as I had been going to school—and for all that time, when school got just too much to bear, I would think about the horses. Quite often on my report card, a teacher would write, *Works hard sometimes, but easily distracted.* That was about me looking out the window or at some picture across the room, or just down at my book, and thinking about Ornery George, or Black George, or Happy, or Jack, or the others who had come and gone. If the ghost was attached to Blue and now to Jack, I couldn't imagine what I was going to enjoy thinking about.

I knew that Brian Connelly, for example, thought about

television and food, and that Stella thought about clothes, and Gloria thought about books and magazines and rock and roll. Obviously, Alexis and Barbie thought about everything. Larry Schnuck seemed to spend his time thinking about how he was going to beat up the seventh graders or get far enough outside the sight of the teachers to have a cigarette (I had seen him do it). Kyle thought about the way things worked, which was a very big subject. And now I was thinking about the ghost, though in a backward sort of way. I shook my head to get her out of there and made myself listen to Stella talk about her new bathing suit, which she was going to wear over break when her family went to Mexico. They were going to Mazatlán, and her dad was going to go deep-sea fishing. "I am just going to unwind," said Stella. Gloria nodded. I tried to imagine this.

In phys ed, we were now going out to the tennis courts and "volleying," which meant making the ball go back and forth over the net. You were supposed to hit it toward your partner so that she could hit it back to you—later, "Mr." Tyler said, we would try to hit it away from our partners. At this point, hitting it away from our partners (into the net, over the fence, way off to the left, way off to the right, over her head, at her feet) was the easiest thing in the world. Actually putting it anywhere near her racket was hard. My partner was Maria. Her backhand was better than her forehand, so we had a little agreement—we would place our rackets more or less opposite to one another and get into a rhythm of back and forth, but we wouldn't try anything because, frankly, I was too tired to run after the ball, and Maria was not interested in sports, so she didn't care to exert herself, either.

After forty minutes of this (which was rather pleasant, since "Mr." Tyler had to pester the ones who weren't hitting it at all), we went to the locker room to change. Barbie, who had been volleying with Lucia on the other side of the court, ran up to me and said, "Guess what!"

"What?"

"Our music teacher changed our dress rehearsal for the recital to Saturday morning, so can I come in the afternoon? We'll be finished by two."

My lessons with Melinda and Ellen began at noon, so I said, "Can you come later? At four? I'm sure I'll be back by then, but maybe not until then."

Barbie nodded. "I've been practicing like mad, and I know my part perfectly, so I'm sure everyone will be in a good mood and I will be able to have whatever I want."

"What's your piece?"

"It's called 'Canon in D.' It's by Johann Pachelbel. It's really beautiful, so whenever we do a good job on it, everybody goes into a sort of daze and everything we ask for afterward, they say yes." She looked dead serious, but I knew she wasn't. I laughed, and then she laughed.

I kept the ghost out of my mind until I got off the bus and was walking toward the house. The sun was shining right on that spot where she had fallen off Blue, and then in spite of myself, I now envisioned her floating up into the air and disappearing into the darkness, her dress or whatever she was wearing fluttering behind her. The thing to do was to go out there right now, before it got dark, or even twilight, and look around the spot. And in the sunlight, I thought maybe I could do it.

I would take Rusty with me. For about one second, I noticed Danny's car parked in front of the house, and Daddy's truck next to it, but I'd seen that twice lately, and it didn't strike me the way it might have.

I went through the door and set down my books.

Daddy and Danny were in the kitchen, and I heard Danny say, "I want to buy the horse. Why can't I buy the horse?"

Daddy said, "I didn't say you can't. I said, I'll see."

I paused. They weren't shouting, but their voices weren't relaxed, either—it was as if they were trying not to shout, but loudness was pushing out around the edges. I paused, and then walked straight into the kitchen and said, "What horse are you talking about? Where's Mom?"

Daddy looked up at me. He said, "She's upstairs, sleeping." And then Danny said, "Happy."

It was startling to see them like that—Daddy was sitting in his usual spot at the kitchen table, and Danny was sitting across from him. Daddy had a half-full cup of coffee in front of him, and Danny had finished his. The sugar bowl was between them, and the milk carton hadn't been put away again. They were both wearing colorful shirts—Danny's blue denim and Daddy's red plaid flannel. Their chairs were turned slightly away from the table. They had taken off their boots, and their feet were flat on the floor. It was like looking at Alexis and Barbie— mirror twins—but as men. In the year and a half that Danny had worked for Jake Morrisson, he had gotten big in the shoulders and the chest, but more than that, his hands were strong, like Daddy's, and his face was tan until you looked at his forehead, which was white because he always wore a hat. Just like

Daddy. They were both gritting their teeth, and the only difference that I could see was that Daddy had a few gray hairs, but you wouldn't notice them except that Danny's hair was glossy, thick, and dark—no gray hairs. Daddy drank up the rest of his coffee and opened his mouth, and I said, "Happy is perfect for you. All she wants is cows cows cows, all day long."

Daddy opened his mouth again. I said, "What was the name of that horse you had, Daddy, that mare who cut cows without a bridle on? Whenever I look at Happy, I think of her."

Daddy said, "Josephine. Josie."

I said, "Yeah, her. Happy could be like that."

"She could be a nice horse," said Daddy. "That's why I bought her. But—"

I said, "Too bad we don't have any cows. It's kind of like it was with Black George. I miss him, but I realized finally that he wasn't going to be contented with jumping a few straw bales every so often, given how much he enjoyed himself."

Daddy said, "Are you finished?"

Danny said, "I need a horse of my own. I want to start her."

Daddy said, "She's started."

"Well, she's started with the saw cow. I would—" And then, "Jake has a few calves—"

"She's been up to the Jordan ranch."

Daddy was getting stiffer and stiffer.

Danny looked away, out the window.

There was a long moment of silence, and I thought how I could just keep going, right through the kitchen and out the back door. Rusty would meet me or find me, and we could go look in the pasture or chase coyotes or something.

251

Daddy cleared his throat.

Danny cleared his throat.

I said, "Well, Danny, can I show you something? Out in the pasture?"

There was another long moment of silence.

Danny pushed back his chair and stood up. He said, "Sure." He looked completely like he didn't believe me. He said, "Let me get on my boots. I did ride Blue today. We went down the road, but I think the arena should be dry by tomorrow."

"Oh, sure it will," said Daddy. "No more rain until Monday or Tuesday, they say."

Danny and I went out the back door, which I closed carefully, so as not to seem as though I were slamming anything.

Sometimes, after a lot of rain, the sky where we live is so bright that you have to shade your eyes. All the leaves on all the trees are washed clean and the grass seems to have grown another inch in the last hour. The trunks of the oak trees are dark and damp, too, and a sort of greenish lace hangs down from them that Mom calls Spanish moss. Some of the horses are clean, because the rain sluiced them down, and they haven't yet rolled in the mud. Horses are different in their enjoyment of mud—we had one gray horse a few years ago who raced Daddy to a mud patch—Daddy had hosed him off and turned him out in the arena to dry in the sun, something that he was used to doing with the other horses. Then, as Daddy turned to walk back to the barn, he realized that there was one puddle in the arena that had still not dried from a storm four or five days before. He turned and ran to catch the horse—Smoky George, we called him—but the horse had already arrowed straight for the puddle and was just getting up from a good roll when Daddy came back around the corner of the barn.

Danny blew his nose and put his bandanna back in his pocket. I said, "How was Blue?"

"He was okay."

"Did he do anything bad?"

"No. Little tense."

We walked on.

"Did you ride anyone else?"

"Happy."

I sniffed, then said, "Was she happy?"

He cleared his throat. We got to the gate. I decided to drop the subject. Danny rested his arm on the top railing of the gate and said, "What are we doing here?"

"Enjoying the weather."

"I don't really have time to do that, I have to be . . ."

"Do you believe in ghosts?"

"Didn't you ask me that before?"

"Yes, but I saw one, and I heard one. It's the ghost of Blue's old owner. She was riding him in the middle of the night last night."

"You were dreaming."

"I wasn't. I was out here. It was about three. She fell off." I suddenly thought about that kid Freddie, in Alexis's story.

And of course, Danny said, "Don't be an idiot."

"Rusty saw her, too."

"How do you know?"

"She ran to the house and pushed her way in."

"Last night?"

"No, a few nights ago, when I came out to check on the horses. The ghost tapped me on the shoulder and whispered in my ear that Blue was her horse, and then I ran to the house and Rusty was behind me when I started, but she was ahead of me by the time we were on the porch. She HAD to get in."

"What did she see?"

"The GHOST!"

He shook his head.

I opened the gate and walked into the pasture, shooing away the horses. Danny stayed at the gate, obviously not intending to take this seriously, and for once, I was pretty mad at him. And Rusty did come over. As Danny was closing the gate, she slipped through and ran toward me, but she didn't look around and sniff anything, she just galloped on, bellied under the far fence, and ran up the hill.

I don't know what I expected to see—ruby slippers? Glittery dust? Of course there was nothing. The pasture was a muddy mess, and my rubber boots were sticking everywhere. By the time I got back to the gate, I was as crabby as Danny, so I said, "I don't know what's going on about Happy, but you know he's got a price in his head, and if you don't have the money, well, good luck. This is a business!" That was something Daddy said a lot.

Danny said, "Great!" and tromped away, and good riddance, I thought. He walked around the house, and a few minutes later, I heard his car engine start, and then I could see him on the road for a moment.

I let the horses come back to me. Blue and Jefferson were clean, Jack and Lincoln were dirty, Happy, Sprinkles, and Foxy were clean, and Amazon was like one giant dusty ball—she had rolled several times and the dirt had dried and crusted, not only over her back and haunches and neck, as with most horses, but under her neck and under her belly and all the way around her head. She looked very proud of herself. When she shook, the dust flew. I petted her on the tip of her nose and backed away.

Inside, you could tell Daddy was grumpy and Mom was fed up, and whatever it was that they had been talking about (Danny, most likely), they had decided to drop the subject. Mom didn't look great—she was sitting where Danny had been at the table, and Daddy was rearranging the dishes in the dish drainer, which he only did when he was upset, because otherwise, why would you care if they were arranged according to size or not? And I thought, Why are we always dropping subjects around here? Why do we keep our mouths shut and hope for the best and check the Bible and stay patient at all times? And then, as I was walking past the refrigerator, I stumbled and fell with my broken wrist right against the corner of the refrigerator, and of course it throbbed, of course it did! So I barked, "I am really tired of being *patient*! Really!"

Mom said, "Well, honey, I—"

And Daddy said, "Abby—"

So I stomped through the living room and stomped up the stairs and I made sure they knew I was stomping, and I didn't care one bit that stomping was worse than shrugging and even worse than eye-rolling. I thought, Stomp stomp, so what? Stomp, stomp, who cares? And when I went into my room, I slammed the door.

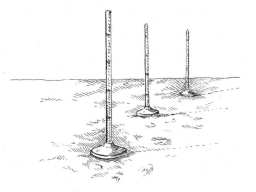

Poles in Arena

Water Trough

Chapter 21

Everyone knows that you can be bored at school. What you sometimes don't realize is that school can be relaxing. When I was in seventh grade, for example, I didn't know this at all. Every day, I was nervous when I got on the bus in the morning and nervous when I got off at school. My instinct was to go around the outside of everything and sneak in when no one was looking, but of course, when you are in seventh grade, everyone is looking. So when I was in seventh grade, I was always glad to get home again after school. I used to think, Well, okay, maybe my family is weird and we don't have television and we go to church in a mall and we spend a lot of time talking about the Bible, but if the kids at school are the alternative, then being weird is fine.

Eighth grade had been different. For one thing, the kids at school just seemed normal—they were doing what they were doing, and that was just what they did. It's like the teachers— Madame dressed very well every day, and if you sat and watched her through class, you'd see that she spread her fingers a lot and flared her nostrils when she took a breath before she said something. You could think that she was being weird, or you could think that surely if she knew how strange the kids thought she was, she would stop flaring her nostrils, but, really, she just did stuff. If we didn't have to look at her (*"Attention, s'il vous plaît!"*), we wouldn't notice and wouldn't care.

On Friday, I was so glad not to be at home that I enjoyed school all day. It made me laugh to watch Stella and Gloria discuss the pennies in their loafers—should they be dimes, in case something happened and you needed to use a pay telephone? Should the heads be up or the tails? And if it was the heads, should the top of the head be pointing toward the toe of the loafer or the heel? When I was in science, I enjoyed watching Mr. Ramirez drill us on some laws about motion, because he always raised his voice when he said "MMMAAASSSS" and "FFFFORRCCCCE," as if we couldn't hear him. And maybe some of us couldn't. I always enjoyed Barbie and Alexis, and at lunch I sat with them. They were nice, but they discussed their recital piece the whole time, except when Barbie was offering me a deviled egg or a celery stick or a piece of apple, "I love Jonathans!" The day went on and on and I didn't want it to end, because I was nervous about going home the way I used to be nervous about coming to school.

But the bus took me there. The good thing was that when I

went through the gate, the car was gone, the truck was gone, and the trailer was gone. The bad news, which I discovered when I changed my clothes and went out to see Jack and Blue, was that some horses were gone, too—at first I didn't see who, but then I did. It was Jefferson and Foxy. In the gelding pasture, there were only Jack, Blue, and Lincoln, and in the mare pasture, there were only Amazon, Happy, and Sprinkles. Six horses didn't seem like very many, especially since Foxy was so little and bright and because of that filled up almost as much space as Amazon, who was big and dull.

Here I was, with another chance to be patient! I had to be patient and wait for Daddy or Mom to come home and tell me what happened to Jefferson and Foxy, and then I had to be patient about whatever that was, and then I would have to be patient about whatever was going on with Danny, and of course, I had to be patient about my broken wrist—four more weeks for that. And because I was thirteen, I had four and a half years to be patient until I was eighteen and could do things my way, which would be to keep the horses around maybe for the rest of my life, and even though they were expensive (I always had to listen to Daddy say, "Abby, horses are expensive, you know that"), I would get some kind of a job and support them, rather than having to sell them all the time.

Well, I went upstairs to my room, and I lay down on my bedspread and I made myself think about all of the things I had to be patient for until I started crying, but I don't know if I was crying from being sad or being mad.

Then I went out and got Jack's halter and took him to the pen. It was muddy, but not as much as it had been, and he slopped around, splashing a bit. I stood in the center and got him to do everything I knew he knew—he trotted big and he trotted slowly, he turned toward me and went the other direction. He backed up. He let me snake the end of the rope around his feet, and then pick his feet up, hold them, and drop them, including the back feet. I walked around him with the rope, wrapping him until he remembered to turn away from me and unwrap himself. I had him step his back feet over about six times on either side. I asked him to duck his head again and step back and he did, four steps, then five steps. I turned my back on him, and waited until he approached me, and he did, but he didn't check my pockets, because he knew we were working. I asked him to turn his head in both directions, and hold it there for a moment. I asked him to stand quietly, with the lead rope dropped, while I stroked him along his back and sides. And he did everything properly, and I thought, Well, patience is good for something at least, but it was a Jem Jarrow sort of patience, where you were waiting for the horse to learn something, rather than a Mom and Daddy sort of patience, where you were waiting to learn something yourself. It seemed like the horse's job was to learn good things and my job was to learn bad things. I took him and put him back in the pasture. Then I carried the hay out of the barn flake by flake, because it was too muddy for the wheelbarrow.

I was finished with the mares when Daddy came out to help me. I said, "What happened to Jefferson and Foxy?"

I must have sounded sassy, because Daddy gave me a look.

I changed my tone and said, again, "What happened to Jefferson? What happened to Foxy?"

"I sold them."

"Why did you sell Foxy?"

"Someone wanted to buy her. A rancher down by Harley with a kid."

Now I was very careful. I said, "Who is Barbie supposed to ride? And Mom really liked Foxy."

He said, "You'll think of something."

Well, that was one thing I was really tired of, but I knew not to say it. When we finished throwing the hay and putting a few things away, we went in for supper. It was macaroni and cheese. At least no one had to cut it for me.

I did have a lot of homework, so there was an actual reason for me to go to my room. And I didn't mind my homework. I was maybe the only kid in my class who liked *Ethan Frome*. I read the whole book, which was short, that night, and though I didn't understand it completely, I knew that it was about being trapped—first in the snow, and then in the town, and then in everything else. I thought the book showed what it felt like to be trapped, and how after years of being trapped, there wasn't much to you anymore, and you couldn't do anything about it, either. I sort of wondered why we were reading this in school. If there was anywhere in the world that people were trapped, it was in junior high, but I liked the book, and not even Alexis and Barbie liked it. I thought that I would spend a lot of time on my paper and would get an A, because if no one likes some book, then the teacher is always happy when one person does.

Downstairs, I could hear something going on, first in the living room, then in the kitchen, then back in the living room. I did not want to know what it was.

But of course, I found out. When the time came to go to

bed, I put on my pajamas and opened my door to go to the bathroom. When I came back five minutes later, Mom was sitting on my bed. I said, "Oh, hi."

"Hi, honey."

She moved to the desk chair when I pulled back the bedspread. She let me get all the way into bed, and then she pulled up my covers and tucked me in. She still hadn't said anything, which was not like her. Finally, I said, "How do you feel?"

"Feel? Oh, I'm fine. It was a very light case, if that's what it was. Just some napping. Your grandmother always said that the more people that have something, the worse it is, but that didn't happen with this, at least."

"Well, that's good." I didn't know what to say. Then I said, "I guess you were having a fight?"

"Did it sound like that?"

I kept my mouth shut.

I closed my eyes. I thought maybe if I pretended I had gone to sleep, then we wouldn't have this conversation.

But she just went on. "You know, honey, when you are married to a person, sometimes you do have fights. Your dad and I don't have many of those, really."

I opened my eyes, accepting the inevitable. "Stella's parents fight all the time. She says it's 'cleansing.'"

"But that's not our business, either, is it?"

I shook my head.

"The thing is that sometimes when you are married to someone, they have a fight with themselves, and you end up being part of it because you have to say some of the things that the other person doesn't really want to say to himself."

"Is that the kind of fight you were having?"

She nodded.

"About Danny, right?"

She nodded, then sighed.

"Well." I sat up because I was a little mad. "He should just give him the horse. Happy and Danny are perfect together, and he doesn't have to make money on every single thing that sets foot on the ranch."

Mom smiled.

I sniffed.

Mom crossed her legs and said, "Then you and Daddy agree."

"We do?"

She nodded. "The thing is, Danny wants to pay for the horse, and your dad can't stand that."

I said, "Oh, good grief." And I slid down under the covers and turned toward the wall. Really, grown-ups, and in this group I was including Danny, were way too weird.

After a moment, she leaned toward me and touched me on the shoulder and said, "Okay. But I think it's important that you understand how each one of them is thinking."

"Why?"

I thought she would say that it would be good for me, because maybe someday I would be married, and all that, and I was thinking, I don't think so, but she said, "Because it's interesting."

I rolled over. I said, "Okay."

She scratched her chin and pushed her hair back, then said, "Danny wants to pay for the horse because that's what grown-ups do, and that's what men do. And your dad doesn't want him to pay for the horse, because that's what strangers do, not family members."

"And if Danny pays for the horse, he'll never come back here and do what Daddy says he should do."

Mom nodded.

I said, "He's not going to do that anyway."

"I know that."

"But Daddy doesn't know that?"

"Well, he knows it, but he hates it."

"Is he mad at you?"

"Have you ever heard the expression 'kill the messenger'?"

I said, "Mom!"

"Oh, I don't mean that literally. But sometimes the person who gives the bad news has to hear the first reaction to the bad news. He went out for a walk. He promised not to get in the truck."

"Oh, Mom!" I said this because she was half smiling. Then she said, "Do you know the difference between funny and absurd?"

I kind of shrugged.

She said, "Well, some things are bad, but they don't make any sense. I mean, after you think about them for a while, you understand how they came to be, but when you first experience them, they don't fit in with the way you understand the world, and so your initial reaction is to laugh."

"That's how I felt that time Ellen Leinsdorf threw herself off the pony so she could show her mom that falling off the pony wasn't so bad. I guess that was absurd."

"Well, maybe to you and me, the idea that Daddy thinks

that Danny is going to move back into his room here and go back to being told what to do, and ask for permission to go places seems absurd, but it seems to Daddy like the right order of things, and so if Danny pays him for the horse, that's like the final message that the right order of things can't be. Do you understand that?"

Of course I did.

I said, "So I guess we aren't going to see Danny again, riding Blue and Happy and stuff?"

Mom stood up, then leaned down and kissed me. She said, "Oh, I think we will."

The weirdest, or maybe the "absurdest" thing about the ghost was that when I woke up in the middle of the night (twenty after two again), I wanted to get up and go outside and see if she was riding Blue. I wanted to do it so much that I wasn't thinking about anything else, and I pushed back the covers and put my foot on the floor before I remembered that I was scared of the ghost and that maybe the ghost would do something to me. What happened was that the floor was so cold that it woke me up, and the first thing that came into my mind was Alexis's story about Freddie and Larry—when their ghost was coming to them all the time, Freddie was scared, but when the ghost stayed away, they got more scared, so scared that they really wanted to see the ghost, if only to keep an eye on her.

It was really cold, in the forties or even in the thirties. Out the window, there was a little bit of moon—it wasn't as dark as it had been a few nights before. By that very little light, I could see glittering here and there—on the top railing of the fence, along the curve of the geldings' water trough. It was even beginning on my window, pale and hard to see. The frost seemed to change shape when I shifted my position. I could look through it, and then I could look at it, but I couldn't do both at the same time. I touched the windowpane along the bottom where the frost was forming. It was gritty and cold. My finger wasn't warm enough to melt the frost, but the window was cold enough to chill my finger. I scratched it a little bit. Even while I was doing this, I started to shiver. I tiptoed back to bed—not because I didn't want to make a noise, but because I didn't want to set my feet on the cold floor. I couldn't see any frost on the floor, but it felt cold enough for it.

The horses and Rusty were out there, I knew, but Daddy always said that as far as being warm was concerned, a horse's body was a big engine, many times bigger than a person's body. Even in places like Oklahoma, where it gets really really cold, a horse can make himself warm by moving around—the soles of his hooves sort of bounce the blood back up his legs, and make the engine run faster, and if his coat is dry, it fluffs up like a blanket. Heat is much more dangerous for a horse than cold, but horses are made to deal with heat, too—they can sweat, unlike a dog, and roll their giant bodies in cool things, like mud.

In the meantime, I shivered under my covers for what seemed like hours, and I was glad I hadn't gone outside.

Which didn't mean that the ghost didn't come inside— when I was finally warm, and almost asleep, the ghost walked around my room, sat down in the chair where Mom had been sitting, leaned toward me, and made me colder than ever. At first I wasn't even scared, but then she opened her mouth, wider and wider, as if she were screaming, but there wasn't a sound, not even a whisper. Then she raised her arms, and she lifted out of the chair and rose above me, and went out through the ceiling of my room, right through that water stain that Daddy wanted to fix but now opened like a door, and you could see the sky through it, the sliver of moon, the sprinkle of stars, and bits of frost floating in the air. Her hair was down, and it was longer than she was; it seemed to drag behind her like Spanish moss dangling off the oaks. If I had dared to reach up, I could have touched it, but with each thing she did, I got more scared and more paralyzed until I had my eyes shut and my hands under the covers, and I could not move.

Saturday morning there was frost everywhere, but the air was so bright that we knew it would burn off in an hour. That meant that we could enjoy the way the frost reflected the sunlight and made every surface whitish-gold. Even the horses had frost on their whiskers when Daddy and I went out to feed them—very delicate pale flecks of ice that sparkled through their foggy breath. They were actively keeping themselves warm—their ears were pricked and they were snorting. They trotted to the piles of hay and made a big deal of working out who was going to get which stack, but they really didn't mean it—they were only charged up by the cold. Just watching them woke me up. Rusty was excited, too, maybe because all sorts of scents were rising on the air as the frost vaporized in the slanting sunlight.

As for Mom and Daddy and me, we said nothing important. Mom would have said that there was nothing like a long walk in the cold to get a man to think about things, and maybe that was true. For thinking, she always said, walking was way better than driving or even riding a horse. At any rate, Daddy did have his Bible at the breakfast table, but he didn't open it for us or quote anything. Maybe he thought the Golden Rule would show up again, and the Golden Rule was clearly on Danny's side, because if Daddy was going to buy horses, then he had to let others buy horses from him.

All this did not mean that I was in a good mood when I went out to the stable to give Melinda and Ellen their lessons. I wasn't. I thought it was a long trip and a lot of saying the same thing over and over, and yes, the money was good, but some days you were so lazy that even money seemed boring. I was in such a bad mood that I could not think of a single thing to buy with my money (if and when the time came to spend it) that might make it worth the trouble to earn it, but I didn't say any of these grumpy things to Mom, because if I had, then I would have to be patient while she talked about being reliable and doing a good job no matter what and life is toil, and those sort of things, which are the sort of things that every person in the world who has horses already knows.

I was there before Melinda, who was five minutes late, so Rodney had already given Gallant Man to me, and I was sitting on the mounting block scratching his ears when the limousine drove up with Melinda in the backseat. The chauffeur let her out and she came running over and hugged me and then hugged the pony, and then she petted the pony very carefully along the bottom of his mane, and took the reins, and pulled down her stirrups, and then stood him up next to the mounting block and got on without being told to or whining. Then she picked up her reins and lowered her heels and settled into her saddle. She looked me in the eye and said, "Ready?"

I burst out laughing, and Melinda laughed, too, and the whole lesson was like that—nothing new, because you can't have something new in every single lesson. Sometimes you just have to practice what you already know until you are doing it automatically, and that is what we did. The surprise was when she waited with me for Ellen, and then handed the reins to her when Ellen came running from the parking lot. Ellen scowled when she first saw Melinda, but Melinda smiled, and so Ellen smiled, and Melinda did a smart thing—she held on to the reins for just an extra second until Ellen remembered to say "thank you." Melinda said, "You're welcome." And then, "Have fun!" And she hugged me around the waist before running away, I suppose, to find Jane.

As we walked to the arena, Ellen said, in a very grown-up voice, "Did Melinda have a good lesson?"

I said, "Yes, she did. Very good."

Ellen's heels immediately went straight down and her chin went up and her chest went out. I said, "Remember last week when you rode bareback, and you had to sort of relax and sink into yourself and the horse in order to stay on?"

Ellen nodded.

"Well, try to have that feeling for your whole lesson today."

Ellen relaxed, and her position improved.

We walked into the arena and I closed the gate. She said, "My mother dropped me off. She has to get her hair done. That could take hours."

I pretended not to know what this meant, but in the end,

she did jump for about ten minutes—figure eight over a crossbar and then four cavalletti, which is a grid of poles that the pony trots through. Those got to be about six inches high, which was high enough to make Gallant Man arch his neck and use his back a little, and to give Ellen a big smile on her face. Ellen had evidently gotten a lecture about manners that week, because she "pleased" and "thank youed" the whole lesson, and then when Mom showed up while we were walking toward the barn, and she was still on the pony, she held out her hand for me to shake, and said, "See you Tuesday, then."

I thought this was so cute that it was me who kissed her on the cheek before I left. And so I was in a better mood when I got in the car than I had been when I arrived at the stable, just the way it had been with school the day before. And why not? As we were driving home, I listed all the things we were driving toward: Daddy and Danny circling one another like boxers, no Foxy for Barbie to ride, days upon days of no riding for me, homework, upset at church and probably conversation about that, and a ghost. I felt my good mood vaporizing through the roof of the car just the same way that the frost had melted in the morning.

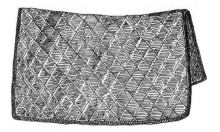

Quarter Pad

Horse Head Pad

Chapter 22

AND THEN BARBIE WAS LATE—IT WASN'T HER FAULT; HER MOM
had had a flat tire on the way home from the music lesson, and
they had to wait for a truck to come, and then she had to
change out of her music clothes and into her riding clothes,
but, she said, "I told them I had to come, so here I am." We
were standing in front of the barn, between the two pastures.
She said, "Where's Foxy?"

"Well. Well, my dad sold her. She's gone."

Barbie's eyebrows lifted, then she said, "Good."

"Good?"

"I can ride—"

"I thought Lincoln would be good. Amazon is easygoing,
but she's a little—"

"Blue."

I started shaking my head before she even finished saying the word.

She said it again. "Blue."

My wrist started throbbing. I cleared my throat. I had never actually said no to Barbie when Alexis wasn't there. Finally, I got it out. "He's not trustworthy. He's spooky and sort of worried about things. I can't let you—"

"Sure you can." I had seen this Barbie in school—the Barbie whose smile just got bigger when someone said "no." Whose eyes twinkled more because now there was a challenge. Who put her hands on her hips and said, "Come on. It'll be fun."

I said, "I thought it was Alexis who was the daring one."

"Comparatively, yes. Come on, let's just go pet him."

She took my hand and walked me toward the gate of the gelding pasture. Of course, Blue was there to meet us, with his ears pricked and a very intelligent look on his face. He even beat Jack to the gate, because Jack was busy playing in the water trough. His forelock, which was pretty long, fell over his left eye, which made him look even cuter, and Barbie reached up and gently smoothed it down. She said, "You will like me. Everyone does." And who was I to disagree with her? One of the things I liked about her, of course, was that she would say anything, and you only thought you knew if she was serious. She continued smoothing his forelock, and he dipped his head and softened his neck. She said, "Let's just get him out. I want to pet him all over."

"What are you doing?"

She looked at me and pushed her hair back. She said, "It's

called 'the thin end of the wedge.'" She put her hand on the lock and said, "Don't you remember when we learned about the five elementary machines, the lever, the pulley, the wedge, the screw, and the wheel?"

I said suspiciously, "I only remember the wheel."

She laughed, then said, "You use a wedge when you want to open things. You get the thin end in, then you push."

She had that halter on Blue in about two seconds and was opening the gate. I had to wave Jack off, because he cantered over to us, ready to come out, too.

I knew she would like him, and she did, because he walked along beside her at just the proper distance and speed, as always, pausing when she paused to unzip her jacket, speeding up when she sped up, and also moving over when she sidestepped a puddle. Someone like Barbie, a twin who played music, would certainly notice this, and she did. After they moved over to miss the puddle, she said, "Does he dance, too?"

I wondered how to put my foot down. Finally, I said, "I'm going to get Lincoln." I turned and ran back. But, of course, Lincoln did not come to the fence, and then he avoided being caught, and then when I had him, I dropped the halter because I was so awkward putting it on, and when I dropped the halter, he backed away, and I had to catch him again. I could see from where I was standing that she had put Blue in the pen and that she was carrying the saddle out of the barn, so I unclipped the lead rope from Lincoln's halter and ran for the gate, because, really, with a Goldman twin, you never knew what she would do, and didn't they tell you that over and over from the first time you talked to them?

Barbie threw the saddle up onto the top rail of the fence and turned back to the barn. I ran right up to her and was about to get mad, but she said, "Oh! Great! I brushed him off, and he was really sweet, and I think he's such a nice horse that we can actually teach him to brush himself off, I don't see why not, and then to clean the barn, hang up the tack, and make sure the doors are closed." I paused too long before answering, and she turned and trotted toward him, the bridle in her hand. I ran after her. When I caught up to her, I was about to say, "So why are you the boss?" but Blue interrupted me with a big whinny, and Barbie said, "You are so right. I was just thinking that very thing," and petted him down his neck.

Finally, I managed to put my hands on her shoulders. She turned with her biggest smile. I lowered my eyebrows in a deter- mined Ellen Leinsdorf sort of way and said, "You are doing a dangerous thing!"

She said, "Am I?"

I nodded.

She said, "Then make it less dangerous."

I realized I could do that. Then I felt that thing that people dealing with the Goldman twins must have felt for years, that sense of being overcome, of saying, okay, have it your way. So they weren't perfect after all. I stared at Barbie with my hands on my hips and then I said, "First we have to make him move and buck in the pen to see if he's tense in his body, and maybe this is going to take a long time."

"That's okay."

"It might get dark."

"That's okay, too. Just doing something is fun." While she

was grinning at me, she did a little Irish jig and made me laugh all over again.

So then I went to the middle of the pen while Barbie untied Blue, and I made him trot and canter and turn and trot out in bigger strides and halt and step under. Barbie watched me, and then came into the middle and took the flag and tried it herself, and he went smoothly and willingly. When he trotted, she smiled, and when he cantered, her eyebrows went up, and I saw that his special grace was visible even to someone who had only had two riding lessons. We made him work until he was breathing hard—that was the safest thing; for her lesson, she would certainly only walk and maybe trot a little, so that could be his cool-down period.

I held him while she tacked him up, and then while she mounted, and there we were, doing the thing I thought we'd never do. I said, "I'm going to lead you around for a minute or two while you get used to him."

She said, "Okay. Thanks."

So I led him around the pen while Barbie arranged herself. As before, she was good about her hands—not too high but high enough, thumbs up—and her legs—relaxed, heels down—and her back and shoulders—straight—and her neck and head—loose and floating. We walked along. She seemed to settle into him. His ears were not pricked and not flopped, but in working position. His steps were relaxed. I kept my right finger on her left rein, but I moved a bit away and walked along beside them. Blue's eye was calm, but he was looking here and there. When a branch over by the arena creaked, he glanced at it but kept walking. Then he did a strange thing. Barbie shifted her weight toward me, I don't know why, but maybe to get comfortable, and Blue shifted, too. He shifted his balance to get himself under her. I said, "Wow."

Barbie said, "What?"

"When you shifted your weight—"

"I had a wrinkle in my jeans."

"Well, when you shifted your weight toward me, he moved to come under you."

"Is that unusual?"

"I think so."

She shifted her weight to the outside, and he moved to come under her again. She said, "That's very considerate."

"Yes, it is."

I backed toward the middle of the pen a step or two, and let them go around me. It wasn't getting dark, but it was thinking about getting dark, so the shadows were longer, and everything around us was more mottled and spotty, just the sort of atmosphere where I would expect to see a ghost—where I would expect Blue to see a ghost. The ghost. I shivered. But the two of them walked around, and then Barbie picked up her reins and asked Blue to trot. Her posting wasn't great, yet, and she bounced for a couple of steps, so Blue slowed his pace to a jog. When she got her balance and rhythm, he sped up. Pretty soon they were going around the pen very nicely. Barbie said, "Very good!"

I said, "Yes, actually. Very good."

Barbie's hand crept forward on the rein, and then she asked him to turn. He made a smooth loop and went back the other way. Every time she lost her balance a little, he slowed down, and then went on. His eyes and ears kept track of leaves and acorns and even Rusty, who trotted by on her way to the house, but he never changed his attentiveness to Barbie. I just stood there. They kept trotting, made a few more turns, and then she said, "Whoa," and they came down to a walk and then to a halt. She said, "I do like him better than Foxy."

I said, "That is the least selfish horse I have ever seen in my life. My dad isn't even going to believe he exists."

Barbie leaned forward and petted Blue in front of the saddle. She said, "I'm glad you said that, because I wouldn't want to think I was crazy thinking this horse was reading my mind."

"Well, he's not reading your mind. He's reading your body."

Barbie said, "What's the difference?"

I watched while they worked for another five or ten minutes—nothing strenuous or beyond her, but very interesting to me. Finally, I said, "He's behaving much better for you than for Daddy or even Danny. Maybe it was them he was scared of and not the ghost."

Barbie said, "What ghost?"

I said, "Oh."

Barbie said, "What ghost? Come on and tell me what ghost."

I went over and took Blue's rein and scratched him on the forehead. Barbie sat there in the saddle looking down at me. I said, "It's really stupid."

"Alexis told her ghost story, so you can tell yours."

"Well, let's put him away first. I'll tell you while we're giving the horses their hay."

"Oh, I love that," said Barbie.

The ground had dried up some, but not enough for the wheelbarrow, so as we walked back and forth to the haymow beside the barn, I said, "Did I tell you that we got Blue because his owner was killed in a car crash on Highway 1? She ran into a tree."

Barbie shook her head.

"Well, she had only moved here at Christmas, and she didn't seem to know anyone. Jane, my friend out where he was boarded, tried to find out if there was someone back in Ohio, but there wasn't, so we got him because there was no one to pay his bills. He came with lots of stuff." I waved my hand toward the trunks. "And I didn't change his name—"

Barbie said, "So she found him!"

She meant the ghost. I hadn't thought of that as a reason to change his name.

We headed toward the mares with flakes of hay in our arms. I nodded toward the arena and said, "I saw her the first time, just coming around the barn like a regular person, walking. I could barely see her, but I knew she was wearing high boots. And she was tall and slender, with dark hair. She just walked around the corner of the barn and disappeared, but Blue was really afraid of that end of the arena."

"Why did you think it was her?"

"It wasn't Mom, and it wasn't anyone else we knew. Besides—"

"What?" said Barbie.

"The next time I saw her, she was floating in my room, and she had Spooky in her arms. Or Spooky's mom, because it was a full-grown cat. I think she was wandering around here, maybe riding Blue late at night, and she found a dead cat, and she kept it."

"Who's Spooky?"

"Our kitten. Our kitten that Rusty brought in from somewhere and can't be related to any of the barn cats."

"Why not?"

"The black one has been spayed and the other one is a tabby."

"What color is the kitten?"

We walked along the fence and threw the hay over to Amazon, Happy, and Sprinkles.

"Black. He's in the house."

"Rusty didn't kill it?"

I shook my head. "I was sitting in the barn thinking about the ghost and Rusty brought in the kitten and dropped it just inside the door."

"Mmm," said Barbie. We turned back toward the barn.

"The ghost has come to my room twice."

"Wow!"

"But that wasn't the scariest thing."

"What was the scariest thing?"

"Well, there were two. The first was that the ghost of Spooky's mom, I guess, got under my covers in the middle of the night and was gone by morning."

"That gives me the creeps."

I nodded. "And the second was that the other night, when it was rainy and windy, I was out checking the horses because Daddy had that virus, and she touched me on the shoulder and whispered in my ear, 'He's still my horse.'"

Barbie took a deep breath.

"And I might not have noticed or believed that, but Rusty, who never goes into the house, ran up behind me and just had to get in the house. Just had to."

"What did she see?"

"I was too scared to look!"

"Wow!" said Barbie again.

I was getting pretty impressed with my story. We picked up more hay, armloads. I said, "I know what she saw."

"What?"

"She saw the ghost riding Blue, because I saw that the other night, when I was almost over the virus. I slept so much during the day that I woke up around two in the morning, and I put on some clothes and came outside, and she was riding him bare-back, kind of lying along his neck with her legs hanging down. She had the boots on and her hair was hiding her face. This time he saw me in the night, and he spooked, and she fell to the side and slid off. But I couldn't find anything in the morning."

"You never can with ghosts."

We came to the geldings' fence. I said, "I guess not."

"Weren't you terrified?"

I shrugged. "Well, yes. But it was like with Alexis's story. I was terrified, but I didn't want to miss it, either."

"Yes, I always wonder in monster movies why they don't just run the other direction. You know, why do they open the door of the haunted house and go in, even though Mom is calling them home for dinner?"

I laughed, but I said, "You don't believe me."

"I do, in a way."

We tossed the flakes over and Jack and Blue came first, then Lincoln. I thought Lincoln looked a little lonely. I wanted to finish my story, but I couldn't help saying, "Why are you so nice?"

"Habit."

"What do you mean?"

"Well, you know when Mr. Ramirez says that for every action, there is an equal and opposite reaction?"

I nodded.

"For twins, for every mean action, there is an equally mean reaction."

"You're kidding."

"Not kidding. When we were little, we specialized in hair-pulling. I could get her down and actually put my knee on her hair and sort of work it until she was screaming. She just ran over and grabbed handfuls and yanked. She could have me before I realized what was happening. Mom thought the fighting was going to drive her crazy. So we learned. It's easier this way."

I said, "More fun, too?"

She nodded, then said, "So tell me more."

We went into the barn to put away our riding things. I turned on the light because it was almost dark and said, "Those are her trunks." Barbie glanced over at them. Then I said, "Okay, and something happened last night."

"Last night! You're kidding! You seem so sane."

"Last night I woke up and looked out at the frost, and then when I was lying in my bed, she came in the window and floated around. She sat in my desk chair, and screamed, and then floated over above me, and the ceiling opened up and she

283

rose through the hole. Her dress was trailing behind her. It seemed to leave frost sparkles on the blanket. I thought I was going to freeze to death."

"So now that I've ridden Blue, she's going to follow me home?"

"I don't know."

"What did the scream sound like?"

"I don't know. Either I can't remember, or there was no sound."

Barbie walked over to the larger of the two trunks and stood in front of it. She said, "Is there anything in here?"

"Lots of stuff. Blankets. Things we don't use."

"Let's look through it."

My heart started pounding for the first time. I shook my head, but of course Barbie didn't see me, and being Barbie, she just lifted the lid of the trunk. She stood there staring, but her eyes didn't get wide or anything. She didn't open her mouth to scream. She said, "It's dusty."

I took one step toward her.

I turned around—I couldn't help myself—to see if any slender ladies were entering the barn. The answer was no, but it was almost completely dark out there.

She leaned forward.

A skeletal arm did not reach out and grab her. Instead, she reached in and pulled out an oval-shaped pad with two holes in it. She said, "What's this?"

"A head protector. Sometimes horses wear those in trailers. His ears go through the holes."

She set it on the ground beside the trunk and pulled out a blue square of wool trimmed in white. "What's this?"

"A quarter pad. In places where it's cold, they put that over his haunches behind the saddle in the winter to keep him from getting stiff."

I took another step.

She pulled out a girth, padded with sheepskin.

I said, "English-style girth. I guess she rode English."

Now I could see into the trunk. Barbie pulled out the bridle, English style, nice brown leather, snaffle bit, braided reins. She shook it a little and then handed it to me. It was curled from lying in the trunk, and someone (namely me) had not cleaned or oiled it, so it was a little stiff. But it was just a bridle. I took it and hung it on the bridle rack.

Now Barbie leaned over and lifted out the saddle using two hands. It was a little stiff, too. I picked up one of the saddle racks and carried it over to her. She set the saddle on the rack. I said, "It's an expensive saddle. I think it's English. I mean, made in England."

Underneath the saddle were some folded-up saddle pads, the kind that English riders use, that are shaped like an English saddle. I reached in and picked these up. There were two of them, and underneath them a paper bag. Inside the paper bag were two dried, oily sponges and a tin of saddle soap. I opened it. It was almost empty—that was the creepiest thing, because I could imagine the slender dark-haired lady patiently cleaning and oiling her saddle, taking good care of it. You could, in fact, see faint indented streaks in the soap where the sponge had been rubbed across it. I said, "I wonder sometimes if he knows she's dead."

"If she's a ghost, I'm sure he knows the difference."

I nodded.

The last thing in the trunk were three brushes, all with wooden backs: a dandy brush, a body brush, and a soft brush. They were still sort of new.

Barbie said, "How come you never unpacked the trunks?"

"We've got all the stuff we need. Maybe Daddy didn't know where he was going to put it. Anyway, I just didn't. I'm sure Daddy is waiting for me to take responsibility."

I didn't say that I'd been avoiding the trunks ever since we saw those black boots the first time we looked in them.

She opened the lid of the other trunk. This one was mostly blankets, but I knew the boots were in there. She took out the top blanket. It smelled musty.

She took out the second blanket—the thicker one. She set it aside. Underneath it was the fly sheet. Underneath that I could see the shape of the boots. I said, "I guess it's the boots that give me the creeps."

"Why?"

"Because they're hers, not his."

She picked up the fly sheet and set it on top of the heavy blanket. Something flopped over from the end of the trunk, an envelope that I hadn't noticed before. Barbie picked it up and opened the end flap, which wasn't sealed. She drew out a piece of paper and turned it right side up. She said, "Oh, a photograph." I looked over her shoulder.

There she was, Blue's former owner, standing with him under a sign that said HIGHLAND HILLS RIDING STABLES. She was holding him by the reins with her right hand. Her left arm came under his neck and her fingers were touching his left cheek. She had her hard hat in her right hand, with the reins, and I could see the boots, too (though only the high tops). She had on a white shirt and a big smile. She was blond, with short, thick hair, plump cheeks, and bangs. She didn't look a thing like the dark-haired slender lady. Even though it was a black-and-white picture, she looked like she had blue eyes. Judging by where she came up to next to Blue, she was about my size, but heavier—a woman, not a girl. In case I wondered if this was really her, she had written in ink along the bottom of the picture—*Me and Blue, August 23, 1965. OUQT.*

I said, "What does that mean?"

Barbie said, "Oh, you cutie."

I said, "That's not the ghost."

She glanced at me, then reached into the trunk and took out the boots, one in each hand. They had plastic boot trees in them, and they were beautiful, just as I remembered. But they were just boots.

Barbie said, "There must be some kind of resale shop where you can sell these sorts of things. They look expensive." She set one beside her foot. It was too small. Then she set it beside my foot. Also too small.

She said, "Well, you're right, this stuff is sad."

I thought it was, too. But not scary.

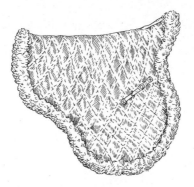

Sheepskin Saddle Pad

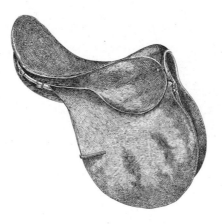

Jumping Saddle

Chapter 23

WHEN WE SAW MRS. GOLDMAN, SHE WAS COMING OUT OF THE house with Mom. They were chatting away and Alexis was behind them. They all came down off the back porch, and I could see Mom gesture toward the ground, which I knew she was saying was muddy and maybe slippery. They all walked toward us, and Alexis seemed to be carrying something. We went to meet them.

I said, "We fed the horses and put some stuff away."

Mom said, "Good. Did you have a nice lesson, Barbie?"

Barbie said, "I was great."

I said, "She was pretty good, and she rode Blue."

"Did you really?" said Mom, and it all sounded so mundane.

I said, "He took good care of her."

"He did," said Barbie. "He's great." And I thought how hard it is to say what you really mean—to get other people to understand how you feel and to really know what that feeling is.

"Look!" said Alexis. She lifted her hand, and I saw that she had Spooky on the crook of her arm. Barbie said, "Oh, he is cute! Look at his white toes, two on each foot!" She stroked him. "Is he eating solid food?"

"Oh, sure," said Mom. "He's a good eater. Does his job in the litter box, too." Both girls smiled all of a sudden, right at Mrs. Goldman. She threw up her hands, and shook her head, then said, "If I didn't have twins, I could be a cat lady. That was going to be my destiny."

We all laughed.

Alexis said, "Mom even had a cat in her dorm room in college. She took him for walks on a leash."

"In college!" said Mom. "Weren't there rules?"

Mrs. Goldman said, "I pretended not to know. It was Antioch College, so breaking rules was a way of life there." We all went around the house to their car, and as we did, I felt the ghost disappear, drop by drop, the way the frost had disappeared that morning, simply rising and evaporating, without even a good-bye. Yes, I felt stupid to have never looked in the trunks and found the picture, or even to have never asked Jane what the owner had looked like—Jane would have told me.

Alexis said, "Is he old enough for a new home?"

Mom nodded.

Mrs. Goldman said, "What's his name?"

I said, "Spooky."

Barbie said, "Can we change it?"

I said, "I wish you would."

Then, simultaneously, Alexis said, "Joe," and Barbie said, "Bliss," and Mrs. Goldman said, "Well, this will go on for days," and they opened their car doors and got in. I ran to the gate.

As they drove through, Barbie put down her window and said, "Staccato! That's his name."

When I told it to Mom, she said it was a musical term meaning "short and sharp." And then she walked into the house singing, "'Tis the gift to be simple, 'tis the gift to be free," in bright, short notes, and we hummed it all through making dinner, because that is a song that gets into your mind and stays there.

That night Jane called to tell me that I had forgotten to get paid, but that she would keep my lesson money in an envelope in her office, and I could pick it up on Tuesday. I told her how Blue had been with Barbie.

She said, "Well, it stands to reason that he understands how to take care of beginners. His owner rode him around everywhere, and she seemed to think she was perfectly safe. I asked her very early on if she planned to take lessons, and she said that she had no 'larger ambitions.' I had a horse once, a mare I got off the racetrack, who was a real stinker, just as bossy as she could be. Once she pinned my groom against the wall when he was trying to blanket her. Then I lost track of this mare for a year or two, and when I ran into her again, she was owned by a girl about your age, and the parents came up to me and thanked me for starting this mare, because she was 'wonderfully safe.' I thought that was so strange, so I snooped around, and finally, one of the other girls in that barn said that this mare was still a stinker, except with this girl. She was a one-girl horse. So you never know what they know, do you?"

"I guess not."

"The other thing is—" She lowered her voice.

"What?"

"Some horses just don't like male riders. When do you get to ride him?"

"A few weeks."

"Well, we'll see. You've only had him what, three or four weeks? That's such a short time."

Maybe it was. Hard to believe, though. I said, "Was she blond?"

"Mary Carson?"

"Yes."

"Yes, she was a blonde. Let's see. I think she was about fifty. If you saw her in the grocery store, you'd think she had five kids and some grandkids and a lawyer for a husband, but none of that. Sad, really. All she had was Blue."

I said good-bye and hung up. In the living room, Mom was cleaning up Spooky's box and litter box. Everything seemed really normal. Daddy was reading his Bible. Mom went and got the broom, then came back and started to sweep the corners of the hall. When she had a pile of grit and dust and kitty hairs, I knelt down with the dustpan, and she swept the pile onto it. Then she took the pan away from me and carried it and the broom and the boxes into the kitchen. That was the end of Spooky. Especially since he was "Staccato" now. I thought I should miss him, but given all the creepy thoughts I'd had about him, I was glad to see him go.

Homework was waiting. I went over and kissed Daddy on the cheek. He said, "Are you going upstairs?"

I said, "*Mais oui,* Papa. *Je dois lire mes devoirs,* Le Petit Prince." I added, "*Maintenant.*"

Daddy looked up at me, then said, "Tell me why you aren't taking Spanish again."

"*La classe d'espagnol est complete. Moi, j'aime la belle* France."

Daddy nodded. I said, "Do you know what that means?"

Daddy shook his head.

"It means, 'I have to do my homework now.'"

Mom smiled and picked up her knitting.

I decided that whatever was going on with Danny wasn't my business. I went up the stairs, saying, "*Au revoir!*"

My room was normal, too. Most importantly, the stain in the ceiling was just a stain, and not a very big one, at that—a faint outline in the paint. In fact, the place was a bit of a mess, and it was nice to walk around, straightening the rug and the covers on my bed, and sitting the books upright, and plumping up my old stuffed animals. I even went into the closet and picked up some clothes I had dropped on the floor and hung them up. I straightened my desk. My broken wrist wasn't that bad anymore. Nothing was that bad anymore. It was a strange feeling.

The first thing we saw when we got to church the next morning was that the Greeleys were back. Bart was sitting on Carlie's lap and Brad was playing with a toy in the toy corner, and Mrs. Greeley was bouncing the baby on her hip and chatting with Mrs. Larkin, who was holding out her finger for the baby to grab. We were the late ones, so as soon as we sat down, Mr. Hazen started a hymn, and it was not "Simple Gifts," which was fine with me. It was "I'll Fly Away," which was one we didn't sing often. Then we went on to "Farther Along" and "How Can I Keep from Singing?" Then Mr. Hazen stood up with his Bible open, and was about to start his lesson, when Mr. Greeley said, "Excuse me, Brother Hazen. Before you begin, I would like to say something."

Next to me, Mom took Daddy's hand.

Mrs. Greeley was looking up at Mr. Greeley. The baby had fallen asleep and was in a kind of carrying bed at the end of the row. Bart was rolling a truck along his knee, and Brad was sitting in Mrs. Greeley's lap. Mrs. Greeley nodded, and Mr. Greeley smiled, and then he said, "Well. This isn't easy. We felt, though, I mean Rhoda and I . . ." He looked around and smiled a small smile. "We didn't want to just disappear without a word, because you have all been very kind to us, especially you, Carlie, and you, Abby, but everyone else, too."

The sisters started clucking.

"Um, well. We have decided to depart the church, here, in spite of your kindness because, I think we made a little mistake, and as we have kept coming, the mistake has loomed larger for us, rather than smaller."

Daddy cleared his throat. I looked at him, but his face was blank. Nevertheless, he always liked it when people admitted to their mistakes.

"Our mistake was in thinking that because this is a simple church with no pastor and no connection to a larger hierarchy, it would be like the church we left behind in Philadelphia when we came out here."

The clucking got louder.

"No one back home knew anything about meetings out here, and so that was our first mistake, and then you all were so nice and welcoming, but really, you aren't Quakers, and it would seem that your thinking is not along that line, and so as the time has gone by, we have had to accept that we, um, find it difficult to conform to your beliefs, even though we do see all of you as friends, and that's friends with a small *f*." He glanced down at Mrs. Greeley, who nodded.

He went on. "It now seems like such a silly mistake to have made, and in talking about it I am really quite embarrassed, but I guess I would say that looks are deceiving, and then you get yourself into things and don't see a way out because you have made friends and have failed to speak up and just let things go along, and all of a sudden it's a year and a half or more, and we just thought we should admit our mistake and give all of you brothers and sisters a fond farewell. So we brought along a couple of pies that Rhoda made as a parting gift, pecan, one is, and banana cream, too."

Bart looked up at his dad and said, "Are we having pie?"

And then we all laughed.

Mr. Greeley said, "Later, Barty boy." He turned to the rest of us again. "So, that's all I have to say. Thank you again for your kindness and your welcome. We don't plan to stay for the rest of the service." He cocked his head, and Mrs. Greeley set down Brad and stood up.

We all stood up.

Daddy said, "We wish you wouldn't leave."

There was a long silence, and then Brother Abner said, "But we understand your reasons, and honor them."

Mr. Greeley picked up the baby bed, and they started walking toward the door. I shouted, "Bye, Bart! Bye, Brad! Be good boys!"

Bart turned his head and then waved, but Brad came running back and threw his arms around my knees. I bent down and picked him up. He kissed me and said, "Miss you, Abby. Miss you!"

Then he struggled to get down, and when I set him on his feet, he ran for the door and went out with the others. The door closed behind them.

I heard Mrs. Larkin say, "Dear me," and then Mr. Hazen stood up and continued with his lesson.

I never thought I would miss Brad Greeley, but I did.

As for Daddy and Danny, you would have thought that there had never been any problem about the horse. When we got home from church that night, Danny was there with Jake Morrisson's truck and trailer. It was a nice evening, almost April now, so we sat on the front porch and drank some glasses of lemonade. Danny said that he'd ridden Blue up the hillside, "Nothing strenuous, but he was good." Also, he had met a guy on the other side of the valley who was looking for a big horse, and he had mentioned Amazon to him. If someone called named Wayne Kingston, that was him. Danny said, "He has some money to spend, and she's a good-looking mare."

"Lucky fella," said Daddy.

At this point, Danny reached into his pocket and pulled out a folded piece of paper, his check, and handed it to Daddy. Daddy smoothed it out and looked at it, and then, after a long pause, said, "Fine, then. That's fine." He nodded. He put the check into his shirt pocket.

Then there was another long pause.

At last, Daddy said, "What's your schedule this week?"

Danny said, "I can be here Tuesday, Thursday, and Friday."

And Daddy said, "Well, then, why don't you plan on staying for supper Thursday night?"

And Danny smiled and said, "I'd like that."

I realized right then that Mom was standing inside the door, and I'm sure her ears were as big as plates, just like mine. Maybe she let out a long breath, just like I did. What I thought was that it was really weird the way that things are very very hard until all of a sudden, they are easy again.

About the Author

Jane Smiley is the author of five works of nonfiction, as well as many novels for adults, including *Horse Heaven*, *Moo*, and the Pulitzer Prize–winning *A Thousand Acres*. She was inducted into the American Academy of Arts and Letters in 2001.

Jane Smiley lives in Northern California, where she rides her horses every chance she gets. Her first two novels for young readers, *The Georges and the Jewels* and *A Good Horse*, also feature Abby Lovitt and her family.